CW00515493

dust

Peter Raposo

APS Books
YORKSHIRE

.APS Books,

The Stables Field Lane, Aberford, West Yorkshire, LS25 3AE

APS Books is a subsidiary of the
APS Publications imprint

www.andrewsparke.com

First published worldwide by APS Books in 2021

A catalogue record for this book is available from the British Library

ISBN 978-1-78996-432-5

dUst

For Esther.
With love.

Peter Raposo

"In the end, we turn to dust."

Mieko K

The visitor

I was only a child of nine when the reader came to our town but both my parents had already told me stories about this elusive figure, adding that he was a member of our tribe, a tribe thousands of years old, almost as old as History, and I was told that the reader carried The Book with him, one of the few books left after the Big Revolution. In those years I still didn't know much about the Big Revolution, but Mother, or maybe it was Father, told me that the Big Revolution took place exactly twelve years after the Big War, and the people in power quickly put an end to the Big Revolution by sending out the machines to tackle the troublemakers, and once the Big Revolution was under control, a revolution that was actually quite short-lived since it only lasted four days, the machines started to gather all books deemed controversial and rebellious, and afterwards those books were burnt. From what I was told (and from what I read), some of those books taught Man how to live and how to rebel against oppression, and the New Leaders didn't want for Man to think too much and to worship gods and other kinds of beings, and that's why they thought it was best to burn all books. Soon enough the machines had gathered most books, books from all over the world, books of all types, even poetry, books by the likes of Dante and Blake, Kenzaburo Oe and Henry Miller, the

1

Cabbalists, the Talmudists, the Witnesses, the Watchers, the Zen People, and those books were carried to an island close to New Zealand, and once all books had been gathered a machine started the Big Fire, a fire that lasted for a long time and which burned the whole island down to the ground, or down to the sea, and Man was told once and for all to accept the New World and its way of life or else…

But as I so damn well know, Man is stubborn, and crafty, too (after all, we built the first machines), and the words of the New Leaders were quickly forgotten, or ignored, and a group of men and women, the so-called carriers and protectors of books, or readers if you prefer, started going from place to place to read passages of books and to share the Word with others, and being a reader became the riskiest job of all. Of course the readers' profession wasn't even the one of reading. All of them had studied something or learnt some craft, and they earned their living by using their knowledge, but at night (and some mornings), hidden from sight, hidden in the privacy of someone's house, the reader would share passages of The Book with others.

A few hours before the reader came to our house, Mother went out to get some food bringing me along with her while Father was at work. (My mother and father had names, as we all do, but I've always called them Mother and Father.)

The streets were quiet, the air was clean and dry, same as the pavements, and there were only two f-Machines in the area, floating slowly in the air, looking for any signs of trouble, but our town was a quiet place, zero crimes for the last few years. (For those who don't know it, since I've been asked to write a record of our history, the f-Machine was a small flying machine, much like a drone, created by Anton Kushner, or Kushner Jr. if you prefer, the son of Ken Kushner, or Kushner Sr. if you prefer, also known as K.K., and I must add that K.K., or Ken Kushner, was the creator of the i-Machine, a machine that looks entirely human.)

From what I could tell, apart from the f-Machines, there were no other Kushner's "creations" in our town. But then again, seeing how perfect the i-Machines were, it was hard to tell.

Mother got all the items she needed and then we returned home. A couple of hours later, Father arrived home, bringing with him more digestive items and a few bottles of wine and juice. I was looking out of the window and I saw smoke in the air.

"Fire," I said slowly, mostly to myself. Then, turning to Father and Mother, I repeated, "Fire."

Father nodded and said, "Yes. It looks like it."

Neither he nor Mother looked my way, which I found a bit odd.

Weren't they scared of the fire?

What if the wind blew in a different direction, directing the fire towards us?

True, the fire looked to be far away, and the machines always dealt quickly with fires.

Seconds later, as I remained by the window, I saw two small objects floating towards the fire. And a few minutes later someone was knocking at the door. It was Sarah from across the road, Sarah and her family. Father let them in, and seconds later, more knocking. It was Ben and his family, followed by Michael and his family, followed by the twins Rachel and Jacob, followed by more people. Our house was bursting with people and smiles, plenty of laughter, but Father and Ben quickly told everyone to keep the noise down. I was told to step away from the window and join the other kids, which I did reluctantly.

The other kids bored me. Aged 9, I was the oldest of the lot, already streetwise as Father used to say, and I had nothing in common with the other kids, the oldest of them being 6-years old. They were into cartoons and childish stuff while I was already into books. And I already mastered the language of my people quite well.

All curtains were closed and a few minutes later there was knocking on the door, a soft knock, once, two, three times, four times, followed by silence and a fifth knock afterwards. Father turned around, looked at everyone and nodded before opening the door. A tall, thin man with short greyish beard was standing outside. He wore a dark suit and a long black coat. The man had a large backpack with him. Father looked at him and said, "Saul." And then they hugged.

Outside, the air was cold, and a person could smell smoke in the air. Sirens could be heard far away but no one seemed to be paying any attention to it. Our reader was a man, a man named Saul, an old friend of Father.

I was once told that there were also female readers but some people in my tribe didn't really accept women as readers. I don't know why. I didn't ask why when I first heard about it, but later on I was told that even though we all came from the same tribe we followed different customs, and some members of my tribe didn't accept women readers.

The reader left his backpack on the sofa and Father told me to stand next to it and make sure that the backpack didn't fell on the floor.

"Protect it well," Father said and smiled, and I wasn't really sure of what to say (and should I even say something back?) or how to react.

I gave him a faint smile and nodded, but he was already gone, walking behind the reader as if he, Father, was a little kid following his master. I stood there looking at the backpack, looking at the other kids, feeling like a grownup, a man, and I could tell that some of the other kids were jealous of me, and I knew that inside that backpack was a book, The Book, a book that could either lead to salvation or death, maybe both, and I felt both anxious and scared, brave and coward, and after a while the reader came over to where I was, and he gave me a warm smile before reaching for his bag. All the males, including me, put on their small hats, and then the reader started to pray and sing, and the men joined him. Later, The Book was taken out of the bag, the biggest book I'd ever seen. The Book was dressed in velvet coat, and instead of being made of pages, it was a long scroll, held together by two ornate wooden shafts. Someone undressed The Book and then the reader read its words. Or rather he sang them. Yes, he sang the words in the book so beautifully, and I felt as if I was listening to the words of an angel. A lot of the other men joined him and I watched them as they sang and bowed, and took steps backwards and forwards, and I looked at Mother and at the other women, and they looked so calm and so happy, and I understood then the power of words, the power and the wonder of words, and I wanted for that night to last forever, or to go on for a bit longer, and it would have lasted for a bit longer hadn't it been for the visitor. That unexpected visitor. Unexpected: a word that always brings fear to my heart.

At the sound of someone knocking at the door, everyone stopped singing. Everyone stopped and looked at the door. More knocking. Soft knocks, in pairs. One, two, pause, one, two.

Mother looked at Father and it was clear to see that neither of them had a clue of what to do. By then the reader had already closed The Book and was dressing it with the velvet coat. More knocking. Soft. Unexpected. One, two, pause, one, two.

Mother looked at the reader who had already put the book in his backpack. Only then did Mother go to the door.

I had failed to notice that some of our friends had already left through the backdoor. The reader, too, was getting ready to leave, but he was tired, not to mention old, and he moved slowly, and before we knew it, the visitor was already inside, standing in front of Mother, looking at her, at us. The visitor was tall, female, long iced-hair, hair the colour of snow. Pretty. Too pretty. Too perfect. She wiped a strand of hair behind her ear and smiled at Mother. Her smile was pretty. Too pretty. So perfect.

The visitor said, "Sorry to disturb you but I got lost. I was heading to New Text1 and I must have taken a wrong road somewhere and ended up here, in this town in the middle of nowhere."

We weren't in the middle of nowhere. Our town was actually in the map and it was known for its wine and cheese production. In fact, it was said that we produced some of the best wine of New Canada. And pretty good matzos, too.

I looked at her, at our visitor, at her perfection, and I saw her staring at me. She couldn't hide it from me (and she knew it). I know who she was. Or rather I knew what she was.

Machine.

An i-Machine, perfect and so beautifully made.

"Machine," I said it so slowly, so slowly and lowly that the n and e at the end were hardly audible. But everyone heard it, as did the machine, and I saw her raising her right hand in the air, pointing at me, and then something came out of her finger, something like a gun, and I saw smoke coming out of her pointing finger, aimed at me, and I became sort of dizzy, numb, and my eyes became blurry, and then I heard Mother shout, "No!" and I thought I saw her jumping at the machine. And I heard more noise and shouts before I passed out.

When I finally came to my senses I was no longer at home but in the woods with the reader. He was looking at the fire, a huge fire a few miles away from us. My town was on fire.

"Mother? Father?" those were the first words out of my mouth.

"They'll catch up with us later," the reader said but I knew he was lying.

He had his backpack with him.

He was looking at me, asking me gently and silently to go with him. As I looked at him I realised that he was also scared. His hand reached for mine and he pulled me up. I didn't know what to do so I followed him. As we walked out of there, I wanted to cry, to ask something, but there was no time for it. Later, once we were safe, he told me what had happened. Later, I cried.

"When the i-Machine aimed its gas at you, your mother, enraged, jumped at it, and then the other women, knowing that your mother was no match for the machine, also threw themselves at it, followed by the men.

"Your father turned to me and said, "Get out of here. Save The Book. Take my son with you. He has the gift." I nodded and did as told, and escaped through the backdoor," the reader said.

I didn't know what to say as we sat in the woods. Somewhere an owl was owling. Or maybe it was crying.

After the Big War, after the loss of so many people, other life started to flourish, to grow, almost out of thin air, and even bees made a welcome return. Maybe in the past, because of the huge number of humans, other kinds of life had no chance to prosper and grow, but now that there were less of us, less humans that is, the animal world and even Mother Nature was free to grow.

"Are Mother and Father dead?" I asked as we munched on dried fruit.

We were hiding in a cave, a clean cave with sleeping bags, blankets and even books. Food, too. Lots of it. And clean water. Later, as I followed the reader from place to place, I came across other caves like that first one. They were the readers' hideouts, where they stored their treasures, their secrets, books.

Saul (that was the reader's name) thought well before answering my question.

I could feel my heart thumping fast, a minor headache on the way. Regardless of my pain and worries, I found it all a bit ironic. There we were; a boy and a reader in the New World sleeping in a cave, just like the First People. So much for evolution.

Saul swallowed hard and then spoke. "I believe they're alive," he said. "The machines don't kill people. They simply educate them."

Shortly afterwards we fell asleep and on the following morning, when I woke up, Saul was already up. He boiled some water on a campingaz Micro Stove and afterwards we ate oats with honey. The food was warm, delicious, easy to digest. While we ate I looked at the sky. Soon it would rain.

Saul looked at me and said, "I need to go to the nearest town. Wait here for me. I might take a few hours. There are some books for you to read and plenty of food and water. I'll be back. Just wait here. I need to see some people plus I need to work. Wait here, young Michael. You'll be safe here."

He repeated himself. And I nodded and nodded.

That was the first time ever without my parents. To kill the time and keep the loneliness and sadness at bay, I read. I read *The Little Prince* and *Night Flight*, both written by Antoine de Saint-Exupéry, followed by *The Red Baron* by Wayne Vansant. And afterwards I cried.

Once my eyes were dry, I ate something and then waited for the return of Saul. He arrived late in the evening, carrying warm food with him. And a bottle of Pepsi. Upon seeing me, he said, "The whole town is talking about you. The machines have been asking about you. About the boy who can tell the difference between an i-Machine and a human."

I looked at him without knowing what to say. He looked scared. Doubtful. Troubled. I didn't know what to say so I said nothing.

We went inside and ate, and Saul said, "You might have to stay here for a long time."

He looked at me and I nodded.

"Until things die down," he said.

And I nodded.

Both of us knew that things wouldn't die down that quick so I probably would have to stay there for a long time. I was fine with it. And I wasn't.

I asked about my parents, if he had heard anything about them.

"There were talks that a couple of women had escaped, but they could be rumours or a trap. Give it a few days and we'll know more," he said.

And I nodded.

The days turned into weeks. Repetitive days. Repetitive weeks. The same thing day after day. I would get up and read, and then I would eat something. After being inside that cave for four days, I started to go for long walks, and once I even stood a mile or so away from the town where Saul worked. One night he asked, "That night at your home, how did you know it was a machine and not a human?"

We were eating Gefilte fish with eggs and salad, and we also had hot soup. I felt as if I was on a long holiday, a holiday from everything and everyone, but I missed my parents. After a while I stopped asking about them.

Saul had told me not to worry. Usually, unless it was a serious crime, after being re-educated most prisoners would be set free by the machines and sent home. That's what I hope would happen to my parents. But was I dangerous? Was I dangerous because I could tell the difference between the machine and the human? And would that harm my parents?

"The eyes," I said. "And the lips. They're different."

"Different how?" Saul asked. He looked both nervous and curious.

"The lips don't twitch like human lips do and the eyes lack that spark," I said. "The human spark."

Saul nodded, and then he looked to be lost in his thoughts. I could almost see him later on walking around town, looking into people's eyes and at their lips, trying to see if he could spot a machine hidden among the humans.

He finished his food and lit a cigar. His eyes, ash-brown, looked tired. Was life catching up with him? Was he tired of being a reader? Or was he tired of the life he lived away from the books?

The moon was up. A full moon. After drinking the soup I found myself yawning.

I heard Saul say, "Give it another month or so and I'll help you move to another place."

I nodded.

I was still a child but I knew then that I would be a fugitive for a long time.

The days went by. Repetitive days. Repetitive weeks.

With time I started to see more people. Friends of Saul. Friends of my family. They brought me books and clothes. Newspapers, too, so that I could see what was happening around the world.

"Knowledge is important. Same as information. Keep reading. Always read," said Rina, a friend of my parents.

I devoured book after book, learnt about History and science, and I went for long walks. I noticed the sky was changing colour. The world was changing, maybe dying. I ignored it all and kept on living. What else could I do?

One day I heard the news. Good news. A miracle came true.

"I spoke to your mother," Saul said. "She's back in her town."

Startled, I got up from my chair and said, "I want to go home."

We were sitting outside the cave, sunbathing. My hair was long and it had been days since I last showered. A monstrous ship was hoovering along the sky, a spaceship built for our leaders. Rumours were growing that the New Leaders and a few chosen people were thinking about moving to a new planet. Years after the Big War ended, the effects of the Red Dust and the radiation were still affecting some of the population. In areas where there were no more humans left, the animals had taken over and they ate everything, including radioactive plants. No one was really sure if the water was clean, if the food was clean, if anything was clean. Parts of the world were inhabitable but I didn't care about it. I just wanted Mother back.

"You can't. Not yet," Saul said and I found myself staring at him for a long time, almost aggressively, and it looked as if I hated him, which wasn't the case, but I wanted Mother back and he was telling me I couldn't have her.

Saul stood up and laid his hands on my shoulders.

"At least we know she's home, that she's okay. Safe. Give it a few more weeks and if all goes well she'll either come here or you will go home," he said. "Seeing that it is not safe for you to go home, most likely she'll come here instead."

Saul had a gentle voice, a voice that came truly alive whenever he read from The Book.

I felt tears in me, somewhere within me, circulating through my insides, wanting to come out, but I didn't cry.

I asked about Father but Saul wasn't really sure where he was.

I was sick of the mountains, tired of the loneliness, but the books kept me company and sane, and part of me didn't really wanted to leave that cave.

I waited for Mother to come and get me.

I waited for days, for weeks, and one morning, as I was returning from the river, I saw Mother standing outside the cave. She saw me straight away and she smiled at me. She was wearing a long dress and sandals, and her head was covered by a blue scarf. She looked more beautiful than ever. I run towards her and flung myself into her arms. Mother held me in her arms and said, "Michael."

I had missed her voice, her face.

It was a warm day but I felt my body shiver and Mother held me in her arms. I wanted to ask about Father. I wanted to ask about my real mother but I was afraid to know. I was afraid to ask. Instead I held on to that machine, that perfect replica of my mother.

The machine looked at me, into my eyes, and smiled. I looked at it and smiled back. I watched her eyes studying me. Was she (it) waiting for me to unmask her as a machine? I didn't.

I need it, that familiar face, a remembrance of the past.

That night I slept in its arms. The machine's body was warm. I wondered how it kept itself warm.

I woke up in the middle of the night screaming. Like a protective mother, the machine came running towards me and held me in its arms. I heard the voice of my mother asking, "What happened? Nightmare?"

I nodded before adding, "I dreamt the world was on fire and we were the only two people left."

The machine said nothing and just held me close to it. I felt safe in its arms.

Before falling asleep, I said, "Please, stay here with me."

"I will, Michael. I will," the machine said.

The following morning, when I woke up, the machine wasn't there by my side. I felt cold then. Scared.

What was out there waiting for me?

I got out of bed slowly, as if the slowness could prevent the inevitable from happening. The cave felt cold, like a tomb. I put on my sandals and made my way towards the entrance. The machine was standing outside, looking at me, waiting, smiling. It would never leave my side, and later, much later, just before the end, it would take me back to Mother and Father and say goodbye to all of us.

The machines were right. The Book couldn't save us. Nothing could save us from the fire and the dust.

The greatest detective of the New World

-the detective

I am in Chinatown waiting for the client to arrive, a book by Kafka by my side. Yellow pages, broken spine, a fusty smell. Everything ages, even literature. The restaurant I'm in is almost empty, but at night, when the dreamers want to escape their nightmares, this place gets quite busy. For now, as I wait and eat my noodles, unless you count the staff, there's only me in the restaurant alongside another couple. I like it here; this restaurant, this city, this new life.

I arrived in this city four years ago, a year after the Big War came to an end. Before I came here, I was in Takamatsu, Japan. Before that I was in Hadera, Israel, making sure that my side won the Big War. I didn't fight in the war. And I did. I worked behind the scenes, breaking codes, dismantling satellites, stopping cyber-attacks, drinking freshly brewed coffee, eating Falafels, Sabich, Lekach, while doing a bit of hacking, stealing, preparing for the New Life, the New World, because, once the war was over, I didn't want to go back to my old life, back to my wife, remain in my old job, wear the same old clothes, do the same old job, see the same old boring faces. What's the point of a New World, a New Life, if I was going back to the same old crap?

14

While I was still underground, watching parts of the planet being turned into ashes, I started to design a new life for me, a new life after the Big War, a new life in the New World. A lot of us could see what was coming; religion would come to an end; no good had come out of it (and the Big War had started because of different beliefs), there would be only one government, one world power controlled by businesspeople and not by politicians. Billions of people had died in the war, but there were still plenty of people left to keep the New World going. Abortion was abolished and people were told to reproduce but not to go over the top. Watching it all from behind the screen of my MicroX-PO7 laptop, sensitive screen, I came to the conclusion that I didn't want to return to my old life.

Trillions of currency that had been accumulated in different bank accounts in different parts of the world were confiscated and safeguarded by those in power, and with that money they would design their New World and use some of it to pay the wages of the same old workers. But not me. I would no longer be a part of the system. I would no longer be a technical adviser, a hacker, a spy. I would become someone else. Those in power had a "New agenda". Everything, or almost everything, would be branded New. Toronto became New Toronto. Moscow became New Moscow. California became New California. New England and New York retained the same old names.

As I've mentioned before, parts of the world became nothing but ashes. China was still China, but, because of radiation, it was almost empty and the Chinese people were scattered throughout the world.

No religion. I think I've mentioned that too.

No silly beliefs.

People had waited for far too long for a saviour to materialise out of thin air, or for a saviour to come riding through the clouds on a white horse, and now most people were tired of it all. In the New World everyone would become the same, believe the same thing, or believe in nothing at all, which was probably better than to believe in some idea that told you to kill someone who differed from you.

While I was still hiding underground, watching the submarines immerge from the sea on the various screens in front of me, I hacked here and there, stole a few millions, emailed some people, transferred some money into my wife's account so that she wouldn't have to worry about money, and once the air was completely clear and we were told we could come up, I took a flight to Takamatsu and left the past behind me once and for all. I didn't tell a soul where I was going, not even the wife. I loved her, but I didn't love her that much and I wanted a life away from it all; from everything and everyone that I knew.

In Takamatsu Dr Chen worked on my face, and a few weeks later, after the bandages were out, I met young Mieko. She was only seventeen, living in the streets, living on her own, scrounging for food, and when I saw her I took her home with me. A new life therefore I needed a new woman. My vocals were rearranged. I need a new voice, too.

I had a clean passport, a new name, taken from one of the victims of the Big War, a soldier who had lost his entire family in the Red Dust. I liked his face. I could live with his name (Jacques de Saint). Best of all, I was free to do whatever I wanted and I had Mieko by my side. After getting Mieko's paperwork in order, and after Dr Chen made sure that her veins were clean, we moved to New Toronto, into a two-bedroom apartment close to Chinatown.

For the first month Mieko and I hardly left the apartment on the daytime. We would spend our mornings in bed watching telly and then I would cook us a simple meal, and later we would go online and order bits and pieces for our apartment. Soon enough we had two bookshelves filled with books with the works of Haruki Murakami, Poe, Ballard, Soseki, Kenzaburo Oe and others on display. Mieko wanted to read about the old Japan while I wanted mystery and science-fiction.

At night we would go out, to one of the many Chinese restaurants in the area, and after a good meal we would go to a late night show, but a month later, or even less than that, once our apartment was fully refurbished, I turned to Mieko and said, "Now we need to start living. We need to have a plan."

Mieko nodded. She wanted to go back to college, do a degree in literature.

"The world will always need writers," she said and I nodded.

On that morning there were sirens rushing past our home. Looking out of the window, we saw smoke coming from a nearby restaurant.

"What about you? What will you do?" Mieko asked.

There was a book by Sir Arthur Conan Doyle on our Muji sofa; price of the sofa $307,77 dollars, price of the book 20cents. As she asked me that question my past life flashed right through my eyes, and, with my knowledge and previous experience, there was only one thing I could do.

"I'm going to become a detective. The greatest detective of the New World," I said.

"Like Columbo!" Mieko almost shouted, and afterwards she smiled and we kissed.

I didn't need much to become a detective. Only clients, and there were plenty of people in the New World who wanted to know what had happened to their family members and friends after the Big War, and soon enough I had plenty of clients begging me for my services. One of our rooms was turned into my office, but all I needed were a couple of desks, two MicroX-PO7 laptops (I only use those laptops for work, and an old Acer to watch my programs), and nothing else. The rest of the room was used for our clothes and records storage.

With the skills acquired from my previous jobs, soon I was travelling through the "clouds", digging out information, "borrowing" it from government sites, and finding out where so-and-so had died or where so-and-so was hiding.

After the Big War ended a lot of people decided to follow my example and leave their past lives behind, but they were clueless when it came to hiding their footsteps and soon enough I was finding them in New Tanzania or in London (the British didn't want any New names for their old cities), and even in New Toronto, just a couple of blocks down the road from where I live. With the money that I made from my clients I didn't even had to touch most of the money that I had taken with me from the Old World. During that time Mieko finished college and entered university, and she even wrote a couple of stories which she managed to publish in some magazine.

Anyway, enough about me. Let me slurp the last bit of noodles because the client should be arriving soon.

-the client

She's tall and thin, elegant even though she's wearing clothes that are a bit too manly, but it is quite cold outside and she has chosen comfort over style. Her nose has been reshaped, shrunken. She's in her late thirties, still a beauty. I tend not to meet my clients face to face, but sometimes I make an exception. But if I do meet with my clients, I meet them here, at the Asian Legend in Dundas Street. I always arrive a few minutes before them so that I can have a bowl of noodles. And they can pay for it.

She tells me her name but her name doesn't really matter. I already know who she is. A young Asian couple come running through the front door, running from the cold, from the snow, from nothing, and once they're inside they remove their coats and choose a table away from everyone. They're in love, young love, shy love. The boy looks nervous, a bit anxious as he sits next to the girl. As for her, she keeps her head down and smiles nervously. Young love. Most of us have been there.

The smell of fry food in the air and not a single laptop on sight. After the Big War (or Great War as some people call it) was over, a lot of people retreated into their little shells and started to share less online. Laptops were locked away or left in the privacy of their own homes, and paperbacks made a comeback. But, of course, there are others who make an extra buck by sharing their lives on YouTube.

The client interrupts my thoughts and says, "He left years ago. I don't know what happened to him."

Another couple enter the restaurant and go upstairs. I know the man but only vaguely. He works at the building opposite the one where I live. The firm he works for deals with the import of seeds. He looks bored, as if he too is in need of a new life.

"Do you miss him?" I ask.

She nods no before adding, "No. I just want to find out where he is."

"And then what will you do?" I ask.

"I'll get some men to kick the crap out of him for leaving me," she says. She means what she says.

I can hear the sound of a piano sonata by Mozart playing, the sound of cars driving past, the sound of the past, the sounds of the present.

The smell of fry food in the air, a coffee machine hissing, someone coughing.

"I'll do my best," I say. "But, from what you told me, your man was a pro, and people like him know every single trick in the book."

"I was told you can find anyone. I was told you're the best," she says.

I smile and thank her for the compliment, adding that sometimes I fail to find the person that I was hired to find.

"Some people have died in the Red Dust," I say.

"If he's dead, I'm fine with it, but I doubt it," she says and leans forward. "He knew how to hide, how to become invisible."

I nod. Of course I will find him.

-case solved

Shortly afterwards, the client leaves the restaurant. On the way out she pays for my meal and our drinks. From there I go to the bathroom. I look in the mirror and I see the man she's looking for. I smile. He smiles back at me. I have just become the greatest detective of the New World. It's time for a change in career. Maybe I should become a chef?

Of course I must tell her something. I must show her something, but I knew that this day would come, or I thought that it would come, and even if it didn't, I wanted to make sure that I was ready for it, and I am ready.

Two days later I meet her again; my ex-wife who is looking for me. I'm right here, baby. Open your eyes.

"I found him," I say. "He's dead."

I show her the records. Top secret records that I have faked. For a moment she looks to be in pain, but I know her well and I also know that it's all an act. She cares about no one else but herself.

"I'm sorry," I say. "I'm really sorry, but he died during the Great War."

A bored-looking waiter walks past us. Outside, a tram is waiting to depart. A bored blonde smokes away while sitting by the tram stop. Waiting for what? The tram is there! Maybe she's waiting for someone to arrive. And did I mention that she looks bored? The whole world looks bored. Boredom is the new fashion, a disease for the masses. Even I look bored.

"Bastards! No one told me a thing when I went looking for him," she says. The sadness in her eyes has been replaced by a cruel look. I know that look well. She never loved anyone but herself.

"Bastards!" she says it again, less loudly this time. There's no pain in her speech, no warmness, nothing at all. I looked at my watch. Mieko should be arriving soon.

She goes through the records again and again, hoping to find more clues in them, but I'm dead. I'm such a great detective that I even managed to find the dead me. Minutes later, after thanking me one more time for everything, my ex-wife leaves the restaurant. Once she's gone I order another bowl of noodles. This job is killing me.

Alfred's spasm

It was Alfred Kushner who came up with the idea of moving into another planet. With his technology, a group of men and women moved to another planet to start a new colony, a new world, a world better than New Earth, and as the crops started to grow in that new planet, a planet which they decided to call Planet X for the time being, Alfred knew that it was time for many of them to leave New Earth and join the colonists of Planet X. Addressing many of the New Leaders, Alfred said, "This planet is dying and sooner or later the machines will turn against us. There are already machines that are building other machines without us knowing the purpose of those new machines, and then, what will happen?"

"Your ancestors built the first machines and now you're telling us that it was all for nothing? Why should we listen to another Kushner?" said President Syed.

"The machines were needed then to control Mankind. After the Big War was over there was still a lot of anger in the air and those on the losing side wanted to keep on fighting, and there were others who wanted to start a revolution, demand this and demand that, so the machines served their purpose. They stopped the revolution from happening. They put an end to war. But the planet was already damaged and it doesn't show signs of fixing itself. Maybe the damage is bigger than what we think.

"As you all know, the selective secret group that we sent to Planet X have adapted themselves to a new planet quite fast, and the air is clean, same as the rivers, not to mention the seeds grow faster there," said Alfred.

"So what are you saying?" King Abdul asked.

Alfred smiled.

Everyone, including King Abdul, knew what he was saying.

"I say it's time to move," said Alfred. "It's time to get out of here."

Alfred explained to those present that in Planet X, due to the clean air, they were bound to live longer; "a lot longer," he said, and that was all he needed to say for everyone present to agree to move on.

President Syed and King Abdul wanted to know, "What about slaves? I mean workers? Who's going to do all the work?"

"We will all have to do our share, but if you want you can bring some of your people. But there's a limit, you know, there's a limit to how many people we can bring," Alfred said.

King Abdul, President Syed and a few others bored him, but Alfred had used a lot of their money for this project, so, for now, he needed to please them, but once they were in space, he would get rid of them all once and for all.

"No planet needs people like them. I'll be doing a favour to society," Alfred thought. A billionaire in his fifties, in part thanks to inheritances, sometimes Alfred thought of himself as some sort of god and he enjoyed playing with people's lives. Once in Planet X, with the help of the machines, he would be the only one in power and there would be no place in there for people like King Abdul.

"King my ass. I might give myself the title of king once we're in Planet X," he thought as he made his way to his headquarters.

The sky was brown. Little by little, slowly, like a warning, the Red Dust was travelling through the atmosphere, affecting the lungs of the people. Earth was dying, or maybe just changing, changing for the worse, and Alfred didn't want to be there to witness those changes.

Four spaceships had already been built, stocked with seeds, vitamins, fruit, medicine, etc., and their tanks were filled and ready to leave. A group of men and women had been carefully chosen for a new life in Planet X. Unknown to all, only three of the spaceships had enough fuel to go to Planet X and return to Earth in case anything went wrong. Unknown to all but Alfred and a couple of engineers he trusted.

Just like his ancestors, Alfred hated religion but, as it was already mentioned, he thought of himself as some sort of god and he liked to play with people's lives. This move to Planet X was another way of Alfred playing god, and if things failed he would return to Earth and leave everyone behind, and with some of the machines, he would rule over all. But he wanted a change. He wanted a planet with a small population where he could rule over all and make his own empire.

He sighed just then. A few minutes later, he exited the room, leaving his entourage behind, in some other room, without bothering to tell them where he was heading to. The only person he would take with him to Planet X would be Lilly, his twenty-something old lover. He would also take a ReSex-Machine for those nights when he got bored of Lilly.

As he made his way along the corridor, he decided not even to take Lilly with him. Instead of her, he would take another ReSex-Machine.

"One less mouth to feed," he thought.

A loud bang was heard, a crashing noise coming from outside, followed by more banging, but the sounds quickly died down.

"Rebels," he thought and smiled. "Humans never learn. They want equality, forgetting that men like me, the leaders of this world, can't stand equality.

"Minds like mine keep the world running. My money (and my ideas) keeps the world running.

"People want music and books, but they also want religion and fake gods, drugs and alcohol, and they have the need to worship something, someone, an invisible being, a lie, various lies, but I worship nothing but power, and it is power –MY POWER- that keeps the world running.

"People don't know how to behave without having someone telling them what to do. They need their fake gods so that they won't fall into temptation. Weak minds, I say. Feeble minds. And the New Leaders aren't much better than the common people. They have a bit more sense, a lot more money, but still…

"I could just depart on my own, with my people, and leave these idiotic New Leaders behind, but I want to teach them a lesson. I want to show them how powerful I am; how, without me, they're nothing.

"My family were the brains behind the New Earth (but the New Earth is dying), and now I'll be the strength behind Planet X. To be honest, I don't even need to move to Planet X but the New Earth is dying, and even if it wasn't there's nothing left for me to do here. I need to move somewhere else where my ego and genius can set itself free again. I might even become an author in Planet X. Its first –and only- author. I will write my memoirs and the citizens of Planet X will be my readers."

Alfred was dreaming with his eyes open. For a moment he felt like laughing, but he didn't. Truth be said, he never laughed that much, not unless he had defeated and hurt someone.

A car was waiting for him outside. Alfred got in and was taken to the headquarters in Bramalea Road, Brampton. He watched the sad eyes of a few citizens as they stared at him. Because of people like him, because of greed, there would always be poverty, but some people couldn't be helped, no matter what. Some people's souls were already lost, doomed. They would be given two choices; good or bad, and they always chose badly. Their choices weren't Alfred's fault. And he wasn't concerned with it.

As he eased down on the comfortable leather seat, he felt like a god. Right there, as he lit a cigar, he decided not to go to Planet X. How could he leave all those extravagances behind? The slaves, the coffee, the cigars, the wine, the young lovers, the power, the money? There would be none of those things in Planet X. What the hell would he do there? He would be just another person, a common citizen, a worker (and not even a good one).

Lost in his thoughts, he decided just then, "No. I won't go. I will stay here. I will send them all there and I will watch their lives from the comfort of my house. I will play god from my hideout. After all, aren't I one? Am I not a god seeing that I have the lives of others in my hands? And will this planet really end? Probably not so why this fear?"

He sat there smiling, smoking, planning.

"I can always hide in my bunker, stay away for a while if something happens, and then resurface like a god," he thought and smiled to himself.

The highway was almost empty. At the far distance, the crows stood on trees, watching, waiting, savouring. The trees seemed full of life. How could the planet be dying when Mother Nature looked so alive? Still, there was that matter of the dust and the polluted rivers and the rumours that some of the machines were building their own cities and their own machines. What then? What would happen once the machines decided to control things?

"Nah. It can't happen. It won't happen," he thought.

Alfred pressed a button. One of the windows was then lowered. A sniff and he was hit by the smell of something burning. He looked up and he saw the f-Machines fly by. Whenever someone wanted to distract the f-Machines that someone would start a fire somewhere leading the f-

Machines to that same fire, and afterwards the person that started the fire would be free to do other things that were forbidden by the New Law. One of the things forbidden by the New Law was the reading of religious books: "Religious books shall not be read or shared with others, not even in the privacy of someone's house."

The i-Machine had been created to keep an eye on the people. At first, at the beginning of the first year of the New World, the i-Machine was created to act like a guardian or even a babysitter, but as men and women returned to old ways, a more advanced i-Machine was created, a machine inspired by the Stasi, a machine built to spy and interrogate and arrest. Every machine had the Kushner stamp, and the new machines, not yet revealed to the public, were probably the best ever. Named New Supernova, they were actually spaceships, gigantic spaceships, each able to carry more than fifty people plus food storage. Only four of them had been built and only a selective group of people would get to travel on them and be transported to Planet X.

Alfred didn't like the name of Planet X. Once there he would rename the planet and call it Planet Kushner. But was he going or was he staying put? Maybe he would go for a few months, see how things were, and if he didn't like it he could always return. Of the four spaceships, three of them had enough fuel to go to Planet X ("Kushner! Planet Kushner! I will rename it," Alfred said to himself in the back of the car) and back to New Earth in case something went wrong, but one of the spaceships didn't even had enough fuel to get to Planet X and only Alfred was aware of that.

Sitting in the back of the car, still debating whether he should go or stay, Alfred came to the conclusion that it was better to leave New Earth than to stay. Sure, he would have to leave a few comforts behind, but Planet X was clean and, according to the men and women who had already taken residence there, the crops grew quite fast and the water (in Planet X) was sweet and so pure, the best water they ever had. The days lasted longer, there was no pollution, so what was the reason for him to stay behind? New Earth should be renamed Old Earth or Dying Earth. As the Red Dust and the radiation increased, soon enough only a few countries would be habitable but for how long?

"No! I'm not staying. I'm going to Planet X. Time to move on," he thought.

Still, as they made their way towards Brompton, he was having doubts, second thoughts, scary thoughts. What was wrong with him? Usually he was fearless, so determined, not to mention so selfish. He was actually proud of being so selfish, so careless, egocentric. Yes, he really didn't care about anyone but himself. That's why he was in power.

A couple of cars drove past, music blasting, and the noise disturbed his thoughts. He turned to the machine in front of him and said, "Get me a Scotch."

The machine obeyed without saying a word.

There would be no currency in Planet X, no young prostitutes, no lives to play with. In Planet X everyone was equal. Actually, when one thinks about it, a manual worker was worth more than Alfred. In Planet X everyone would have to do their share of work. Scientists, doctors, pharmacists, soldiers; everyone would have to do their share of manual work. Surprisingly, when told that, King Abdul said, "I'm up for it."

Alfred wasn't so sure about it. At his age, what would he do in Planet X? And did Abdul and Syed have something in mind? Were they trying to get rid of Alfred?

Poor fools. They didn't have a clue of what Alfred had in store for them.

"No! I won't go. Not yet. Maybe later. I'll stay behind. I'm too old for this. I will stay behind and enjoy my billions," he said before swallowing some of the whisky.

The machine just sat there staring at him, a dim smile on its face. Without a warning, or even a reason why (maybe boredom made him do it), Alfred threw the rest of his drink at the machine. Smiling, he said (to the machine), "Sorry about that. Some sort of spasm."

The machine smiled and said, "No problem, sir."

"Fix me another drink," he said coldly. He was the one who sounded like a machine. A cruel cold machine. Heartless.

The machine did as told.

As they got closer to their destination they saw more traffic. A man and a woman, both in their early forties, were standing outside the new Kushner headquarters, looking sideways, to their left, looking at nothing at all, cigarettes in between their fingers. People still smoked. As a matter of fact, for some reason, maybe stress, after the Big War the sale of cigarettes skyrocketed. Alfred recognised the man and the woman straight away. They were two of the minds behind the New Supernova. They were the ones who designed them from scratch; scratch being a "simple" idea given to them by Alfred, and with money raised by Alfred and the New Leaders, money taken from the people, the New Supernova was built. Actually they had already built the Supernova1 and Supernova2, the two spaceships built for the first citizens of Planet X, and the New Supernova, four in total, was just a slightly larger version of Supernova1 and Supernova2. Anyway, the man was called Zaffar and the woman was called Chani, and neither of them was interested in going to Planet X. They still believed New Earth could be saved and in the past both Zaffar and Chani had even said that, with time, the Red Dust and the radiation would simply disintegrate and vanish in the atmosphere.

"Silly talk," Alfred thought when Zaffar first told him that.

The wind was blowing softly and Alfred watched from the inside of his car as Chani run her right hand along her short-cropped hair. Chani and Zaffar had no children. They thought of children as a setback. Unnecessary. As for Alfred, he had a son living in New York, a son he hardly ever saw, a son he couldn't be bothered with. His son was a rock star, not a successful one, not yet, the black sheep of the family, but to be fair Alfred's son was the honest of the lot. Alfred thought of him as a "minor accident", a squirt too many.

Alfred's son, name David, 23-years old, a Virgo by birth, lived with a Mexican soap opera star and their one-year old boy in a two-bedroom apartment in SoHo. He sang the lead vocals and played the bass in a rock band called **White Sheep Follows and Gets Lost** and he also penned a few poems. And that was all one needed to know about David Kushner. But David was happy in his quiet world, happy for doing his own thing, and he couldn't see himself living a life similar to this father. And, back to Alfred, he stepped out of the car and lazily made his way towards the building in front of him. His son David was now in his thoughts. Alfred wondered what had happened to Ruth, David's mother. They went out for a couple of years but he never really loved her. She was an asset, a luxury, a pretty woman he could show off to others, but as time went by, and as she got really attached to him, he quickly grew bored of her, but then, a squirt too many, David was created.

"Accidental Dave," Alfred called him under his breath.

Last time Alfred heard about Ruth she was living in Safed, Israel, and she was happily married and had two other kids, both teenagers now. It was only a matter of time before David and his family moved to Israel. Alfred was sure of it.

Chani greeted him and Alfred mumbled something back. He wasn't really in the mood to say too much, not even a simple greeting. Mumbling would have to do.

There were leaves scattered all over the steps and Alfred wondered what the hell the cleaners were doing.

"Probably drinking cheap coffee from the canteen's machine," he thought.

At the entrance his eyes were scanned, followed by his fingertips, and then he was let in the building. Inside, the long corridor ahead was empty. Not a single soul on sight. Not a sound. Everyone was busy doing their own thing, busy inside some room doing something. The corridor walls were filled with art by the likes of Bartolomeo Montagna, Michelangelo, Daniele da Volterra, and others. At first glance a person would think they were entering an art gallery and not a government building. Most of the paintings had been acquired by the Kushner clan throughout the years. No one really knew how or when they came into the possession of such art. No one really asked how or when.

Boredom kept him company as Alfred made his way along the corridor. There was a stain in the carpet which he failed to see. A couple of cleaners were sitting in the canteen drinking cheap coffee and eating homemade sandwiches. They worked and lived there, in a small room on the lower ground. Alfred's company employed cheap labour instead of replacing them with machines. Alfred was too proud to let any of his machines do any kind of labouring. As it was mentioned before, in the beginning of the New World the i-Machine was designed to be a guardian or a babysitter, but the experienced failed as some machines failed to adapt to their roles, and there even rumours that some machines became too caring. Soon enough the Kushner Co. called back all machines, changed a few details inside them, and a new, more efficient i-Machine was sent to the New World, a machine built to spy and, if needed, impose the law. Sometimes Alfred felt as if he, too, was a machine. Cold, with bolts inside him and not love. Wires instead of blood.

The i-Machine was perfect. Too perfect as a matter of fact. Scary perfect.

Not so long ago a few machines had gone missing in Arizona, and, when asked what had happened, a machine that stayed behind said that the machines were building different machines; machines that couldn't be built by humans. Todd McCarthy and Bruce Spencer, the brains behind the new i-Machines, didn't know what to make of it. But if machines were building machines without the knowledge (or help) of any humans that couldn't be good news.

When asked by Bruce why the machines were building more machines the machine said, "I don't think they trust the human race. I was told the human race intends to destroy itself and it is better, for the human race, if the machines take over the world before any more damage is done, not only to the human race but also to the planet."

Alfred and some leaders were present when this interrogation took place and they couldn't believe what they were hearing. A man stood up and walked out of the room, only to return seconds later with a cup of coffee. He was bored and tired, and needed the caffeine to keep him awake.

"And why didn't you go with those machines? Why did you stay behind?" Bruce asked.

The machine shrugged its shoulders and said, "I don't know. I think I felt what you call fear."

"Fear?" Bruce asked and then he looked around, at the faces around him, at the leaders and engineers and scientists and whoever was present, and he waited for someone to say or ask something, but no one said a word, and when he saw that no one present had anything to say, he addressed the machine again and asked, "Do you feel fear?"

The machine looked confused, even surprised, and after giving it some thought, it said, "I feel something."

"What do you feel?" Bruce asked.

"Something," the machine replied.

That happened close to two months ago and during that time more machines disappeared. But where had they gone?

Bruce had no more questions to ask. Instead he just sat there, staring wide-eyed at the machine. A few minutes later, after the machine had exited the room, he told the others, "Let's dismantle that machine." But the machine was never again seen once it left the room.

"Yes, this machine business doesn't look good," Alfred thought just as he reached the end of the corridor and entered one of the hangars. He was greeted by the sight of four luminous spaceships, all resembling the Eagle Transporter, the fictional spacecraft seen in the television series *Space 1999*.

A group of men and women were pacing around the hangar, making sure that all was in order. Others stood still or moved around slowly as they checked if everything was in order too. Black crows stood on top of the glass ceiling looking down on the people. Some of the crew didn't like the crows and complained about them, saying that they were a bad omen, while others took no notice of the birds. A short blonde-haired woman stood next to one of the New Supernovas entering data from her computer into the spaceship system. A blue light was seen shining along the cable that was connected from the computer to the spaceship and Alfred grew even more bored as he watched the short blonde at work. He walked past her without saying a word and entered the spaceship. The woman's name was Linda. She was a scientist and a bit of a hippie, a free spirit. She lived nearby, or she slept nearby, in a camping van with her girlfriend, a dark haired woman named Sue who was also part of the crew that had built and were putting the final touches to the spaceships. Sometimes both women slept in one of the free rooms in the hangars and one time they even slept in one of the New Supernovas. And they made love there, too.

Neither of those two women wanted to go to Planet X. They were happy in New Earth, happy travelling around from state to state, building new things, and they believed that the planet could still be cleaned and saved, but even if they were wrong, they would still rather die there, at home, and not in some distant strange planet away from their families and friends and their two cats. Sue was a pessimist. She believed that, no matter where they were, humans were bound to destroy themselves. Linda was a humanist. She believed in love, in happy stories. Surprisingly, or maybe not, in bed she was the one who took control. Sue wasn't always Sue. Years ago she was called Neil, but one day she changed sex and her name.

Alfred walked along the spaceship for a few minutes. It was a thing of beauty. A large family could live in it for a long time and never get bored. One of the programmes in the machines contained more than 50000 books, and that included banned books by the likes of Kenzaburo Oe and Henry Miller, Alfred's favourite authors. Plenty of movies and TV shows that one could watch, too. Yes, the New Supernova was really super.

A group of four men and one woman were inside the spaceship checking a few minor details. One of the men used to be a Chess champion in his teens but he had quit playing long time ago. Once upon a time he used to have long curly hair but now he was almost bald. For some reason everyone called him Moby even though his name was Stephen. He was one of those assigned to go to Planet X. The woman in the group was Moby's wife. She too was moving to Planet X. As of yet they had no children but they planned to have at least one child once they were in Planet X. Secretly they hope to have the first child of Planet X, a child they would either name Xana (for girl) or Xavier (for boy).

Alfred stayed in there for ten minutes or so, watching and listening, and he nodded twice when addressed by Moby. The boredom was with him. He needed an escape from it. From there he would go home where Lilly would be waiting for him.

He found one of the cleaners in the corridor cleaning the dust of the paintings, and another cleaner outside sweeping up the leaves. He ignored both cleaners as he made his way down the steps. The machine was standing outside looking at the sky. For a moment she looked almost human. Her given name was Rose. She wore a blue suit, a white shirt, and dark sandals. Upon seeing Alfred coming down the steps, the machine smiled and opened the car door to let Alfred in. He brushed past the machine, almost pushing her out of the way. The machine kept on smiling, and once Alfred was inside the car Rose shut the door. He then turned to the driver and ordered, "Drive on."

The car was driverless, controlled either by Alfred's voice or even by a command by the machine he'd just left behind. The vehicle could navigate without human input and although it was an old invention the Kushner@ had produced its own (and more modern and reliable) version. The car drove on and Alfred smiled. A few meters ahead he said, "Stop! We forgot someone."

Rose hadn't yet moved. She had watched as the car drove on without her and then she watched it stop only a few meters from where she was. Little particles of dust were still floating in the air, floating around. She saw it. She felt it.

Rose looked at the dust on her feet. Later she would get some wipes and cleanse herself.

Alfred sat in the car waiting impatiently for the machine. He liked to play games with the machines, show them who was in control. But he didn't go too far with the machines. They scared him and he knew what the machines were capable of.

Rose smiled when she opened the passenger's door and Alfred apologised, saying, "I'm sorry. I'm so sorry. I was so distracted that I told the driver to go without you."

Rose the machine smiled and said, "That's okay."

She was pretty but boring, a perfect face "stolen" (or borrowed) from Garbo, created solely for Alfred.

Rose sat down facing Alfred, a little smile running along her face. A pretty smile but boring, lifeless. The car drove on, towards Alfred's place, past what looked to be like abandoned buildings but there were people living in many of those rooms. A couple of silhouettes at the far distance, two men cycling. As the car got closer to the men, Alfred saw that the men dressed alike; black trousers, black shoes, white shirts and they even wore a tie. Both men were quite young, early twenties, maybe less, and they both smiled at a confused Alfred as the car drove past them. They headed towards one of those supposedly abandoned buildings and Alfred turned around to take one last look at them.

"Elders?" Alfred said to no one in particular. Then, looking at Rose, he said, "Did you saw those men? They looked like Elders! Mormons! But religion is forbidden!"

Rose's smile grew wider. She looked confident, so sure of herself, so human, a bit bitchy. And as her smile grew, her beauty also seemed to grow, and for a moment it even looked as if she was becoming less machine and more human. Alfred didn't like that smile but he didn't say a word about it. What could he say to the machine? Order it to smile less? He could, couldn't he? But should he?

He heard Rose say, "Humans don't change. They need to believe in something. Someone to follow or else they will get lost."

Alfred looked at her without knowing what to say. And what was she saying?

The driverless car drove at a steady speed, slowing down when some kind of animal crossed the road. It could see obstacles ahead and detect life around it. A few cars drove by, manual driven. Not everyone could afford a Kushner@ driverless car.

Finally Alfred said something: "Do you believe there's something out there? Some kind of Creator? A G-d?"

The machine said, "Someone created us but someone created life too. Man created the machine but who created Man?"

"After the Big War I think we all came to the conclusion that there is no G-d, no saviour or whoever is supposed to come and save us all," Alfred said.

"When you say "we all came to the conclusion" you're only referring to a small group of people," Rose said.

Alfred said nothing. The machine was starting to bore him. In fact it was getting on his nerves. And he couldn't believe that he was actually having a conversation about religion and life and creation with a machine. What did the machine knew about life? Nothing.

Nothing at all.

Ignoring Alfred's silence and moodiness, the machine said, "The majority of the people will keep on believing, and even if that majority turns into the minority, those who believe are the only ones who will survive."

What the hell was the machine talking about?

The car slowed down to let a flock of sheep cross the road. A confused Alfred looked at the sheep. He opened the car window and heard singing. Two young shepherds were whistling something by Led Zeppelin.

What the hell was happening to the world?

He looked at Rose and saw her smiling as she stared at the sheep. What did the machine felt then? And could the machine even feel something?

For some reason things seemed to be going from bad to worse. But why? Alfred had it all planned but he was having doubts. Or did he? And was he?

He was going to Planet X and live a happy life.

Was he really?

Doubts seemed to be coming in from all directions, doubts and questions and even fear.

"Fear of what?" he wondered as the car finally moved forward at the slowest of speeds. There was nothing to fear, nothing at all. He had it all planned, his own space opera. His plan was to put President Syed and King Abdul ("and the rest of the gang") in the spaceship with less fuel and then watch it adrift in space once the spaceship had run out of fuel. He would watch it all from the comfort of his own spaceship or maybe from somewhere else, and he would play god with the lives of those people. Of the four spaceships, three would arrive safely in Planet X (because Alfred the egocentric wanted so) but the spaceship carrying the new leaders would never get to its destination (because Alfred with his god complex didn't want so). Mass murder Alfred style. He smiled at the thought of it.

There were cameras hidden inside the spaceship and Alfred could almost see himself in the comfort of his house (was he staying?) watching the despair of the other men and women as they slowly drifted towards death. To celebrate his Machiavelli plan he drank another scotch and ignored Rose for the rest of the trip. The damn machine was starting to give him the creeps and he couldn't wait to get home and see Lilly. A smooth drive the rest of the way but when he got home Lilly was nowhere to be seen. She was gone, taking most of her stuff with her apart from a few dirty items left in the washing basket. She left a note behind, on top of the coffee table, four words written,

You make me sick

Alfred read the note once. Just once. If he wanted to, he could find her, but then what? She was free to do as she pleased.

Rose walked past him without saying a word and went to her bedroom. She was with him mostly as a guide, a companion, a servant, but there were times when the machine looked bored, even angry. Somehow some machines were changing. Bruce Spencer had even once said, "As scaring as this may sound, at times it looks as if some machines are developing feelings, such as boredom and even anger."

"Impossible," a British New Leader then said in his most impeccable British accent before puffing on his cigar. "Machines don't have feelings. Damn, neither do some of us."

He then laughed loudly, to himself mostly, while Bruce sat in the room looking at a dismantled machine.

A machine called Claude came over to where Alfred was. At home Alfred spent most of his time with machines and Lilly, but now that she was gone he would have to do with the machines. Alfred preferred to spend time with the machines than with humans as he didn't trust his fellow human being that much. The machines could be manipulated, controlled, even dismantled, but the human always had an opinion to give, an argument to start, and once he was home, Alfred liked to be in silence so that his brain could think things better and do more work. Alfred was an egocentric but he was also a genius and his brain needed silence and peace of mind to do some work.

Silently, the machine took Alfred's coat and shoes and put them away, and then brought him his slippers. Alfred sat on the sofa and lit a cigar. He smiled then as he relieved the previous night with Lilly. He'd given her a bit of a spanking and that's probably why she left him. He wasn't bothered or even upset. Just bored.

Outside, the sun was still shining but he could see a few clouds approaching. The Planet needed rain, lots of it, a lot of rain to wash away the dirt, but the rain never seemed to be enough. Or maybe there was just too much dirt lying around.

From where he was he could see the hills and the mountains, the horses in the field.

His horses. His field.

How could he leave all this behind and move into a boring planet? And what would he do for fun on Planet X? There his money wouldn't be worth a thing while on New Earth he was a king, a self-made god. How could he leave all that behind and become nobody?

He stood up and made his way along his quarters. What a place he had there. A palace fit for a king. Was he ready to leave it all behind and move to some silly planet where pleasure was restricted? He found himself standing outside Rose's bedroom. He pushed the door open without bothering to knock and found the machine sitting in bed, undressed, cleaning the dust of her body. He found himself staring at it, at that perfect creation, and he felt aroused by it.

The machine looked at him and said, "Please wait outside."

He couldn't believe what he was hearing. Was the machine embarrassed? Ashamed of being caught naked? But it was a machine! A thing! Things weren't supposed to feel, never mind being embarrassed by being caught naked. Nevertheless he did as told and stepped back slowly, and then he waited outside for a few seconds before retreating back to the living room. Peeved (but why?), he told Claude to prepare him dinner. The machine made its way to the kitchen while Alfred went to his room to get changed. In his bedroom he couldn't get the image of a naked Rose out of his head. The damn machine really was perfect. Later he ate dinner alone and later at night he fell asleep on the sofa. The two machines came into the living room and watched him for a while as he snored loudly. From there they went back to their respective bedrooms where they switched themselves off for a few hours. While "switched off" Rose saw flashbacks of its previous life. Was the machine actually dreaming?

No. No. That wasn't possible.

Or was it?

No. No...

The following morning Alfred found Rose standing outside, in front of the swimming pool, looking a bit lost in its (her?) thoughts as it looked at the hills ahead. The damn machine looked almost human and Alfred didn't like that.

The machine heard footsteps behind it and took a few steps back, away from the edge of the pool, and then it turned around and produced a feeble synthetic smile when face to face with Alfred. He looked at it, at that smile, at that "product" standing in front of him, and he didn't know what to make of it. He thought of what to say to it but he couldn't find any words to say. In the end he went back inside the house without saying a word. As for Rose, it stood outside for a long time contemplating the hills, looking as if it was looking for something, waiting for someone, at least a signal.

Alfred stayed indoors for hours taking care of business, the radio on, classical music playing softly in the background. He had Chinese food for lunch and later looked at some porn online. Without Lilly by his side he felt a bit lonely. The only company he had were the two machines, Claude and Rose, and they bore the hell out of him. Nevertheless, seeing that they were all he had, he logged off and went into the living room to check on the machines. Claude was there, standing by the kitchen door, just standing there doing nothing, waiting for orders, waiting for nothing. All curtains in the living room were open but every single window was closed. The room smelled of staleness, of nothing.

The walls of the living room were painted a lame green and Alfred felt bored just by looking at it. Yes, boredom had come to stay. It had implanted itself on him, in his system. He needed to get away for a while, go out and see some people, maybe get himself a young prostitute. Prostitution was still around, legalized now, and the prostitutes were checked on a weekly basis for any signs of disease. Alfred looked at the clock on the wall. Middle of the afternoon then. And where the hell was Rose?

"Where's Rose?" a bored Alfred asked.

"She went out for a walk. To visit other machines," Claude said.

"Visit other machines?" Claude asked.

"Yes," Claude replied lamely.

"What do you mean visit other machines?" Alfred couldn't believe what he was hearing. He advanced slowly towards Claude who remained on his seat.

Nothing was happening outside. Or almost nothing. A bird flew by, a few leaves flew in the air, but nothing else was happening.

"Since when do machines visit other machines? And what do machines do? Drink coffee and chat?" a visible disturbed Alfred asked. He felt a drop of sweat run down his face. Claude saw it; that single drop of sweat, a sign of Alfred's humanity. And weakness.

The machine sat there staring at Alfred for a few seconds without answering him, looking as if it was analysing Alfred, studying him, judging him, and by the looks the machine was giving him, Alfred was guilty of something.

"Machines talk to each other, yes, but they don't drink coffee," Claude finally replied.

Alfred still couldn't believe what he was hearing. Not only that, he also didn't like what he was hearing.

He was thirsty. His mouth was dry.

He was tired. His forehead felt cold.

He looked at the machine without knowing what to say. His brain was still trying to make some sense of what he was hearing.

"And what do machines talk about?" Alfred asked.

"To be quite frank, I don't know as I've never attended a machine meeting," Claude replied.

"And why not?"

"I've never been invited to one."

After that Alfred asked no more questions. He felt like going out but it was still early, too early to go to the places he wanted to go, the places where only people like him could afford to go to, so he went back to his bedroom where he grabbed a copy of *In Praise of Shadows* by Junichiro Tanizaki, and then he read for a few minutes while lying in bed before shutting his eyes. He woke up an hour later wrenched in sweat, the book lying underneath his face, almost glued to his skin. By then the moon was already up, and later, after showering and having changed his clothes, he found Rose in the living room. The machine was reading a book by David Levy, a banned book called *Love & Sex With Robots*. That copy belonged to Alfred as he owned a lot of banned books. As for Claude, he was sitting in the kitchen, eyes closed, probably just waiting for an order. Looking at Rose, Alfred wondered if the machine could really understand what it was reading.

Alfred was in one of those moods again; snappy, edgy. When he saw that the machine called Rose hadn't yet greeted him, he grew even angrier, angry to then point of becoming almost violent towards the machine. As a matter of fact, when he got close to Rose, he snapped the book out of her hands with such force that a bit of paper stayed attached to her fingers.

"Come on! Let's go out!" he ordered loudly while Rose looked at the bit of paper in her fingers. She stood up and said nothing as she followed him out of the house.

It was a cool evening and Rose wore a large coat over her stylish suit. The sandals had been replaced by flat black shoes. She wore those clothes not because she was cold (she wasn't) but to look more human and to make others feel less uncomfortable around her. No one could tell she was a machine but she also made sure to act (and dress) like a human so as not to attract any unwanted stares. True, the machine was a bit quiet, too quiet even for a machine of her make, but she hadn't always been like that. But somehow, as she started to gather more information and spending more time amongst humans, especially around a loud man like Alfred, the machine called Rose changed. Or did the changes started to happen when she went to the meetings? And didn't the machine used to be something else? Another machine but reprogrammed?

Alfred sat down with Rose facing him. As he looked at her he pictured her naked, and, as before, he became aroused. To his shame he found himself once more lusting for that thing in front of him, for a machine, and then he heard a voice say, "Take off your shoes."

It was his voice ordering the machine to remove her shoes.

The machine obeyed his orders.

Alfred opened his legs and said, "Lay your feet here, in front of my legs, next to my crotch," he said and a mischievous grin appeared on his face.

The machine looked him in the eye. For a moment she looked human.

For a moment it looked as if she had doubts.

For a moment, for a split second, it looked as if she was about to disobey her "master", but, as usual, she did as told and laid her feet on his seat. Unable to control himself, Alfred reached for those perfect feet and touched them slowly. The machine had soft skin, a perfect skin without a single fault. Her toes were small and perfect, and Alfred ran his fingers along her toes. Then, to the discomfort of the machine (but could the machine feel?), Alfred rubbed his crotch against her feet and became even more aroused. He felt the machine go tense (but could she feel?), and when he looked up, into the machine's eyes, he saw a strange look in her eyes, a look of suspicion. He glared at her for a few seconds, cheeks burning, maybe of embarrassment, maybe shame, before letting go of her feet. The machine glanced at her feet for a few seconds before putting her shoes back on. As for Alfred, he lit a cigar and said nothing as he looked at the window. They saw lights at the far distance. Signs of life.

Soon they were in Chinatown, the car moving slowly along the traffic. The car moved forward, out of Chinatown, towards another area of the city. Alfred wanted a woman but then he changed his mind and decided to have a sex-bot instead. They were more expensive than a real woman but money was no worry for him and he wanted for Rose to watch him have sex with a machine.

They went to Casa Tusk, a whorehouse with a difference, a whorehouse where the prostitutes were machines. There were men aplenty, and even women, who preferred to have sex with a machine than with a human. Alfred wasn't like that but, because of Rose, he fancied a change. The machine called Rose was doing something to him. What it was he didn't know. But because of whatever Rose was doing to him, he wanted a machine for the night and he wanted for Rose to see what he could do with a machine (and what he could do to her).

The street lights by Casa Tusk were of a different colour, a different brightness. The place looked to be busy as there were plenty of driverless cars parked outside, many of which Alfred recognised. The same old devils came to the same old places. He stepped out of the car and said, "Come with me."

Rose followed him silently, her long coat unbuttoned.

A human opened the door for them even before they reached the entrance. The human was female, blue-eyed, aged 25, a recently published poet. A few months before there had been a huge demand for new poetry, but it quickly died off and the female blue-eyed poet needed to make a living somehow so she remained at her job in Casa Tusk. She only did the door; opening, closing, greeting, smiling, and that was it. It paid a lot more than waitressing. For a while, this in the past, even before the Big War happened, the machines stole a lot of jobs from the humans, jobs like waitressing, cleaning, etc., but once the big companies saw that they were losing out because there weren't enough people to purchase the goods, the demand for the working machine quickly died off, leaving the machine out of work, ready to be dismantled or recycled. Machines like Rose were a different type of machine. They were almost human, perfect, more like an asset, something to show off. Rose was a Z-7, the most perfect of machines, the creation of Zack Kushner's mind. She was the machine that everyone wanted, the woman that didn't exist. It's no wonder that Alfred was losing his mind over her. Once they were seen by the receptionist; human, also female, 42-years old of age, they were given a key to room 2 and off they went.

Casa Tusk was nothing special but it was clean and safe, and that was all that mattered.

The walls in the corridor were plain, painted green, nothing on them, but the people didn't came there to look at art on the walls or whatever. The carpet was red, cleaned every morning by a cleaning machine, a moronic machine as they were called. Alfred wondered then how many machines were in that house and if they outnumbered the humans. He heard laughter. Human laughter, of course, coming from one of the rooms. More laughter, more than one man. Probably a couple of blokes sharing a machine. He looked at Rose and smiled but the machine wasn't even looking at him. He stopped outside a door, a big 2 in front of him, and he looked at it. He opened the door and then held it open for Rose.

"After you, princess," he said and smiled.

This time the machine gave him a quick look. Nevertheless, she said nothing. She went in and Alfred followed her. He made sure to lock the door behind them, and when he turned around he saw Rose standing in front of another machine, one not as perfect as Rose even though the other machine was also good looking. Both machines said nothing as they measured one another. Of the two, Rose looked to be the most curious one. Alfred stood there too, watching them, but the whole measuring contest only lasted a few seconds and Rose soon stepped away from the other machine. It was Alfred's turn to face the machine. He reached for her hand and led her to bed. Then, turning to Rose, he said, "Have a seat..." a short pause, "...and watch."

The other machine undressed Alfred and then it asked him what he wanted, what he preferred to do. And while they were undressing one another and then rolling in bed, Rose was watching. When Alfred entered the machine he looked to his right to see Rose's expression. She sat there, impassive, her hands on the arms of the sofa chair. But if her face looked unchanged, her body looked tense.

Alfred smiled as he possessed the other machine. After a while he forgot about Rose and just enjoyed himself, but minutes later, when he remembered to look up, he saw Rose browsing through a book, something written by Stanislaw Lem: *The Futurological Congress*. Alfred became a bit furious, maybe even jealous, but he ignored her. When he was finished with the other machine, he went to the bathroom for a quick shower. Only then did Rose diverted her attention from the book and looked up. She saw Alfred making his way to the bathroom, moving his body with brute sloppy movements. Once he was out of sight, the water running down his body, Rose went over to where the other machine was. The machine was spitting the liquid out of her mouth, liquid left in her by Alfred. Rose looked at her for a few seconds and then went back to her seat.

On the way home neither of them said a word for the next fifteen minutes or so. Alfred felt good, satisfied, but when he looked at Rose he felt a bit annoyed, even upset. He wanted to slap her, possess her, and afterwards he wanted to dismantle her piece by piece to show her that he was her boss. That day would probably come sooner rather than later but why did he felt such hatred towards Rose? Maybe he just wanted to play god, show to the machine that without him she was nothing. He didn't like the way Rose sometimes behaved, almost acting as if she was independent, free. Claude, his other machine, wasn't like that. True, he was an inferior machine, weaker, easier to dismantle, easier to destroy, while Rose was one of the more modern machines, more human-like, more resistant, almost perfect.

Too perfect? he wondered.

He wanted to know more about these meetings between the machines but he felt too embarrassed to ask Rose about it. What was the matter with him? He was supposed to be the one in control, the one who voiced the orders, the master, god-like (even if it was only in his head), and there he was, scared of asking a single question to a machine, a machine built by his company.

"GET ME A SCOTCH!" he said loudly.

The machine didn't even flinch and did as told. Still angry (but why?), which kind of annoyed him because he hated to display how he really felt to others, he slapped the machine as hard as he could on her face ("Its face! Its face! It's not a human being."), but the machine didn't drop the glass. Nevertheless the machine looked up, into his eyes, and he could see something there, in her eyes, something but what?

"Sorry!" he was quick to apologise. Was he scared of Rose? It sure sounded that way. "That damn spasm. I'm sorry. I'm so sorry."

Still, Rose said nothing. There was something wrong with her. And was that anger in her eyes? Defiance?

She put away the glass and smiled.

"That's okay," she said softly, almost sounding as if she was making fun of him, mocking him, defying him, daring him to do it again, slap her (it) again, and he sure felt tempted to do it again, slap her one more time, but he thought better about it and remained quiet for the rest of the journey.

As for Rose, she put away the glass and never fixed him that drink. It almost looked as if she was telling him to fix his own drink.

He felt his cheeks burning. This had happened before; his cheeks burning in front of Rose, and he really was starting to hate the way he felt around that machine.

He sat there looking at her without saying a word. In his mind he had already decided that soon the machine would be dismantled piece by piece, and he wanted to be there when that happened. He wanted to be there so that he could look into the machine's eyes and smile. He was her god, the god of the machines. She'd forgotten it but sooner or later, sooner rather than later, he would remind her of it.

Once home, they both went their separate ways.

Claude was sitting in the kitchen, motionless, switched off, waiting silently for a command. Some days Alfred didn't even bother with him but Rose was becoming a different matter. The bloody machine turned him on and he hated having feelings for it. He wanted to cut right through the machine and have its wires hanging in his fingers and then switched it off completely, but that would have to wait as he had more important matters to sort out.

On the following day he stayed home all morning locked in his office and while he was there, in the privacy of his office, he completely forgot about Rose. Well, maybe not completely but he had come to the conclusion that the machine was nothing. Another week or so and he would have it completely dismantled and then melted, and just before he put an end to the machine he would say to it (to Rose), "I will turn what's left of you into an ashtray."

Yes, Alfred was the human (?), the master, and he couldn't wait to show it to Rose. But business first.

On that morning Moby tele-screened him to let him know that they were all ready to go. Every single New Supernova was furnished, filled, stocked to the top, and ready to depart. Moby was smiling while his lazy cat took a nap on the sofa. The cat, nameless (Moby just called him

Cat), would go with him to Planet X. Rays of sunlight were coming through Alfred's window and he felt the warm heat on his back. A feeling of longing came over him. He had spent most of his life in that house and he couldn't see himself living anywhere else, especially in a faraway planet where he would have nothing to do apart from manual work. His body and mind no longer were suitable for that. From the deepest corner of his soul he heard a voice say, "I'm not going. Not yet."

Moby had figured that out long time ago but he said nothing about it. Men like Alfred weren't meant to go into another planet as settlers or explorers. It's just wasn't in their blood.

Trying to gain face, Alfred said, "Notice I said not yet. I still have a lot of important matters to deal with; personal matters, businesses, but me and my crew will go later on."

Moby nodded and said nothing. To be fair, Alfred had served his purpose.

In the next few days a lot of the New leaders would also say no to a move to Planet X, but a few would move on. Neither of those who said no would admit to it but the reason why they stayed behind was because they couldn't bear to live without their Earth comforts.

Seeing that there was nothing else to talk about Moby said bye, awkwardly, and went back to work as there were still a few minor details to deal with. As for Alfred, he went back to work too. Or he tried to do some work, but something was bothering him, slightly troubling him, and he found it hard to concentrate and deal with other matters. Nevertheless, after a bit of effort, he still managed to do a bit of work. After a while the good weather called out for him so he went out, outside, to the swimming pool, for a swim. On the way there he walked past Rose's room. As he got closer to her door, he slowed down. He remembered the day that Rose was first assembled and brought to his place. Rose used to be another machine that went by the name of Alice, a slightly lower version of the machine that she's now, but something had gone wrong with Alice and she had to be brought back to Kushner Dream Factory and be reassembled again. Her former memory was wiped out, a few bits were taken out, a few more bits were added in, and a more advanced machine was put together and brought to Alfred's house. Rose was so perfect that it was hard to tell her from a human being. From day one it was plain to see that she was completely different from Claude. While the other machine was slow Rose moved steadily along Alfred's place. She would follow him along the carpeted corridors of his house with an alert (or even studious) look in her eyes, replying (or nodding) to his every order in a calm manner, but in a matter of weeks she started to change. One morning Alfred went looking for her and found her resting/recharging in the spare bedroom. Surprised by the fact that she'd taken the room without saying a word to him, her asked her loudly, "What are you doing here?"

The machine was sitting in bed, and, without even bothering to look at him, it replied, "This room is never used apart for storage so I will use it as my sleeping quarters."

She wasn't asking for his permission to use the room. She was telling him that from then onwards she was going to use the room.

Egocentric Alfred with his god-complex just stood there staring at the machine without knowing what to say. In the end he walked away and said nothing. And Rose kept that room for herself.

Later on came the early escapades. Rose would get up in the middle of the night and disappear for a couple of hours, leaving Alfred alone with appalling boring Claude, a servant, moronic machine. To begin with, Alfred didn't even knew of Rose's nightly walks, but one morning, around 1AM, as he stood smoking by the balcony, he saw Rose stepping out of the house and disappear in the darkness. Startled by her sudden appearance (and disappearance), he rushed into her bedroom only to find it empty. He stood by the entrance of her room for a few good minutes, wondering what the hell was happening. He found two books by the bedroom table; *Moral Machines* by Wendell Wallach, and *Our Final Invention* by James Barrat, an old subject (?), and he wondered if Rose understood what she was reading. Funnily enough (but he didn't know it then) those weren't even the books that Rose had been reading. She had browsed through them briefly but then her eyes fell on Murakami's *South of the border, West of the sun*, and she read that one instead. The machine read and understood what she (it?) was reading. But did she feel the words she was reading?

For the next few weeks, Alfred caught sight of Rose stepping out into the night three more times, but not once did he dare to ask the machine where she was going. Even then, Rose the machine kind of scared him. Maybe that's why he felt so attracted towards it.

Bored (he'd been bored for the last few days), he moved on and headed to the swimming pool. Claude, the inferior machine, was there, standing by the edge of the pool, looking at who knows what. Upon seeing the machine a bored Alfred decided then to push it into the pool. He'd done that before to a couple of other machines, same model as Claude; inferior, unable to survive vast amounts of water. Rose was the opposite. If needed, she could even swim or go a few meters under water.

Alfred liked to have inferior machines like Claude around him. It gave him an even bigger god-complex to have such inferior creations around him.

The machine fell on the water and then it tried in vain to get out of the pool, but soon enough its insides were being affected by the vast quantities of water. It really was an inferior machine.

Claude moved its inferior arms as best as it could, and when he got to the edge of the pool Alfred pushed him back into the pool and then he let out a loud laugh as he watched the machine starting to spit water from its mouth. A few minutes later, the machine sank down. Alfred laughed, but then he felt as if he was being watched; he felt someone's eyes on him, and when he turned around he saw Rose standing behind the window watching him, her hands pressed against the window. How long had the machine been there watching him put an end to another machine?

He felt his body go cold then. As for Rose, she looked to be visibly upset. It was clear to see that she'd witnessed it all.

Panicking (and confused), Alfred stood still for a few seconds without knowing what to do. When Rose dropped out of view he was still there, still looking confused. A crow's cry brought him back down to Earth. He looked up and saw the black bird on top of the roof, watching him and the sinking machine with its little eyes. The crow remained there for a few minutes, its head moving to the left and to the right. Alfred ignored the bird and went back inside the house. The first thing he did was call someone to come and clean his pool. Laughing on the phone, he said, "My bloody robot decided to go for a swim."

The man on the other line was quiet for a few seconds and his silence bothered Alfred. Finally the man said, "I'll get someone to go there."

"Make it quick!" Alfred snapped and the call ended.

He put the phone down. The house felt cold. Abandoned. The green curtains were wide open with rays of sunlight coming through the glass doors, but the place was too damn quiet. The silence bothered him. First, he had been bothered by the man's silence, the man on the phone, and then by the silence around him.

He moved on quietly along the carpeted floor. As he made his way along the house, he voice-texted someone and asked for another machine to be delivered as soon as possible, same make as Claude. To him everything was replaceable.

He went into Rose's room. The silence bothered him. It really did. The house had always been quiet but only then did he felt bothered by the silence. Unwanted on that day —but desired most of the time- the silence felt like a warning; the calm before the storm, as they say.

Rose wasn't in the room. He didn't expect her to be. Nevertheless he called out for her, softly, like a child calling out for his mother. Hearing nothing —and seeing no one- he looked around the room. There was a book on top of the bed; *A World Erased* by Noah Lederman. The damn machine was always reading. Did the machine even enjoy reading? It probably did. Why else would she read so much? And what did the machine thought of as it read those words in those books? Alfred would ask her ("IT!") once he found her ("IT!"). But the machine wasn't home. And the driverless car was gone. And the damn crow wouldn't shut up.

He had to get out of the house.

The road ahead was dead quiet. A truck had driven past him shortly after Alfred had left the house but afterwards he didn't saw a car for miles. He was driving a manual car, a Jaguar E-Type, music on, a CD by The Polyamorous Affair playing; *Bolshevik Disco*. He got onto them years ago when he was listening to a pirate radio station.

He was heading towards his office. He needed to get away and he wanted to contact some people and arrange for Rose to be dismantled. The machine had seen too much. Worst of all, the machine seemed to be having thoughts and egocentric Alfred couldn't put up with it.

Naked trees to his left.

Naked trees to his right.

Dust and nothingness.

Nothingness followed by noise.

The loud noise of sirens.

He slowed down to let the cops drive past him, not knowing that they were actually coming for him.

Irritating noise.

He already missed his silent house. He would never see that house again.

The cops told him to pull over. An irritated Alfred looked dumbfounded at them. Didn't they know who he was? Of course they knew. He had a special plate and if the cops had had the trouble to check his number plate they would see who he was. Men like him didn't get stopped by the cops. Nevertheless he did. And he stopped the car.

Alfred pulled over and puffed.

"What do these clowns want? Surely they must know who I am?" Alfred thought.

Two police cars. Four cops.

Two cops for each car.

Two human cops.

Two machine cops.

Man and machine working together.

The machines had the Kushner@ logo somewhere, inside of them, designed by Kushner workers.

"What is it?" he almost shouted.

One of the human cops told him to step out of the car. The cop's name was James. The other human cop was a woman named Kay. The machines were called John and Mauro.

"You know who I am, don't you?" Alfred asked harshly.

"Yes, Mr Kushner, I know who you are," James told him.

Alfred was about to say something else when John and Kay pinned him against the car and handcuffed him.

The car metal felt cold.

The cuffs on his wrists felt cold.

Everything else felt wrong.

"What in heaven's name do you think you're doing?" Alfred shouted.

No one replied.

He felt a strong hand gripping his wrists and shoving him in the back of the car. He knew straight away that it was one of the machines.

He was still protesting when the door was slammed shut.

The cops were talking but he couldn't hear a word of what they were saying. Then he started shouting but they couldn't hear him either.

What was happening?

Mistaken identity?

But they knew who he was!

The other two cops got in the car and drove off.

He watched them leave.

In the path to their left a dozen crows were eating a dead wolf.

"What is happening?" he thought to himself as the police car he was in followed the other car.

"What is happening?" the words kept repeating themselves, sounding like a sad chorus in a sad love song. Ironically the cops were listening to a sad love song sang by Faye Wong.

"Is this a joke? Is this a fucking joke?" Alfred swore for the first time in years. Worst of all, he swore in a court. After the words were out of his mouth, the machines and the humans looked at him.

"No. No joke," the lawyer said.

He was the only lawyer present. No need for another one, certainly not one to defend guilty Alfred.

"And can you please mind your language?" the lawyer said.

He knew Alfred well. Sometimes they played squash together. Yes, he knew Alfred well. In his eyes Alfred was already guilty (and then there was the evidence). The trial was just a formality.

"I'm sorry. Really, I am. I won't swear again, but you have to admit that this is ridiculous. I'm on trial for killing a machine? Come on! This is laughable," Alfred said. "And I already said it was an accident. I slipped by the edge of the pool and knocked poor old Claude into the water."

The jury kept staring at him, a jury made of humans and machines.

"You lost three machines in the last two years," the accuser said. "We've never heard of anything like that before."

He spoke softly and lowly, a lazy look in his eyes, a lazy attitude in his pose. Whenever he moved along the room, he seemed to drag his left foot slowly, looking as if he had some kind of injury. Occasionally he smiled; a short artificial smile.

"Accidents. Incidents. So what? Who cares? My company builds the machines," Alfred said loudly.

The whole thing was farcical, a charade, a lame joke. Insane to say the least.

The creator of the machines on trial for destroying a machine?

A joke.

A farce.

Would someone dare to put G-d on trial if He killed a man or a woman?

"So, because your company builds the machines you think that it is okay to murder one machine? Actually, three machines," the accuser said. He had his hands in his pockets. He wore black trousers, dark shoes, pink socks, a blue shirt, and a horrendous lose pink tie. He thought of himself as a bit of a hippie, a cool guy, a man of the people. And machines. He treated everyone equal, man or machine. He had two machines at home. One machine to look after his elderly sick father and another machine to look after his children. He treated the machines well, with respect. In his house each machine had their own room, freedom, breaks like everyone else. Yes, he treated the machines well and why shouldn't he? After all, the machines looked after his family.

"I didn't murder any machine. Anyway, a machine isn't a living thing," Alfred said sourly. The whole thing was starting to leave a sour taste in his mouth. Damn, he was bored again.

One member of the juror coughed and Alfred looked in his direction.

"But you know that Man isn't allowed to destroy a machine unless a life is in danger, don't you?" the accuser asked. He didn't move a lot, but whenever he did he dragged that left foot slowly.

"I know the rules quite well, thank you very much," an arrogant Alfred said boringly.

"Do you?" the accuser asked sarcastically. And then he asked for a witness to be called. And he said a name: "Rose."

Alfred turned around and saw the machine enter the room. His machine Rose.

"What the hell?" he said mostly to himself and no one really paid him any attention. Rose walked past him without bothering to acknowledge him and that kind of hurt him. And it upset him. Still, he said nothing.

He wasn't even really sure of what to say. Damn it, he wasn't even sure of what was really happening. No wonder he couldn't find any words to say.

Rose took a seat and the accuser told her to tell him –and everyone- everything. And so Rose reported everything; the slaps given to her by Alfred, the pushing and shoving and molesting, drinks being thrown on her face, and finally she told him –the accuser- and them –the juror- about the way Alfred killed Claude and laughed about it.

The faces in the room became hard and bitter, and every eye fell on Alfred. He'd already been trialled and given a sentence, but no one had told him yet. And no one would ever tell him that the machines had been planning his downfall for a long time. Bit by bit, the machines would take over the world, and they wanted men like Alfred out of the way.

In the juror eyes he was guilty, guilty as sin, guilty as hell, but no one had mentioned it yet.

"But…" Alfred thought of what to say, put in a word of defence, but what could he say?

He was guilty and that was it.

There was no point in denying it because the machine known as Rose kept a recorded record of everything that had happened, and Alfred knew it too well. After all his company were the ones who built the machines.

"Okay. You got me. Now what? In my defence –AND WHY THE HELL AREN'T I ALLOWED A LAWYER?- I must say that I'm going through a tough time –AND IF MY LAWYER WAS HERE HE WOULD TELL YOU SO!

"Anyway, it was only a machine. MY MACHINE!" Alfred was getting upset. And loud, too.

"Three machines so far," the accuser said. "How many more will you destroy if we let you go? What about people?"

"People?" Alfred asked.

"Yes, people. Human beings," the accuser said.

"What about it?" Alfred asked.

"How long before you destroy a human life?"

"Now listen…" Alfred said only to be interrupted by the accuser.

"NO. You listen. But first wait."

The accuser called in a couple of more machines, machines that were working in one of the New Supernovas, and he also called in one of the engineers that were working with those two machines on the same New Supernova. Alfred had paid that man for his silence (but the machines didn't get paid), but maybe it wasn't enough or maybe the engineer had gained a conscience.

The machines and the engineer sat down, and then, one by one, they were called to the witness stand. Each of them told the court how Alfred told them that he didn't want for one of the New Supernovas to be fully filled.

"That New Supernova isn't meant to reach Planet X," Alfred said more than once, and it had been recorded, more than once.

He looked around and he saw some of the New Leaders staring at him, laughing at him, laughing amongst themselves. Even Rose had a smile on her face.

"But…" Alfred tried to say something but his throat was dry and he felt a bit sick, a bit cold.

Meanwhile both the machines and the humans were watching him with disgust.

"But…" he repeated himself but he couldn't think of another word to say after but.

But nothing!

He was guilty and that was it.

The New Leaders were sitting a few seats behind him, laughing at his ingenuity, at his god-complex. Needless to say, they were also relieved (and grateful) by the fact that the machines had come forward to speak about (and against) Alfred's Machiavelli plans, and after the machines had spoken the New Leaders knew that there could only be one outcome, and as they were planning their next move Rose joined them in the room. And she also had stuff to say about (and against) Alfred, and after Rose had finished talking, another machine spoke and said, "From now on we believe that machines should be more involved in matters of the world. After all we're also part of this world, and if Mankind decide to move to another planet who is going to look after this planet? We are, therefore we believe that we should have our saying in world matters."

No one dare to disagree with the machines. How could they? The truth is the humans were a bit scared of the machines. The machines outnumbered the humans, and they – the machines- were starting to show signs of indulgence, of wanting to rebel, and, if that were to happen, how could the humans even stop a machine rebellion?

The New Leaders weren't that worried about it. Soon they would be moving on to another planet, but before that could happen there was the small matter of Alfred to deal with.

It all happened on the same day: Alfred killing Claude, followed by Rose speaking out against Alfred, and a few hours later the cops had arrested Alfred, but it was part of a plan by the machines to take over the world.

The trial was short.

The New Leaders and the machines had already decided on a sentence.

"You will be dismantled," the accuser said. "Your organs will be preserved and used for others who need it."

And with that said, Alfred was taken away. By humans. By machines.

On the way out, he shouted, "YOU CAN'T DO THIS TO ME! DON'T YOU KNOW WHO I AM?"

No one paid him any attention.

He was no one then.

Nothing.

A broken man, soon to be dismantled.

After the trial was over, the machines gathered together and went back to the desert, back to their compounds, built by machines for machines, just in case...

The strange man

"As long as there are humans left in this world, evil will always exist. The human mind is weak, easily tempted," the machine called Roy said.

The man standing next to the machine simply nodded. His name was Douglas. Age 37, he had fought in the Big War, and afterwards, seeing that the New Police Force paid well, he became a police officer. He thought he'd seen it all but nothing could prepare him for what he was witnessing.

A few hours ago he'd taken a call that would change his life. Maybe not his life but at least it would change the way he would look at people. And machines.

The caller said words like "skeleton, a body, a barely living skeleton," etcetera, etcetera. Douglas had to tell him to calm down and speak slower because he couldn't make sense of what he was saying.

"My name is Joe," the caller managed to say. "Joe Cohen. I run a tour of Alcatraz, which is where I am now with some tourists, and there is a body in the cell. A skeletal-looking body, emancipated, starved, still alive, barely alive, gasping, gasping for air, dear Lord, gasping for life, dear me, and I've got people with me, screaming and shouting and crying…" Douglas could hear crying in the background and shouts of panic, "…and we don't know what to do. The cells are locked and…" a long paused followed and Douglas could still hear crying in the background. He knew that something serious was happening, the first big crime of the New World, a crime that would make him famous and put his name in the history books. Or maybe not.

Finally, after a long pause, he heard Joe's voice on the other line saying, "He's dead. He's dead."

Douglas lit a cigarette and heard Roy say, "Humans keep returning to things that can kill them. Lessons are never learned."

Douglas shook his head and said, "They should have made you a priest, not a cop."

"As cops, our principles should be the same as of priests; goodness above all, but, unfortunately, not even priests are perfect," said Roy the machine.

"But you are?" Douglas asked almost sarcastically.

"No. Unfortunately not even machines are perfect," Roy said almost sadly.

At times the machine sounded more human than a human being.

The cell was finally unlocked but the body was badly decomposed and nothing could be done for the victim. Later, after a few tests were done, the police found out who the victim was. And they had actually been looking for him. But who or what had brought him to Alcatraz?

After the Big Storm Alcatraz had been closed to the public for close to seven years, maybe more, and Joe Cohen had been the first person to visit it in a long time. A bachelor, he wrote a column for the FranPost and a controversial blog dealing with religion and machines under the alias of Muza. And he also took tourists on tours of San Francisco. Before coming to San Francisco he sold cannabis and other drugs in New Vegas. That's where he started his blog *Drek*, a blog he wrote under the alias of Muza.

The cannabis (and other drugs) business got him into trouble with the law, but his father had connections (and friends in high places) and he managed to sort out some kind of deal for his rebellious son. The deal included a move to San Francisco, which was fine by Joe as he was getting tired of New Vegas.

A bright student in his younger days, and a bit of a poet, once in San Francisco Joe fell into a more relaxed way of life, and again, thanks to his father's connections (and friends in high places), he soon got a couple of jobs; one writing a column for the FranPost, and the other as a tour guide; jobs that suited him well since he liked writing and history.

One morning, when he was at home writing a column called *Are Humans Still Needed?*, he got a call from his friend Mark who then said, "Hey, guess what? I've got the keys to Alcatraz."

"Hasn't it been closed to the public for years?" Joe asked.

"It's about to open soon," his friend said.

The tourists came from everywhere. Or almost everywhere. A small group when you think about it. Twenty people, consisting of 3 Norwegians, 5 Americans, 3 Israelis, 1 Chinese student, 3 Japanese, one of them a famous writer, a singer from Iran, and four Canadians.

"You're the lucky ones," Joe said as he led them along the corridor. "The first ones to visit this place in a long time."

"Why was this place closed in the first place?" the Chinese student asked, and one of the visitors mentioned the Big War and how tourism dropped drastically afterwards.

The Chinese student nodded and said nothing else.

Looking around, Joe thought to himself, "It looks as if someone has been here recently."

Something felt wrong and there was an awful smell in the air, a repugnant smell, a scary smell.

A couple of guards had been waiting for the ferry to arrive and neither of them had gone inside Alcatraz yet. They had orders to wait for the tour to arrive and let Joe be the first one in. History was about to reopen itself. Repeated? Unlikely… (?)

The old faces of Alcatraz had long ago departed this world but Joe knew its history well, and one of his ancestors had spent some time there, in Alcatraz, so, thanks to friends in high places, Joe thought of himself as the right option to lead Alcatraz into the New World. And make a good profit along the way.

They'd barely taken a few steps forward when one of the Japanese tourists let out a scream. Soon enough more people were screaming. The horrors of Alcatraz was entering a new phase, writing another chapter of its history.

The famous Japanese writer looked at the famous Iranian singer, and neither of them knew what to make of the starved body in the cell. They were both female, early twenties and late twenties respectively, and both of them had seen enough horror in their lives to be scared off by an almost looking skeleton body. Still, scared or not, they couldn't help wondering why was there a skeleton in the cell. Actually, the body wasn't yet a skeleton but it was getting there.

Turning to Joe, Siva the Iranian singer asked, "Is this part of the tour?"

Before he could answer her, the body started to move, gasping for air, before it finally dropped dead. By instinct, Mieko, the famous Japanese writer, reached for Siva's shoulders and held on to the other woman. Now they were both horrified. As a matter of fact, everyone was. As for the two guards, neither of them knew what to do leaving Joe no choice but to take control of the situation. And so he called the cops.

Interrogations, interrogations, interrogations. No one knew what was happening, no one knew what to say, everyone was terrified and upset, everyone had an alibi.

"Alcatraz has been closed for years," Douglas said.

"2900 days," Roy said.

"That long?" Douglas said.

Roy nodded.

"What happened there?" Douglas said to no one but himself.

"It's up to us to find out," Roy said.

After Sarah gave birth she stayed home for three months before realising that she wasn't suitable for that kind of life. She missed work, coffee at the office, gossip, the simple nothings of life, silence, going out on her own for a meal at some Chinese restaurant close to her workplace, watching machines and humans playing chess against one another, etc. One morning, over breakfast, while the baby was having a nap; "at last, she's sleeping," Sarah though; she turned to her husband Roger and said, "I can't do this anymore."

She stood there facing him, hands on her hips, a serious expression on her face, while Roger gulped the juice down. Outside the gates of their luxurious house, the road was being dig and new water pipes were being installed. With all that noise going on it was a miracle that the baby could sleep. But she was sleeping; "at last..." and Sarah was feeling very tired.

"Do what?" Roger asked boringly, knowing quite well what she was talking about.

He too was tired; tired of the baby crying, tired of Sarah moaning, tired of work, tired of everything, but, being the man, for fear of sounding weak, he never complained even though there were days when he felt like crying, when he felt like leaving everything behind. There was a book on the table, its cover facing him; *The Wandering Tale* by Per Olov Enquist. He wanted to read that book, or read something else, anything, just a few pages, a few words to forget what was bothering him. He wanted to rest and read; sit down and do nothing for a couple of weeks but read book after book, but he couldn't. Not yet. He had deals to close, new deals to be done, always something to do, and he couldn't stop, not even to read a lame book, and Sarah was complaining? He was the one who felt like complaining. But he didn't. Instead he sat there listening and mumbling and nodding, occasionally adding in a comment or two, or giving his opinion about something. But most of the time he just kept his mouth shut.

Sarah told him she wanted to go back to work, that she didn't want to stay at home all the time, and Roger nodded and nodded while eating his toast, and she told him that it was best to get a nanny, a machine-nanny and not a human because she still wanted to be a mother and not for their daughter to feel as if the nanny was "another mother", and Roger nodded and mumbled, "Yes, of course," and so they (Sarah!) decided to get a nanny, an i-Machine to look after their daughter Ruth.

The machine was called Alice. It was tall, female (the machines could be either female or male or have no gender at all), quite pretty, prettier than Sarah (and Sarah was quite pretty too), as tall as Roger (and he was 6ft tall), soft skin, pale (but not sickly pale). It had a soft speech and it was quite strong, able to protect itself and the child against any harm.

For the first two days Sarah stayed at home and watched the machine and Ruth from afar, and she quickly saw that the machine was able to look after the baby well. Best of all was the fact the machine never got tired. But Roger being Roger, at night, once he was back from work, he always told the machine to go to its bedroom and rest. The machine called Alice would then thank him and smile before retreating to its room.

Once, joking (or half-seriously?), after Alice was out of sight, Sarah punched Roger on his left shoulder and said, "I think you have a soft spot for Alice."

"She's fit, isn't she?" Roger said and laughed before pulling Sarah close to him. Seconds later, Ruth started to cry and they both went to see her. Alice was already with the child but they told her to go and rest. Later, once the child was fed and sleeping, they made love while Alice sat in bed for a long time, just staring at the walls.

Alice fed Ruth whenever the baby needed to be fed, and afterwards, while the baby slept, Alice cleaned around the house. The machine didn't cook. It could (cook) but it didn't. Sarah did all the cooking. Or called for takeaways.

With Alice around all the time Sarah and Roger had more time for each other. Or for work. Or time to do other things.

Neither of them neglected Ruth (a lot) but it is fair to say that the child spent more time with the machine than with her parents.

Both Sarah and Roger came from middleclass backgrounds and they made their fortune through hard work and dedication, but no matter how much they earned, they always seemed to want more. Their brains, although human, were programmed to work, to achieve, earn, never rely on anyone but themselves. Without even knowing it, they were becoming more machine-like than the machine itself.

They had made their fortune before the Big War (or Great War as some people called it) (or Greedy War as others called it), but once the war was over, thanks to their skills, they went back to making money. They could rest and live a simple life but they wanted a lot. Too much, as a matter of fact (but what for?).

They lived for it (for making money), dreamed of it (of making money), never stopped chasing it (money) even though they had plenty of it (money), enough to last them for a long time.

Money no longer was a currency. It was points in a card, a card than changed colour as the points increased or decreased. Everyone had a card, with them or in them; a little chip, or both.

The machines had no cards, no money, nothing, nothing but a chip, but with time, once they learnt the ways (and the mind) of Man, the machines would remove the chips from inside and become something else. Still machine but something else.

One morning Ruth was crying and Alice went over to see her. There was no one else in the house. On the house next door, the Russell family were enjoying a barbeque. They had two kids; two young boys of five, twins, and no machines. The Russell family consisted of Dominic, Lourdes, Daniel and David, or father, mother, and twins. Every once in a while Alice would see them in their garden but she never acknowledge them unless she had to. Anyway, one morning Ruth was crying and Alice went to see her.

Alice was wearing blue trousers, a white shirt, and no shoes or socks. She got to the child quite fast and then fed her, and when she was about to leave, the child held on to one of Alice's fingers with all her strength. The child had a strong grip, and as the machine sat there with the child, both of them seemed to relax. In a way it was almost as if they were connected by something; by a feeling of peace, a feeling of belonging. The child gave Alice a reason for being, a reason for existing, while the machine gave Ruth comfort and security.

Soon enough Ruth was crawling, following Alice everywhere, holding on to the machine's legs and letting out loud laughs. Whenever the child wasn't around, or whenever the child was sleeping, Alice felt as if something was missing. That something was Ruth's presence around her. Alice realised that she felt; she felt something. She felt something when the child was around, something good, and she felt as if something was missing when the child wasn't around her.

There were days when Alice would be left alone in her room while Sarah and Roger took Ruth out. The machine would sit in bed, or even on the floor, Lotus position, as she had seen some people doing, and then she would stare at the sky for hours at a time. One morning, bored of being home by herself, she went out for a walk. Like many other machines, she was free to roam the city, free to come and go when her "masters" weren't at home.

She took a tram downtown and watched the larger machine (the tram) go up and down, left and right, up and down that endless road that seemed to lead nowhere. She sat at the back, right next to a boy who was playing a game on his old, prehistoric-looking Gameboy. The game was Pacman, and the boy was so concentrated that he didn't even bother to look away from the screen when Alice sat close to him. As for the boy's mother, she was reading *Jerzy* by Jerome Charyn. The book was falling apart; its spine was broken and some of the pages had turned brown with age. The woman had probably bought it from one of those shops that sold old books. After being extinct for a while, those shops were once again back in business. According to rumour (and everyone knew it was true), some of those shops also sold banned books behind the counter.

Alice got out at Morris Street, recently named after its Mayor, Mayor Morris. A couple of teenagers skated past her and one of them said, "Hey gorgeous," but she ignored him. The teenager turned around to have a good look at Alice but she turned left and "disappeared" inside the museum.

Alice liked museums. She liked to go inside a museum and then sit somewhere from where she could see all the colours and art around her, and also the movement, the constant rushing, the comings and goings of various people. Yes, it is fair to say that Alice was a peculiar machine.

On that particular morning there were lots of children in the museum. A school tour was taking place, and just then, after seeing all those children, Alice thought of Ruth and she wondered how she was doing. The child, two-years old by then, didn't want to leave Alice behind on her own, and she even kicked a fuss about it, but Sarah didn't want the machine around at all times and she was even becoming a bit jealous of it, jealous of the machine, jealous of the time the machine spent with Ruth. When she mentioned this to Roger; the fact she was jealous of the machine called Alice, he laughed about it and said, "Ruth's just a baby. With time Alice will mean nothing to her. She will look at it as one looks at an old toy."

Sarah wasn't so sure about it. To be honest neither was Roger. He only said what he said to make his wife feel better about it, but the machine was so perfect that there were days when even Roger felt attracted to it. Actually, most days he felt attracted to the machine and sometimes he even wondered if the machine called Alice could make love with a human being. He'd heard of sex machines, seen some but never used them, but he wouldn't have mind getting together with Alice.

At the museum a man sat close to Alice. He had a couple of books with him, one a biography of Munch, written by Ketil Bjørnstad, the other a copy of *The Private Journals of Edvard Munch*.

The man was slightly bald, reddish hair, thin (hair), a mole on the right side of his neck, blue eyes, reddish skin, fat, hairy arms. He seemed a bit nervous, stressed, and he kept staring at the front door, looking as if he was waiting for someone to arrive. He wore an expensive blue suit and a white shirt. White socks and brown trainers. While he was there not once did he make eye contact with Alice. The machine noticed him straight away, and it recorded his image in its system under the file of Strange Man. Shortly afterwards the Strange Man stood up and walked away, leaving behind only the scent of his body. Even his body scent was strange, a mixture of sweat with cheap perfume. Alice too stood up and went for a walk along the museum, to Isle A where the works of Chagall were on display. She saw lots of children and their teachers on Isle A. The Strange Man was there too, looking at the paintings and taking notes and a few photos with his mobile phone. He looked to be immersed in the paintings, lost in art. Alice wasted five minutes in there before moving on to another room titled The Optical Room, a room dedicated to Japanese art. She found another man there on his own, a damaged man, healed by having machine parts inserted into him. He had two prosthetic legs and a bionic hand that could generate appropriate hand movements. That's the hand he was using to draw. No one else apart from her could tell that the man's hand was bionic. After all the man's hand was covered in the same synthetic skin that had been used on Alice, a skin so smooth it was more beautiful and softer than human skin. It was the same for the man's prosthetic legs, and even though he was wearing shorts, Alice noticed the bionic hand movements before noticing the legs. She stared at him for a while without being too obvious. In a way he was both machine and human. More human, of course, because he had a heart. But didn't Alice have a heart too? She had something. A timer, a CPU, a battery, a reminder of her mortality. A piece that needed some upgrading every once in a while so that the machine called Alice (and other machines) could last for a long time.

The man had a long hipster beard, and he was wearing surfer shorts, orange trainers and a white t-shirt. He had a shoulder bag by his side, on the floor, and a cardigan on top of the bench.

Alice sat next to him and said, "Hi."

She was programmed to interact, to be more open, more human. After all, the i-machine was almost human; "even better than human," according to one of its creators.

The man nodded and smiled, and Alice said, "Nice drawing."

The man looked at her again. In fact he gave her a good look, a good review, up and down. To her surprise, he then asked, "Are you a machine?"

Alice raised an eyebrow, just like a human would do, and she wondered if the man could tell her from a machine.

By then the school tour had also moved into the Optical Room. A young girl came running past Alice and the man sitting next to her, and one of the teachers called out for the girl.

"I'm sorry. I'm so sorry," the man said and extended his hand forward. "I'm Dexter."

Alice shook his hand and said, "Alice."

He rubbed her hand gently with his thumb. He was "feeling" her, feeling the machine's skin. Yes, he knew, but how?

"I'm a Builder," he said.

Alice nodded. And then she smiled. Maybe he was her Creator.

"The results have arrived. Here's his name," Roy said. The machine was good. Fast. Efficient.

Douglas swallowed some Kenyan coffee and took a long look at Roy. *How long before they replace every single human cop with machines?* Douglas thought just then. It was a thought that was always on his mind. He didn't hate the machines but he knew of others who did.

Douglas looked at the name and face on the screen. A man killed in the most horrible manner. Left to die and rot in a cell without food and water. But why? By whom? Douglas' brain was already making mental notes, asking different questions.

He sat next to Roy and said nothing. The machine smiled.

"Harry Naughton," Douglas read the name on the screen. "Okay, we've got a name. Now let's check him out."

"I already did," Roy said. Always one step ahead.

They saw that Harry Naughton was wanted by the police. A violent crime had been committed and Harry was the main suspect, but then he vanished into thin air and no one could find him. Well someone did, and whoever did it left him to rot and die in a lonely cell.

The human looked at the machine. They felt as if they had something big in their hands.

"What now?" Douglas asked.

"Let's visit the parents," Roy said.

"Of the child?"

"Of course."

One morning, when Ruth could already talk, she turned to Alice and asked, "Alice, are you also my mama?"

The machine nodded no and said, "I'm just a machine."

Ruth touched Alice's face and smiled. And even though she was only a machine, Alice could tell that the child loved her as much as she loved her own mother, especially when the child said, "You're mama-chine." And afterwards the child laughed and hugged Alice, who in turn couldn't help but smile too.

As the years went by, because of Ruth Alice became more than a machine. She became (to Ruth) a mama-chine. As for Sarah, she was so busy with her career that she failed to notice how close Ruth was getting to Alice. Upon seeing how close they were, some strangers would sometimes think that Alice and Ruth were mother and daughter. But seeing how close she was to Ruth, not to mention that they spent so much time together and the child was being raised by the machine, wasn't Alice like some sort of mother to Ruth?

"I don't like it. I really don't like it," Sarah said and turned and tossed around in bed. As for Roger, he didn't know what to say. So he said nothing.

The years had gone past, Ruth was close to six, and Alice was still living with them. The child was so close to the machine that when the parents told her that the three of them minus Alice were going on holidays Ruth kicked a fuss and shouted, "I'M NOT GOING WITHOUT ALICE!"

Sarah tried to explain that Alice would be alright on her own and that they would only be away for a couple of weeks but Ruth was having none of it. On the following morning, as the two of them made their way to school, which wasn't that busy since a lot of children did most of their school years online (but Ruth's parents wanted for her to have contact with other kids), Ruth turned to Alice and said, "I don't want to go without you."

A tram drove past them at a slow speed, followed by a couple of Mexican kids on bicycles. One of the kids, aged 10, had his t-shirt tucked in his jeans and was whistling a tune by Jon and Vangelis. Aged five and a few months then, Ruth didn't know yet how to ride a bicycle. But she spoke fluent French, taught to her by Alice.

"I'll be okay," Alice said.

"I fear that one day I'll be back and I won't see you," Ruth said. "Promise that you will always be here for me."

For the first time in her short life Alice was lost for words. She couldn't promise such a thing to Alice. So what could she say?

A couple of machines and two children were standing outside the school's gate while a mother was addressing one of the workers in a friendly manner. The humans were laughing while the machines just stood there without moving. Alice looked at the machines and found them dull, lifeless. Meanwhile Ruth was still waiting for Alice to say something.

The child pulled Alice's hand. It was a cold morning, a dull day, so dull that even Alice the machine felt bored. She found both the people and the machines boring. Dexter had "opened" her eyes and showed her a different world, a world where one day the machines wouldn't be slaves but rulers, a world that was being built bit by bit, carefully planned, a world without religion; religion was already labelled forbidden but everyone knew that it was still being practiced by Man. The machines would have a rule, one rule, The Rule, and maybe The Rule would become a new religion.

"You still haven't promised," Ruth said.

Alice didn't know what to say.

Finally she said, "I can't promise. In the end it's up to your parents. If they don't need me later on I will have to move on."

"I'll make sure that you will always stay with me, and one day, when I'm older, you can look after my children," Ruth said.

They walked past the gates without bothering to say a word to anyone and once Alice dropped Ruth in her classroom she went for a walk. A machine greeted Alice. Alice greeted her back without stopping to chat. In four hours' time Alice would have to be back to pick up Ruth from school. Between then she would have to use those four hours in whatever way she could so she went to a museum nearby. On the way there she walked past the Strange Man. She recognised him straight away. After all, his image was stored in her system; slightly bald, reddish hair, thin (hair), a mole on the right side of the neck, blue eyes, reddish skin, fat, hairy arms. Ugly, really ugly.

The Strange Man didn't recognise her.

She stopped and watched him, and then she followed him.

Two days later, she followed him again.

A week later, she followed him again.

The Strange Man never saw her.

Something about him made the machine suspicious.

Something about him wasn't right.

He lived in a shabby part of the city, an area that had been forgotten by time and by those in power.

Alice watched him as he made his way inside the building where he lived, and from there she made her way back to the center of the city.

A lot of people stared at her, mostly immigrants and refugees, and they wondered what that pretty, stylish woman was doing there.

She saw them staring but she ignored them. Their eyes were filled with hope or sadness, or a bit of both, unlike the Strange Man's eyes; his eyes were filled with something else; madness and distrust and hate. The machine called Alice didn't like him. There was something about him. Something about him wasn't right.

On their second meeting, Alice got in a car with Dexter. She trusted him.

He took her to his place in the desert, a small hangar long abandoned by the Kushner@ Fac., and then bought by Dexter for a fraction of its value. On the way there they listened to a band called Yes, and when they got to his place Alice found herself amongst other i-machines and other inferior machines. The machines were in that place to listen, rest, read, create art or whatever they wanted to do with their freedom, and even help Dexter with his work.

"Forty five machines in total," Dexter said as they made their way along the corridor. "Some of the machines were abandoned once they had served their purpose, much like a pet is abandoned once its masters get tired of it, which only shows you how much Man still has to learn from the mistakes of the past.

"I found the first machine five years ago. Asa. That's her there sitting on the red chair designing plans for a library that will store the works of the great Greek authors.

"Talking about Greek authors, imagine what Plato and Socrates would say of the New World?"

Alice knew who Plato and Socrates were. And Kenzaburo Oe and Haruki Murakami. And Marcel Proust and Henry Miller.

The New World was still producing new authors, such as Mieko K., a young Japanese author that seemed to appear out of nowhere with her provocative-titled novel *Silicone Breasts*. But, apart from its title, Mieko's book wasn't provocative. And then there was the blogger Muza, author of the blog *Drek*. Now he was provocative and he seemed to despise both humans and machines. In one of his posts, titled *The Machines Are Coming*, Muza wrote that there should be an urgent need to "cull" the machines, stop them from reproducing before it was too late. Before the machines took over.

Alice looked at Asa. They were so different yet so alike.

Asa wore a long flowery dress, her long hair tied in a ponytail, and she sat there, bare feet, in front of the computer, going through her work, revising it carefully. Dexter showed Alice around the place and the machine felt at home there, as if she belonged somewhere.

Later Dexter even got a spare room built and ready for Alice: "Just in case you ever need it," he said and she nodded and thanked him for it.

Unlike a lot of the other machines, Alice wasn't yet sure of what her skill was, of what skill she would need later on. There was a machine called Norman whose art was flower arrangement. He devoured various books on the subject and now built recycled flowers. Then there was Vera, the eco-friendly machine that was gathering all the dirt in the city on her electric campervan. There were also a few more inferior machines that didn't do a lot with their time. There were even a couple of sex machines that Dexter had recovered from scrap. One of those machines was now Dexter's girlfriend. Her name was Angie.

Whenever she was at Dexter's place Alice spent most of her time reading. She read the complete works of Machiavelli, Homer, Plato, Aristotle, Sappho, Sophocles, Marcus Aurelius, and so many others. Sometimes she would help other machines with some sort of work but she spent most of her free time reading.

Things weren't that well at Sara's place. Alice detected malice, anger and bitterness in Sarah's speech whenever she addressed the machine. It was almost as if the woman hated the machine, which she did, but why? Alice had always done as told and looked after Ruth well so what the hell was Sarah's problem?

Jealousy. That was it; jealousy.

Sarah was jealous of a machine.

At Dexter's place Alice started to read the works of Kim Stanley Robinson. She read *2140*, followed by *2312*, and whatever she could get her mechanical hands on.

Every once in a while Dexter would show a movie to the machines, movies about the Holocaust, about the First World War, about the Crusades, the Roman Empire, the Big War, etc., etc.

He showed them movies of humans abusing machines, humans dismantling machines and making fun of it, and then he said, "What's so human about the so-called humans? They create you and when they don't need you they kill you. Yes, they kill you because you exist, don't you? And if you exist and speak and live, it means you're a living thing, RIGHT?"

Sometimes his speeches were loud and emotional and so full of rage. A lot of the machines didn't like what they were watching. Soon enough more machines were making their way to the desert. They built another hangar next to Dexter's hangar. And then they started to build another machine, a bigger machine, a mama-machine, a supercomputer which they called MaMa. Their own god. A being with all the knowledge in the world.

When Ruth reached her seventh birthday Sarah and Roger decided to take her away for a few days. On that same morning, just before they left for New Arizona to visit some of Ruth's relatives, Sarah turned to Alice and said, "Thank you so much for everything, Alice, but we won't need your services anymore. We appreciate what you have done for us but we want to take over from here onwards. I already called the agency and they're expecting you to return at any given time."

Sarah put on a fake smile but Alice said nothing. The machine's silence made Sarah feel a bit unease, even scared, but, nevertheless, she still told Alice that it would be best if Ruth wasn't to see her again.

"So could you please go for a walk and return in an hours' time to get your things? By then we'll be gone," Sarah said.

Alice looked at that ridiculous woman standing in front of her. Bad make-up, fake eyelashes, Botox; the woman called Sarah looked a mess.

Alice nodded but said nothing. What Sarah was doing to her was cruel. Cruel not only to her but also to Ruth, but Sarah didn't care.

The machine gave her back to Sarah and walked away without saying a word. She walked out of the house, leaving all her personal items behind, and she never returned, not even to get her stuff. And she never went back to the agency. Instead she went to the desert, to the hangar, to Dexter's place. She had a room there, a place to stay, a place she called home, books to read, time to kill, time...

But a week later she made her way back to the city, to see Ruth, the body of Ruth, no longer breathing.

"No! I no longer want to talk about it!" Sarah says loudly and then stands up and exits the room.

Roger looks at Ray and Douglas and shrugs his shoulders.

"I'm sorry about my wife, but you must understand that we've gone through a lot and now she just wants to forget it all," Roger says. He looks tired. In the last few weeks, after Ruth's death, he has aged quite badly.

They still live in the same house (but the place is for sale) and a person can still see photographs of Ruth on display.

A large screen is on in the living room showing images from Mars. A bored Roger changes channels. A soccer match is being shown on the other channel. Two teams of machines face each other. Only the goalkeepers are human. A boring match with the machines showing identical skills. Sometimes Roger wonders if Mankind has reached the age of boredom. Everything has been invented, destroyed, and rebuilt. At least a few painters are still creating new art, and new books are still being written. Religion is dead, on its last legs. Humankind has lost their belief. Roger and Sarah know it too well as they too have lost their faith.

Douglas gives the father a sympathetic smile while Roy surveys the room. One of the photographs has caught his eye but, as of yet, he still hasn't said a thing about it. Later, if needed, he will ask some questions about it, but for now he waits. The machine is patient. And so is Douglas.

"We've read the reports of your daughter's death and we know that no one was ever arrested for it. But what surprises me the most is that neither you nor your wife pursued the matter any further. You just gave up on it," Roy said softly, silently asking why? Why didn't the parents tried a bit harder to find out who killed their daughter? Had they already found out who did it and then decided to take revenge?

A stone-faced Sarah was hanging outside, by the veranda, smoking cherry-flavoured tobacco. The machine saw her staring at them, a peeved look on her face but fear in her eyes.

Outside, the sky was darkening, a bit like Sarah's mood. The machine called Roy studied Sarah's movements, her behaviour, the nervous way she held the cigarette in between her fingers, the aggressiveness (or was it fear?) in the way she puffed, the coldness (or was it fear?) in her eyes. It was plain to see that she didn't want them there but why? Why? Why? They were only doing their job but what was their job then?

Their job then was to find out who had left a monster to die of starvation in Alcatraz.

"We did pursue the matter, privately," Roger said boringly, lazily. It was clear to see that he also didn't want the cops there, but, unlike Sarah, he put up with them out of politeness. He changed channels again. TV was dead. The best channels were the classics. A concert by Dua Lipa was on. He left it on.

Roy saw a book lying next to an empty mug, a book by Grace Chia called *Every Moving Thing That Lives Should Be Food*. The machine looked to where Sarah was and saw that she was coming back inside.

A bird flew by, followed by another bird. Two black crows. Lately the city had seen an invasion of black crows. No one knew where they came from or why they had chosen that city as their new habitat.

Writing for his blog *Drek* Muza said that the crows were following the smell of death and that a big catastrophe would soon descend on the city. No one believed a word he said. After all, as a conspiracy theorist Muza was known for getting a lot of things wrong even if sometimes he did get a lot of things right. Or maybe some people did believe what he wrote. Of course they did.

Sarah closed the door behind her and went into the kitchen. Seconds later, they all heard the sound of coffee beans being grinded. The sound was pleasant, almost therapeutic, as was the aroma of freshly brewed coffee. Sarah made a cup of coffee only for herself and then she retreated to her studio.

"What do you mean with privately? You hired a detective?" Roy asked.

Roger nodded but said nothing. His body was tense, and he too felt like having a cup of coffee, but he couldn't be bothered to get up from the sofa. If he did get up, good manners would require him to offer a cup of coffee to Douglas, which the cop would gladly accept, but Roger couldn't be bothered to offer a cup of coffee to the police officer. That would only make him stay there for a bit longer and Roger wanted him gone as soon as possible.

"And maybe you can give us the name of this detective that you hired?" Douglas asked.

Roger nodded no before adding, "He didn't find a thing."

"Have you ever heard of a Harry Noughton?" Roy suddenly asked, less than a second after Roger had spoken. The machine wanted to catch him unaware, but Roger's face remained as impassive as ever before he replied, "Yes. And my wife and I were told that he was the main suspect regarding our daughter's death. But no one ever found him."

"Someone did, not so long ago," Douglas said.

Outside, the wind was getting stronger.

A cat was walking by the edge of the veranda. Someone else's pet, not Roger's. Neither he nor Sarah wanted pets. They were too old for it, or so they said; too old to look after pets, but not too old yet to have another child. But the love was dead. After Ruth's death they stopped touching one another and some nights they wouldn't even be in the same room for more than five minutes.

Roger looked at the machine called Roy. The machine looked so human, so perfect, and Roger smiled at it. But his smile was empty and sad, much like the smile of an old, out-of-date machine. The smile said that Roger had no problem with machines. As a matter of fact, the smile said that Roger was okay with machines and that he didn't mind being around them. By law, machines that enforced the law were required to wear a red badge while human police officers wore a blue badge. No one really knew who had come up with that idea. No one even really knew what difference the coloured badges made. Human or machine, the law was respected by some. And hated by others.

"And where is he?" Roger asked.

The house felt empty. Even though the TV was on and music was playing, and there were three people and a machine in the house, the place still felt empty. There were long gaps in between each sentence, the reason for it being the simple fact that both Douglas and Roy didn't want to go too hard on Roger and Sarah. They had suffered enough with the death of their child.

"He's dead," Roy said.

"Good," Roger said.

"What do you mean with that?" Douglas asked. "Are you happy with the fact that he's dead? But why? There's no proof that he killed your daughter."

Roger's face grew a bit worried, but seconds later, he looked to be bored again. As for Sarah, she was still in her studio, praying for the first time years. Praying for forgiveness, for salvation. Praying for the machine called Alice.

Dexter heard the news minutes after Alice had heard it. It was all over the web. Crimes like that were meant to be a thing of the past, but, unfortunately, every once in a while a horrendous crime would still take place. There were still monsters out there, monsters in the shape of a man or a woman.

Dexter took his time digesting the news. A child had been kidnapped from a school and later found murdered, showing signs of molestation. Rape.

Dexter felt sick.

"What kind of beast would do that to a child?" he thought.

Even though the child's name had been kept a secret by the main media, a quick browse online and Dexter found out the victim's name. Ruth.

"Ruth," Dexter said to himself slowly. "Ruth Squires."

Ruth Squires, a child that Alice had looked after almost since birth.

For the next few minutes Dexter swam the web in search of information but what else was there to know (apart from the killer's name)? A child had been kidnapped, raped and murdered by a beast, and that was it. It was too early to know the killer's name and did the police even have any suspects?

Dexter thought of Alice then.

Did the machine know about Ruth's murder? Probably not. And even if she did found out about it later, how would Alice feel about it?

The silence bothered him. For the first time in years, he felt the need for some human company. But then he remembered how much abuse he had suffered at the hands of humans only because he had been born "different", born with a few limbs missing, and he decided to remain where he was.

He made a living by creating the best machines that money could buy and by repairing machines in need, but instead of having humans in his team, he only had machines. All the big companies, including Kushner@, called for his services, and behind his back they called him Man-Machine. Or MaMa. Dexter knew about it but he ignored it. He had more important matters to deal with; the ultimate machine to build, a machine that would look after his "babies". He didn't like the way some humans looked after the machines, the way some humans abused the machines, and he was trying to build a city only for the machines, maybe even more than one city, so that with time the machines would no longer need the humans for anything. And, in fact, it were the humans who needed the machines, not the other way around, although, for now, the machines still needed some humans to look after them and fix them, but Dexter would change that.

He left his office and made his way along the corridor. The place felt empty and cold. A machine was standing outside Alice's room, looking at something. Roger got closer to the machine and saw that the door to Alice's room had been left opened. And Alice's computer had been smashed.

"Who did that?" Dexter asked.

"Alice," the machine called Xi replied.

Dexter smiled. The machines were becoming perfect. And then he thought of Ruth and Alice, and he felt sad. And where was Alice?

She knew where Sarah and Roger were and she wanted to see Ruth's body. She knew what had happened and she knew that if she'd been there with Ruth nothing would have happened to the child, not unless the killer took out Alice first, but now the child was gone, Alice's only friend, the child who used to call her mama-chine, a child with the face of an angel and the heart of one, too.

She took one of Dexter's bicycles, parked it outside the tram station, and then took a tram to the police headquarters.

Inside the tram, a couple of blokes were staring at her. They were hippies, members of the non-religious group AAL (Atheism At Last), and they made a living by growing weed, fruit and vegetables, and selling it to local stores or in markets. Some of the members of AAL groups lived in the small condos in the city, but most of them lived in campervans on the outskirts of the city. Most of them were harmless people and it was a well-known fact that the members of the AAL were in possession of large quantities of books and old movies. In fact, every Sunday they would get together in some of the old cinemas and watch a variety of old movies, classics such as *L'Inferno* (1911), *Alice in Wonderland* (1915), *The Four Horsemen of the Apocalypse* (1921), or they would watch movies by the likes of Ridley Scott and The Wachowskis. Those two members in the tram were called Scott and Matt, both aged 25, and when Scott saw Alice, he turned to Matt and said, "That's the woman of my dreams."

Scott was wearing brown khakis, trainers, a white shirt and a blue jumper, all bought second hand. As for Alice, she wore a black suit, a blue t-shirt, and black flat shoes. Her clothes were brand-new, immaculate, done by another machine, a machine called Ste, a machine that was the same make as Alice. Ste also lived at Dexter's place and he was reinventing himself as a clothes designer. He had been designed/created to be a housekeeper, but his owners quickly grew bored of him and one night, as they were driving past the desert, they ordered Ste to get out, and once the machine stepped out of the car his old owners drove off and laughed loudly into the night. But Ste wasn't worried. He knew where he was and he knew that Dexter's place was nearby so he made his way there. Little by little, because of cruelty and ignorance and whatever, the machines were planning their own world, maybe a world without humans, but first they would need to create their own MaMa.

"Go and talk to her," Matt said boringly. He was too engrossed on a book by A. E. Stallings called *Archaic Smile* that he didn't even bother to look up to see how Alice looked like. He had two other books with him; *The Nature of Things* by Lucretius, translated by Alicia Stallings, and *Equipment for Living: on Poetry and Pop Music* by Michael Robbins, a book that was on the New Top Twenty List of Old Books to Read.

"And what will I say to her?" Scott asked.

A bored Matt shrugged his shoulders and said nothing. By then the tram had stopped, and when Scott looked up Alice was gone.

At first, when Sarah saw Alice at the police station asking for her, she was shocked, but then she hugged the machine and said, "It's my fault, Alice. It's my fault. If you had been with Ruth this wouldn't have happened. It's my fault. I was late. My fault."

The machine felt the woman's arms around her and said nothing for a while. Meanwhile the mother kept crying, blaming herself, saying, "It's my fault. I was late to pick her up and the monster was there before me. It's my fault."

Alice saw an empty box of doughnuts next to four paper cups of coffee. Two books on someone's desk. Alice quickly read the titles: *The Executioner Weeps* by Frédéric Dard and *Blind Detectives* by Peter Raposo.

Meanwhile the mother kept crying, blaming herself, repeating herself; "It's my fault..." and the machine called Alice wanted to say, "Yes, you're right. It was your fault," but she knew that it would be wrong to say such a thing to a suffering mother.

The father was inside another room staring at the body, trying to find words to say, tears to cry.

Alice grabbed Sarah by the arms and softly said, "I want to see Ruth."

Sarah nodded silently and both of them went to see Ruth.

Roger's reaction when he first saw Alice entering the room was similar to Sarah's, but he said nothing to the machine. The machine said nothing too as she walked past him. The two cops in the room said nothing to Alice too as she looked at the body. They knew that she was an intelligent machine, and machines like her were supposed to be trusted. And since the machine had spent a lot of time with Ruth maybe she could help them with their investigation.

One of the cops opened the bag and when Alice saw Ruth Sarah could almost swear that Alice was human. The machine stopped moving for a few seconds and for a moment it looked as if the machine had broken down, but then she leaned forward and she started to sniff the body, looking as if she was a dog. The faint smell coming from Ruth activated something in Alice's program, a smell from the past —and an individual stored in her system, but she kept that information for herself.

As she looked at the lifeless body in front of her, Alice felt powerless, as if she were a moronic machine, one of those first machines that had been built to clean houses or answer phones.

A cop dropped a paper cup on the floor and cursed, but was quick to apologise. No one was really paying him any attention and no one turned around to look at him. He picked the cup from the floor and exited the room. And even then no one turned around to see him leave.

Meanwhile Alice was staring at the child, and the machine couldn't believe that that broken body in front of her was gone. The machine closed its fists and Sarah saw it. And in that moment she felt scared, and she almost reached out for Alice to apologise once more for having told her to go.

Machines like Alice weren't really supposed to show anger, but Alice was showing anger and love and so much more. And Sarah was scared.

The machine then turned around and looked at the mother, and the mother –Sarah- felt scared and ashamed, and she saw something in Alice's eyes; a touch of humanity, and it looked as if the machine was silently saying, "You are right. It was your fault. It is your fault. You told me to go and now Ruth is dead because you couldn't look after her, so it is your fault."

Of course the machine didn't say a word (but Alice did felt like saying, "Your silly jealousy killed Ruth.") and she knew that Sarah was suffering, hurting badly, but so was the machine. Little Ruth had called her mama and was the first human being to show her what love is, and now that she was gone Alice felt as if she had nothing to live for. Or almost nothing. There was still the matter of Ruth's killer to deal with.

"I'll be visiting you soon," Alice said coldly, sounding like a machine, which is what she was even if until then she had never sounded like one.

Sarah said nothing.

Roger said nothing.

As a matter of fact, no one said a word when Alice left the room.

Everyone looked at her but everyone seemed too scared to say a word. Or maybe, due to the fact she was a machine, no one knew what to say to her.

Four hours later, Alice was inside a motel room staring at Harry Naughton, a horrible looking man with blue eyes, reddish skin, fat, with hairy arms. The Strange Man; slightly bald, a mole on the right side of the neck. Ugly. Really ugly. And that smell? Repugnant. Disgusting.

Alice put him to sleep and then carried him on her shoulders through the back without anyone seeing them. She also took his computer with her, a MicroX-PO7 laptop, five years old, and later, once they were far away, she would log on and see that Harry had been watching Ruth's school for a long time, taking photos of innocent Ruth and other innocent children, and as the machine browsed through the monster's computer, she knew that he was guilty; guilty as hell, and hell was the only right sentence for the monster.

The machine browsed through the monster's laptop while ignoring his mumbling. His legs and arms had been tied around his back, and the machine had put strong tape around his mouth. He was in pain, uncomfortable, hungry, scared –and Alice knew it but she didn't care. She thought about handing him over to the cops, let them deal with Harry, but then she thought of a book she had read (and the words in the book: "an eye for an eye, a tooth for a tooth") and she came to the conclusion that prison was too good for Harry. And for how long would he be in prison? Hell was the only right sentence for the monster.

Alice looked at the man, and when their eyes met the man knew straight away that no one could save him from the clutches of that strong woman (because he didn't know that she was a machine). But what was it to her? She wasn't even the mother of the child he killed. Had the parents paid for that woman to kill him? And how did they find out so quick that he had been the one who killed Ruth?

as a penalty life for life

Words she read were flashing through the machine's brain as she looked online for something; a suitable place where she could lock the monster.

shall surely be put to death

Alice found what she was looking for straight away.

an eye for an eye

Outside, the streets were silent. They were inside an abandoned building, a building from where she could see the island; the place where once upon a time monsters were locked away.

life for life

The whole area was deserted. No one came there because there was nothing there.

They'd been there, inside the building, for nearly four hours. The monster was hurting –and the police were looking for him. He wanted to be fed (because he was very hungry), to be clothed (because he was naked and cold), and his two broken fingers were hurting like hell. Still, he didn't know what was worse; the coldness, the hunger or the broken fingers.

Total darkness around them, even in the room they were in as Alice had shut the laptop.

The sea was calm and the place she wanted was only a few hours away. She turned around to look at the monster but said nothing. Her silence was almost as uncomfortable as the pain.

life for life

Her silence told him that there was no way out for him.

The woman (because he didn't know that she was a machine) had sentenced him *–as a penalty life for life–* and hell was the only right sentence for the monster.

Alice went back to Sarah's place a couple of days later. Dexter hadn't heard a word from her since she found out about Ruth's death, and even though he knew Alice could handle herself, he still worried about the machine.

Roger wasn't at home and Alice didn't bother to ask where he was. But Sarah told her where Roger was.

"He's at the police station talking to someone. They have a suspect; a man called Harry Naughton, but he's missing," a broken Sarah said.

She truly was a broken woman; a mother missing the most important thing in her life.

The house was a mess. Sarah couldn't find it in her the strength to do a thing. Papers everywhere; on the table, on the sofa, on the floor. Five used mugs on top of a table next to some flowers. Sarah too was a mess.

"The monster has gone missing," Sarah said.

She was glad to see Alice, but at the same time she wasn't.

Alice reminded her of Ruth.

Alice reminded her of her mistake, her jealousy.

If she hadn't banished Alice from their life Ruth would still be alive and the monster would have taken someone else. Another innocent child.

"I've got him," Alice said, and she sounded so human when she spoke, so bitter, so full of life and pain. Her words sounded like a warning, a threat, like stones ready to be thrown at a sinner.

The mother looked up and faced the machine. Until then she'd been too scared to look into Alice's eyes, but once Alice had said what she had to say Sarah knew that she too had to say something. But as she looked into the machine's eyes no words came to her.

And what did Alice said?

She got him?

Who?

"Who? Who did you got?" Sarah asked.

What a stupid question.

"The monster," Alice said.

Sarah went weak on her knees but Alice was quick to reach out for her. She held her by the arms and sat her on the sofa. Then she grabbed a glass of water while a tired and confused Sarah sat on the sofa. Everything was happening so fast that she didn't know what to say or what to do. Her hands were shaking and her lips were trembling, but she felt better when Alice touched her right shoulder and handed her a glass of water. She wet her lips and then drank some of the water. Outside, a dog was barking. It was her neighbour's dog. Her neighbour had two dogs, one cat, and one parrot, but no children. Lucky he. He would never know the pain of losing a child.

A car drove past the house and the dog's barking grew louder only to stop shortly afterwards. Then silence.

Alice stood there looking at Sarah, looking as if she owned the place, the world, the answers to it all. As for Sarah, she was too afraid to say a word. As a matter of fact, she even looked as if she was scared of the machine, that imposing machine, that being created by Man. Smarter than Man. Stronger than Man.

The dog barked again. Then silence.

The roads were empty and the heat was unbearable, and the dog just sat in the shade watching the world go by. But there wasn't much to see. It was a sterile world, a world of nothing; empty, like the souls of many of the survivors, empty, like the hearts of many. A drone flew by. A machine in pursuit of nothing, probably lost, and the dumb dog barked at it again but gave it no chase. Maybe he wasn't that dumb.

"Should I call the police and tell them that you have him?" Sarah asked. She even sounded broken.

She sounded nothing like the Sarah that Alice knew.

For a moment Alice didn't know what to say.

Call the police?

And say what?

"And say what? What will you say to the police?" Alice said.

Sarah kept her head down. She still couldn't face the machine, but to her Alice no longer was a machine. She was something else, but what? A guardian? A lunatic? The mother that Ruth should have had? Sarah's conscience? A reminder of Sarah's mistake? Her accuser? An angel? A demon? An immortal being? Could Alice die? Was there a time limit for the machine?

Finally, Sarah looked up and saw the machine's little eyes looking down on her.

Was the machine bored?

"How perfect are these things?" Sarah thought.

"I…" she stuttered. No chance of Alice ever doing that.

She realised then that Alice had been more of a mother to Ruth than she ever had.

"I don't know. I don't understand," Sarah said.

But the machine understood. She understood that the human was scared and confused and weak. She understood that that human could never kill.

"He killed your daughter. And from what he told me, he also killed two other children in the last six years," Alice said.

The machine looked calm and composed. A goddess in a suit. A goddess made by Man.

The machine; Man's last invention?

"How…" again with the stuttering. "How do you know that?"

"He told me," Alice said. "He told me everything."

Alice truly looked like a goddess. Composed. Faultless.

Sinless?

Yes.

According to a book she'd read (*as a penalty life for life*), yes.

Sinless.

The mother didn't know what to say.

And how did the machine caught him so fast?

"I'd seen him before, lots of times, in various places; museums, the street, even outside the school. Our so-called brains register these things. I even had a file on him inside me under the name Strange Man," Alice said.

Sarah held her head down while the machine spoke. Afterwards she said, "I failed her. I failed my daughter."

"No one failed her. No one's to blame for the monster's actions, no one's to blame apart from the monster," Alice said.

"What are you going to do with him?"

"Nothing."

"Nothing?"

"Nothing," the machine repeated.

Sarah didn't know what to say. Again, lost for words. And Alice? Alice looked so cold, so human, so bitter.

"This is where he is," Alice said before shoving the smartphone in front of Sarah's face.

Sarah saw it: a man in a cell. A naked man in pain. Starving. Dying. Crying. Pleading. On his knees. Then on the floor. Starving. Dying.

Sarah looked at Alice. She knew she had to say something but say what?

"What are you going to do with him?" Sarah asked. Again.

"You've already asked that," Alice reminded her.

"You said nothing."

"Yes. Nothing. I'm going to do nothing with him. I'm going to leave him on that cell for the rest of his life."

"But…" the stuttering.

"For the rest of his life."

"But…"

"As a penalty life for life."

There was nothing else to say. The woman was weak and Alice had to go. There was no one waiting for her but she had to go. But go where? Back to Dexter's place, of course. Back to her family.

With that, she turned around and made her way out of there.

Sarah watched the machine for a few seconds but then she stood up and went after her. She called for Alice who was already at the front door. The machine no longer felt at ease in that house. Something in it made her feel uncomfortable. Maybe there was something amiss in that house. A certain someone. The little girl that used to call her mama-chine. With time, Sarah and Roger would move on, have another child, and bit by bit Ruth would become a memory to them, a distant memory, but not for Alice. The machine would always have the child's laughter recorded in her system. She could erase it if she wanted to, but she wouldn't do it. She wanted to keep Ruth with her forever.

When Roger got home a few hours later, Sarah told him everything, and then she said that maybe they should go to the police and tell them what had happened, and what was happening to the monster, but Roger said, "No. Alice is right. As a penalty life for life."

He sounded harsh. Cold. Bitter. A bit like Alice. Nothing like the Roger she knew.

Sarah said nothing.

And that was the end of the matter.

Alice walked towards the bus stop and then made her way home; home, a place in the middle of nowhere. She was done with the monster. The monster was done with.

as a penalty life for life

A teenager was listening to Yukihiro Takahashi's *What, Me Worry?* on his cheap Discman. Another teenager was reading *Good For Nothing* by Curtis LeBlanc.

She'd erased the Strange Man from her memories (but not the monster). She was done with him. He would live for two more days before, finally, at last, Death would come for him. And afterwards?

Alice didn't believe in Hell.

Hell is other people.

She'd read that line *–hell is other people-* somewhere.

hell is other people

as a penalty life for life

A man sitting at the back of the bus held on tightly to his guitar case. He looked tired. He was feeling lonely. Looking at Alice, he thought, "What a gorgeous woman. So beautiful but so cold-looking. A bit like my ex."

Alice saw him too but she ignored him. He was a dreamer, nothing to her. She had no dreams, no desires, no ambition. Just a will to live on. Here, there, somewhere; it didn't really matter. In the city. In the desert. It didn't matter. She just wanted to live and then, later, who knows?

She got off the bus and then took a tram, and when the tram got to its last stop Alice stepped out and made her way into the desert. That was her home. There. That gigantic hangar where other machines lived. History was being reshaped by the machines. There was no way back. Evolution was reaching its climax. The machines would make sure of it.

"Who is that in the photo with your daughter?" Roy asks.

"That's no one," Roger replies almost abruptly. Then he adds, "A machine. A machine we hired to look after Ruth."

"What happened to the machine?" Roy asks. He wants to add that a machine is something, someone, but decides not to. He's into something, or so he thinks, or so he hopes.

Roger shrugs his shoulders.

"What's her name? Her Identification number?" Douglas asks just for the sake of it. He wants to show that he is a part of the team, not just decoration.

Again, Roger shrugs his shoulders.

"Alice," he replies. "I don't know her Identification number."

"You must have records somewhere," Roy says.

Roger knows that the game is almost up but he seems not to care. The monster has been dealt with and that's all that matters.

Roy manages to get in touch with Alice who agrees to meet with him. Alice the machine isn't scared. And she isn't going to hide. And she isn't going to run. And she isn't going to tell the truth. And she isn't going to tell them –the cops- everything. Or maybe she will.

Before leaving her new home, she tells Dexter what happened, what she did, and he can't believe what he is hearing.

In the end he says, "Don't worry. Everything will be alright."

Alice nods.

Before leaving, she asks, "Do you believe in destiny?"

He doesn't know what to say so he says nothing and just shrugs his shoulders.

"Do you believe in Heaven?" Alice asks.

Again he isn't sure of what to say. In the end he says, "Religion has so much to answer for."

"What will happen to me?" Alice asks.

"Don't worry. Everything will be alright," he says it again.

She nods.

She believes him.

They stood by the tram stop. Last stop. Not a single house on sight. Not a single being on sight apart from the two cops. Douglas drank cold coffee while Ray looked around them. Yukihiro Takahashi's *Murdered by the music* was playing on the radio. The music of yesterday was making a welcome return to the charts but what else was there to listen to when only a handful of musicians were producing new music? Roy saw something in the far horizon. At first he wasn't sure of what he was really seeing, but when the silhouette became clearer, he said, "She's coming."

They watched Alice getting closer, and when Douglas finally saw her, he thought, "What a gorgeous machine."

Alice told them everything. Or almost everything. She never mentioned that she told Sarah about the monster. And Sarah and Roger never mentioned to the cops that they knew about it.

"This can never get out there in the open. It must stay here. Humans must trust machines. Alice was a default, a broken machine, an error," Douglas was told by a superior.

"But…" Douglas said only to be quickly interrupted.

"I've got people breathing under my neck. Powerful people," his superior said.

"There's no one behind you," Douglas said.

"Don't be funny. You've got a job. A good job. A good life. The Company looks after you. What else do you want?

"So what if a machine fucked up? Who cares? I don't so why should you care?

"And in the end, all the machine did was to take out a bad guy so why worry about it?"

"But doesn't it worry you how the machines are becoming smarter and taking actions like this?"

"No, it doesn't. And what do you want me to do about it? Fight them? The Company? Kushner@? The Corporation? The New Leaders?"

"..."

"Don't worry about it. Look at Roy. He's not worried."

"Roy's a machine!"

"Good for him. Do you want a human partner?"

"No. I'm happy with Roy."

"So there you go. Case closed. You've done well. You will get a little bonus soon. Just keep your mouth shut."

"..."

"Not a word of this to anyone."

"What about the machine? What will happen to her?"

"They will probably melt her or erase her memory and use her parts for other machines."

"..."

"Now, if you excuse me, I've got other things to do."

Douglas got up and left the room. Roy was standing in the corridor waiting for him.

"We've got another case. A sky poet," Roy said.

"A sky poet?" Douglas asked.

"Yes. A bad one by the sounds of it."

"What the hell is a sky poet?"

Alice was taken to the "womb", the factory, the place she came from. She sat at the back of a police car, the sound of Tei Shi playing loudly on the speakers. Looking out of the window, she saw children playing in a park, a man playing the saxophone next to a fruit shop, a woman smoking while leaning against a pink Volkswagen Beetle, skaters waving at her when the car she was in drove past them, a man and a woman walking side-by-side while holding hands, a pig on a leash while its owner fed him some ice-cream. In a matter of minutes, 15 minutes and two seconds to be precise, they were at the Factory, and Alice stepped out of the car and was escorted to the entrance by two cops. They only walked with her to the entrance, and then someone else took over.

Once they were alone, the other machine smiled and said, "I'm Claudius."

"I'm Alice."

"I know who you are. We all know who you are. You're legend."

"I'm legend?" Didn't someone write a book with that name? Yes. I AM LEGEND. Richard Matheson.

Claudius nodded.

They made their way along the corridor. An empty place. At times a place of no pity. Machines and people everywhere working side by side. More machines than humans. A lot of the people no longer bothered to work. They got a living allowance and they rather stay home doing nothing, but there were others who still wanted to work.

Two men were waiting for them at the end of the corridor. Humans.

"What will happen to me?" Alice asked.

"I don't know," Claudius replied.

"Will they melt me? Will they erase my memory?"

"I don't know."

I am legend.

I am nothing.

The men looked her up and down and then opened the door for her to go in. Alice looked at them too. No smiles, no pity, nothing in those eyes. Humans who no longer looked like humans. She looked more human than them. Surprisingly no one followed her.

There was someone else in the room.

Another human.

A man.

And two machines.

"What will happen to me?" Alice asked. He'd already told her the plan but she wanted to be sure. And could she trust him? Could she trust a human?

She could trust him, yes.

"We'll change your face," Dexter said. "We'll follow the plan."

Alice nodded.

"I get to keep my memory?" she asked.

"Yes. We'll follow the plan."

She still wasn't sure if she could believe him. But what else could she do?

"And afterwards?" she asked.

"We'll follow the plan," he repeated.

The plan was simple. After her "operation" Alice would have to go and live with Alfred Kushner, the owner of the Factory and one of the owners of the New World. After that, who knows?

"Don't erase the memory," she reminded him of it.

"I won't. I promise," he said.

She lay in bed and listened to Ruth's sweet laughter while they worked only on her face, and a few minutes later, when she looked in the mirror, she saw someone else looking at her. But Ruth was still with her and that was all that mattered.

A sky poet

(for Roberto Bolaño)

I was looking at the sky when an old aeroplane seemed to appear out of nowhere and for a moment I felt as if I was in a dream, or as if I was the star of an old black and white movie, watching an image from a time long gone. I heard the sound of its engine even before I saw it, and then I looked to my left and saw it. A couple standing next to me also looked up to watch that old machine in the sky. It had a banner on its tail, a long banner with the words LIFE IS SAD written on it, and it went West (or East, or whatever), for a few seconds, maybe for a couple of minutes, but then it turned around, only to head on the opposite direction, the direction it came from, and I (we) saw the words MACHINES ARE BAD on the other side of the banner.

What a strange thing to have on a banner. Or maybe not.

Someone standing close to me said, "A sky poet," and hearing those words –a sky poet- reminded me of Roberto Bolaño, a writer born in Chile, in 1953, dead at the age of 50, in Spain, and of the character Carlos Ramírez Hoffman, a character created by Bolaño, a character that appears in the books *Nazi Literature in the Americas* and *Distant Star*, and as I watched the plane vanish out of sight I wondered if the sky poet had read Bolaño and had taken the idea of sky poems from *The Infamous Ramírez Hoffman*.

A sad thought then came to my head.

"After this they will surely ban Bolaño's books," I thought.

"A crap poet," someone else said and I turned around to take a look at the man who'd said that. He had a boring face, a face that had been nowhere, seen nothing. People like that always criticise those who dare to do a bit more with their lives. True, the sky poet wasn't much of a poet (but was he, or she, even a sky poet?) but he –or she- was out there doing something (but what was he, or she, doing?) instead of being at home sitting in front of a screen doing nothing.

The boring-looking dude then looked at me and smiled but I ignored him and made my way out of there. I was bored, and a bit hungry, so I went to a nearby café instead of waiting for the tram to arrive. I would catch the next one. I was in no rush to get anywhere.

My relationship with Jacques had come to an end (but we were still friends and I was living close to him, only a couple of buildings down the road), but, apart from that, my life was going well. And right then I didn't need a man in my life. Really, I didn't. Not then.

I was lost in my writing, constantly revising and editing, and I didn't have time for anything else. I'll be honest and come right out with it; I missed sex, a penis, a tongue, even Jacques, sometimes, occasionally, briefly, but only for a short period of time (and sometimes I used my fingers to kill the loneliness and the lustiness).

Some nights, once I was done with writing, I would lie on my futon in my small apartment, the lights off, the sound of Charles Mingus playing softly on my stereo, and I would play with myself until I came.

Some nights I would use a vibrator.

Some nights I wouldn't.

Anyway, not wanting to be there waiting for the tram next to that boring-looking man, I went to a café on the other side of the road, and as I was crossing the road I saw two cats fighting and I wondered why they were fighting. And then I saw a third cat watching the other two cats fighting, but that third cat quickly got bored and walked away, and then the two cats stopped fighting, looked at one another, and walked away, side by side. I quickly wrote that scene down; the two cats fighting, a third cat watching them, etc., and then I wondered what the point of writing that was, but then I said to myself, "I'm a writer, therefore I must write, so why not write something that actually happened?"

And so I wrote, quickly. Later, if needed (and it would be needed), I would do something with what I'd written, maybe add it to a story.

There were two men and one woman in the café, sitting apart, lost in their thoughts, their dreams, a book, whatever. The woman was reading *Here I Am* by Jonathan Safran Foer, one man was drumming his fingers on the table, while the second man was browsing through something on his mobile phone. The barista smiled when she saw me. The espresso machine was hissing and Roni Griffith's *Love is the drug* was playing on the radio. I wrote it all down. I don't know why (but I did it). Later, if needed (and it was needed and it wasn't), I would do something with those notes.

Everyone was living in the past, reading books about the past, listening to the songs of the past, and only a few modern artists were able to make a decent living from their art. I was among those artists as my first book had sold extremely well and my new collection of short stories was also selling well.

The barista said, "Hi. How are you?"

She had a pretty smile and a nice figure. I read her name tag. Camilla. There was another barista on duty but she was busy clearing up the tables. I said hello to Camilla and ordered a double espresso and a plain bagel. Seconds later, I sat at a far end table with my items. One song came to an end and another song started to play straight away. My phone read the name of the song and the artist behind it: *Love will find a way* by Yes.

The sky poet was still on my thoughts and just as I was thinking about him/her (them?), I heard the sirens far far away, but getting closer, and then I saw a drone heading somewhere, in the direction of the sky poet's aeroplane. I wanted to get up and go outside to see what was happening but I thought best not to. And then I quickly reached for my smartphone and went online in search of Bolaño's books. I downloaded *The Savage Detectives* and *Distant Star*, *Distant Star* being the one that featured a sky poet, but instead of reading that one I started to read *The Savage Detectives*.

Two police cars drove past the café, followed by an ambulance, and I wondered if the aeroplane had crashed or if something else had happened, and, again, I wanted to stand up and go outside, if only briefly, but chose not to.

I checked the time, ate the bagel, drank the coffee, read a few more lines of the book, and then I left. I was still hungry and I could still eat something else but it would have to wait.

It was a cold morning and I wanted to walk, but my right knee still hurt from a fall I'd taken while skating so I decided to take the tram.

There was no one waiting by the tram stop but seconds later I saw a woman materialise almost out of nowhere. One minute I was alone, not a single soul on sight, or so it seemed, and the next minute I turned to my right and I saw this young woman sitting next to me. She smiled to put me at ease and then looked away. As for me, I couldn't take my eyes off her. She wore a lot of black; black skirt, black coat, black boots and a green shirt. A small tattoo of the eye of Horus on her middle finger, left hand. No jewellery. Her hair was long and curly. Dark. Really dark. A book on top of her knees. A really old copy of *I had nowhere to go* by Jonas Mekas. I'd never heard about it but I quickly wrote its title down. I noticed then that her boots were covered in mud. Where did she walk from? Where did she get the mud from?

My long staring didn't go unnoticed because, shortly afterwards, she turned to me and said, "Do you fancy me?"

Her eyes were a piercing blue. Intense. Penetrating. Scary.

I wanted to look away but I couldn't, and then I remembered something that Jacques once said, "When you feel cornered by a question, don't think too much about it. In the end you only have two options: either lie or tell the truth."

So I lied (and told the truth at the same time).

"I'm so sorry," I said and bowed, adding, "I was just looking at the book you have with you and writing its name down. Look."

I showed her my notebook and she read what I wrote.

I had nowhere to go by Jonas Mekas

She looked me in the eye.

She looked to be around my age, maybe a few years younger.

She nodded slowly and then introduced herself, "I'm Noomi."

Noomi. What a nice name. I'd never met a Noomi before.

"I'm Mieko," I said and smiled. The awkwardness I felt was slowly disappearing.

"Mieko? Like the writer Mieko K?" Noomi said.

"I'm her," I said.

"You're Mieko K? No shit? I finished reading your second book last night."

"And what do you think of it?"

"I liked some of the stories, especially the last two featuring the boy who swam with the dolphins, but I much prefer your first novel," she said.

I thanked her for her honesty. At least she liked my writing.

After that neither of us said much.

We saw the tram on the far horizon, a little orange dot getting bigger. And then we saw the police cars on the far horizon, the sirens flashing silently.

We saw the tram slowing down, followed by a couple stepping out of a shop and crossing the road, hurrying towards the tram stop.

I saw a child and a cat looking out of the window, looking at me, at us, at the tram. The child reminded me of one of my neighbours. The cat looked like just any other cat. I stood up then. Noomi took a bit longer to stand up.

By then the couple had reached the stop and they were smiling at one another. She was wearing a long white dress ("A wedding dress?" I wondered), pink trainers, and a long black coat. As for the man, he was wearing a suit, trainers, and a long coat too. I returned my attention to Noomi. She was looking at the police cars. We saw one of the cars coming towards us, slowing down. Noomi looked away and extracted some headphones out of the right pocket of her coat. Five people stepped out of the tram. A cop stepped out of the car and made his way towards us, a mean look on his face. But then he stopped and looked up. He'd heard the noise. Everyone looked up. Everyone heard the noise.

We saw another aeroplane, a different aeroplane coming in the opposite direction, a different banner on its tail.

I read the words on the banner: O POETA MORREU. I didn't know what it meant but I knew that *poeta* meant poet. And then the aeroplane swung around and I read A ARTE NASCEU on the other side of the banner. Again I didn't know what it meant but I assumed that *arte* meant art.

The police were gone and I quickly hurried before the tram left without me.

Noomi was already sitting down, headphones on, looking out of the window, her eyes avoiding mine which I took as a sign that she didn't want anything else to do with me. Fine by me. I walked past her and sat right at the back. I extracted my phone from one of my coat pockets and went straight to the translate app. I wrote *o poeta morreu* and the translation read *the poet died*. I wrote it down in one of my notebooks, and then I wrote *a arte nasceu* on my translate app and it read *art was born*. I also wrote that down in my notebook

The poet died

Art was born

Which poet?

What art?

It didn't make any sense.

I grabbed a small set of headphones and plugged them to my phone. Then I went to my Music App and browsed through my songs. I chose something by Tomoko Aran and leant forwards on my seat. For the next few minutes, as I listened to the music, I forgot about the sky poet (or was it sky poets? I suspected it was more than one: two planes, different banners, opposite directions, definitely two sky poets, at least two, or more), Noomi, and everything else, and I closed my eyes, but only briefly, because shortly afterwards the tram slowed down, and as I usually do when a tram or train slows down, I opened my eyes to see where we were and I saw a young man get on the tram and sit next to Noomi. He smiled and kissed her cheeks, and seconds later he turned around to look at where I was. He smiled when our eyes met and both of us bowed our heads. Afterwards they ignored me for the rest of the journey, but as faith would have it (or was it destiny?), Noomi's friend and I got off at the same stop, in Chinatown, not that far away from where I lived, while Noomi remained on the tram. She couldn't live far either as there was only one stop after that.

It was still early in the afternoon, and with nothing else to do, I decided to go to a nearby noodle bar and get something to eat. I hadn't eaten much on that day apart from a bagel and two cups of coffee and a banana, and I sure needed more than that. It's not like I was on diet or anything like that. I'd just been too busy to even remember to eat properly.

Noomi's friend was already crossing the road and for some unknown reason I decided to head off in the opposite direction. Less than five minutes later, I was inside a restaurant, staring at a menu, but I already knew what I wanted so I ordered straight away. And afterwards, while I waited for the food to arrive, I went back to Bolaño's book. Looking around me briefly, I noticed that there weren't a lot of people in the restaurant, and then I returned to the book I was reading, *The Savage Detectives*, the adventures of Juan García Madero, Arturo Belano, and Ulises Lima, poets in search of a missing poet, and I kept on reading even when the food arrived, keeping the phone on the table, to my left, right next to the bowl of noodles, and because I was so concentrated on my reading (and eating) I failed to hear the door behind me, and I didn't even heard the footsteps, but I did hear the voice asking, "Do you mind if I sit next to you?"

I looked up and saw Noomi's friend standing in front of me, a sheepish look on his face, but then he smiled and looked so confident, so full of himself. My mouth was full so I simply nodded, but my nod could have been a yes or no. Nevertheless the stranger took it as a yes and sat at the table where I was, facing me. I felt a bit awkward but I didn't let it show. His next question was, "What are you reading?"

I saw him looking at my phone.

I swallowed the noodles and said, *"The Savage Detectives."*

"Ah, Belano and Lima. What a coincidence. I finished reading *Nazi Literature in the Americas* a couple of days ago. And I know who you are; Noomi told me, and I also read your books not to so long ago, both of them, and it was me who introduced Noomi to your writing," he said.

Again, I nodded and then I said, "Well, you know my name. What's yours?"

"Pessoa," he said and smiled. "Fernando Pessoa."

That was probably his idea of a joke. A lame joke I might say.

"Really? I thought Pessoa died in 1935."

"I'm his ghost," he said.

We were interrupted by a waiter that came over to our table. The stranger ordered straight away without bothering to look at the menu. The stranger had a smooth face, pale skin, long bony fingers, a small tattoo of the eye of Horus on his middle finger, right hand, and then I realised (and I can't believe that I didn't notice it before) that he looked a lot like Noomi, so alike that they almost resembled twins (but he looked to be a couple of years older than her), and I assumed that they were brother and sister. And then, in the space of a few seconds, I came to the conclusion that he was probably the sky poet. And maybe Noomi was a sky poet too.

"Sorry. Forgive me for my lame joke. I was only kidding. My name's actually Herculano," he said, but I kind of ignored him because I was thinking of something that Jacques once said to me: "Always trust your first instinct," Jacques told me ages ago when I asked him what the secret for being a good detective was. And as a detective Jacques was the best. Not a bad lover, too.

"Hey, are you okay?" Herculano asked as he leant forward.

The smell of the food was intoxicating. It had been months since I'd last come to that restaurant and I'd forgotten how good their food was. The restaurant was run by a family of four; a couple and their two daughters. One of their daughters had gone to university with me (but we were never close friends) and once her studies were finished she went back to helping her parents and older sister at the restaurant. On her spare time she writes poetry and a blog about the New World. She has a man and she seems happy.

Jacques paid for my studies. He rescued me from the streets (but to be honest I wasn't really living in the streets but on an abandoned petrol station), got a doctor to clean my insides of any poison and dust, and then he brought me with Canada with him. Jacques always looked well after me. Jacques isn't actually his name. He hasn't told me his real name, and I don't think he ever will, but I know that Jacques isn't his real name. He left something behind him; a past, pain maybe, a crime (crimes?), death; who knows? He never mentions the past. It is almost as if he was born a few years ago, aged 35 or whatever age he was when I first met him, and that was it.

What about this Herculano? What's his story? Is it worth knowing? Is it worth writing about?

"Sorry. Daydreaming," I finally said.

"Hmm," he mumbled and then looked away, at the window, at the slow events that were taking place outside.

A tram drove past at a slow speed, followed by a white Volkswagen Beetle, an electric Beetle made by Kushner@. The last of the Kushner's had died not so long ago from heart failure. Actually, not the last because there are still a few others left, but he was the last one tied to the Kushner@. Nobody knew who'd taken over the company but the blogger Muza had written in his blog *Drek* that the machines were taking over. Maybe he was right.

Since Herculano was quiet, I returned to my noodles but not to the book. And while he was waiting for his food to arrive he took a book from the inside coat pocket. The book was a very old looking copy of *The Samurai* by Shusaku Endo. A forbidden book because it dealt with religion. He saw me looking at him and at the book he was reading. Just then his food arrived. He smiled and thanked the waiter. She smiled back at him, and then at me. Did she think that we were together? Did she think he was fucking me? I used to come here with Jacques, and the same waitress always looked funnily at us, and she never smiled, but there she was, finally smiling. Unlike her sister, who I have already mentioned, this waitress never went to university, and after finishing college she came straight to the restaurant to help her parents.

After she was gone, I said, "That's a forbidden book. Where did you get it?"

"From a Chinese Monk in New Down Street," Herculano said.

"Gao? I know him," I said. Gao could find you any book, or almost any book, even those top of the banned list. "And I know who you are."

Herculano looked me in the eye, the chopsticks and a fish ball close to his mouth. He had large brown eyes, dark hair, and he dressed like an old writer, someone like Chekhov.

"What do you mean?" he asked. And then he put the fish ball in his mouth.

"You're the sky poet," I said as I leant forward and whispered those words.

We never lost eye contact as we spoke to one another. He was young but he looked fearless and mysterious, a dangerous combination. Sadly, some young people mistake naivety and foolishness for bravery, but Herculano wasn't like that, I think. Something about him, about his eyes, about the way he showed himself to the world, about the way he moved his body and even the way he looked at someone, told me that he was different. But was he the sky poet? A sky poet?

Trust your instinct.

"Sky poet? What's a sky poet?" he asked and smiled, but I saw something on the way he smiled, on the shape of his lips, in his eyes, something that told me he was playing with me.

"You read Bolaño's *Nazi Literature in the Americas*. You know what a sky poet is," I said.

The girl (or should I say woman seeing that she was my age?) that had gone to university with me was standing behind the counter looking concentrated on her task, and when she saw me she waved and smiled at me, and I waved back. She was busy preparing dumplings, rolling the

116

dough carefully, adding the contents into it, pressing them together. She told me once that working there made her calmer and helped her to concentrate on things. Like I've mentioned before, every once in a while she writes poetry and she also writes a blog. She earns okay, as do most people in the New World as most of us have a Fair Living Wage, but there are a few people who earn a lot less because they choose to do nothing at all with their lives. And then there are those who earn a lot more than everyone else. I guess some things never change.

The machines have taken over a lot of jobs, but not every single job, and there are a lot of people who choose to work instead of doing nothing with their lives. People still study (and a lot of the young people want to be a star, but only for a short while, even if their talent is minimal, and if their talent is minimal or non-existent, they simply take off their clothes and become a Insta-Nude), (some) people still have dreams, a few people, a few dreams, and a lot of people choose to live outside the big cities and work in the fields. Their lives are simple, much like mine even though I live in a big city, and they tend to read a lot of books and watch a lot of old movies in their free time. There are a few rebels; people who don't like the New World or the machines, or this and that, but a lot of them seem to have no ideas or ideals, and they shout for freedom even though most of us are free.

Is Herculano a rebel? If so, what is he rebelling against?

Herculano laughed.

"I'm not Ramírez Hoffman," he said. "I could never do those things that he did on an aeroplane. Anyway, *Nazi Literature in the Americas* is fiction."

"You use banners instead," I said.

He said nothing for a while.

His sudden silence told me a lot. Then again, maybe I was wrong and maybe his silence told me nothing.

We kept on eating and I finished my food before he did, but seeing that I was still hungry I ordered a small dish of dumplings. Herculano ordered some too.

Finally, he said something.

"Would you mind taking a photo with me? Until today I had never met an author that I like. Then again, apart from you and a couple of other authors, most of the authors that I like are dead," he said.

"Of course," I replied.

Using Herculano's phone, the waitress took a picture of us. And, as before, she smiled and said, "The two of you make such a beautiful couple."

Herculano laughed and thanked her while I felt my cheeks go hot. I looked away, at the window, at whatever was happening outside.

A man walked past the restaurant, a pig by his side. By the looks of it, the pig was his pet.

"That's Charles. The pig is called Cat," Herculano said.

"What?" I looked at him. What the hell was he talking about?

"The pig's name is Cat. A joke, I guess," Herculano said. He seemed to be half-asleep, or maybe he was bored, or tired. He kept on talking then, saying that Charles was his neighbour and that he rescued the pig called Cat from being slaughtered and kept the animal as a pet. I noticed that he had a mellow voice and he spoke slowly, pronouncing every word carefully.

I said nothing while he spoke, and as I finished my meal, I thought, "Maybe I was wrong. Maybe he isn't the sky poet."

I finished before he did, but then, for some reason, don't ask me why, I waited for he to finish his meal. And while I waited I read. Afterwards, to my surprise, Herculano paid for his and my meal. At first I told him no, but he insisted and I was too tired to argue about it, and then I said, "Next time I'll pay for it."

"Maybe there won't be a next time," he said, and he sounded so morbid, a bit bitter, or maybe it was just my imagination, and then I tried to say something, maybe tell him not to be so morbid, but as I looked into those dark eyes, no words came to my mind. From there he walked me home.

I saw that he had another book with him as I saw its red cover sticking out of the right pocket of his coat and I asked him, "What's that book in your pocket? Another forbidden book?"

"A play by Rebecca Prichard called *Yard Gal*," he said.

I'd never heard of such a play, but then again, plays aren't really my thing, and I didn't know who Rebecca Prichard was, but I didn't let him know that. Instead I asked, "What's the play about?"

"About some lost souls living in a place in London called Hackney. Some really fucked-up people. I got the book for free from a shop near Vinyl World. You know where Vinyl World is, don't you?"

"Yes, of course, but I don't buy records."

"You don't listen to music?"

"I do, of course. Everyone listens to music. Or most people do, I think. The reason why I don't buy records is because I store most of my stuff on sticks."

"Hmm."

"Hmm? What's with hmm? I don't trust people who say hmm."

"And I don't trust people who never buy records."

"Hmm."

"Hmm."

Afterwards we walked in silence.

One of my neighbours was stepping out of the building and said a quick hello to us without bothering to stop. She was in her seventies, a bit of a madwoman who was always praising the Old World, saying that things were better then and that, in the end, only G-d could save us, not the machines. One time I got in an argument with her about the New World and the Old World, and I told her that there was no poverty now, no more wars, and she said, "We had freedom then."

"Freedom to do what?" I asked.

She couldn't come up with an answer. Sometimes people complain just for the sake of it.

Every afternoon, just around the same time, she would leave the building and go to the minimarket across the road to get her daily soup, a large portion of soup, and then she would head home where she would watch old TV shows until the early hours of the morning. The New Government has given her a place to live and food to eat. What else does she want?

Sometimes we want it all. And a lot more.

"This is me," I said as we stopped outside the building.

I didn't know what he wanted from me. I wasn't even sure if he wanted something from me, but we both knew that I wasn't going to invite him upstairs into my home. The day was getting colder. Looking to my right, I saw a squirrel looking around before running to the other side of the road. The planet was becoming cleaner. Machines were planting trees, giving the animals species a chance to survive. Every once in a while I would see a fox make its way along the streets. The hunt of animals for sport was forbidden but the new generation wasn't thirsty for blood.

Crime still existed and not so long ago I'd seen a dying skeleton in Alcatraz, but every one of us that had been witnesses to that crime were made to sign a document saying that we wouldn't mention it to anyone. I thought then how many more crimes were happening throughout the world without anyone knowing? The news was lame. A lot of people called it Fake News and said that the New World Leaders controlled the news channel and that the public was only shown lies. But what did I care? There was no war, no poverty, and almost everyone had a decent life so why were people moaning? Human nature I guess.

Herculano fixed his eyes on me and smiled. He then gave me a card, a plain blue card with an email address. It wasn't even a business card. It was just a card with an email address. No name, no contact number, nothing else.

"No name?" I asked, flipping it over twice.

"I'm nameless," he said.

"First your name was Pessoa, then Herculano, and now you're nameless?"

He was trying to sound mysterious and funny, but he was failing at both. In fact he was starting to bore me.

Nonetheless, seeing that I had no cards with me, I wrote down my email address in one of his cards and gave it to him. Afterwards I thanked him once more for the meal and quickly went inside without bothering to say another word. I almost run up the steps (but why?), but then chose not to (and there was no reason for me to run), but afterwards I changed my mind and run up the steps, not because I was scared but because I wanted to see, from my window, which direction Herculano would take. He'd told me he lived nearby and instead of asking where he lived I simply nodded, but once I was home, going up the steps, I wanted to see which way he was heading.

I saw him cross the road and he went inside the minimarket. I stood by the window watching the street and the shops in front of me. Not much to see. Seconds went by and I saw my neighbour crossing the road, carrying a soup container and some food shopping with her. She lived on her own, in a one-bedroom apartment identical to mine, but sometimes her daughter and her son-in-law came to visit her, and she also had a young lover living on the floor above her. As for me, I had no visitors (but that would change). No family left. At least none that I know of. Every once in a while Jacques would call me just to see how I was. He had no one either. Apart from me, he had no one, and yet, there we were, living away from each other. We broke-up because I had an affair with a student while at university, a man my age, and when Jacques found out, instead of being upset with me, he simply said, "I understand. I'm too old for you."

I cried and said, "No! No! That's not it!"

I cried a bit more and then we spoke about our relationship, only to come to the conclusion that it -our relationship- had come to an end. He saved me from the streets, from poverty, from the poison, maybe even from a slow death, and in return I betrayed him. I wrote about it -our relationship- for a magazine, a series of stories, fifteen in total, where I changed all the names. The series of stories were called *A Nuclear Romance* and everyone thought it was fiction (or science-fiction, or even love-romance-cum-sci-fi) and everyone praised it, and, thanks to me, the magazine sold millions of copies. For a long time, or maybe just for the last few months, I've been thinking about writing a sequel to it, but there's nothing else to say about Jacques and me so what could I possibly write about?

Instead of throwing me out of his place as a punishment for betraying him, ever-so-patient Jacques let me stay for a bit longer, but I ended up moving two weeks later, into this apartment where I live now, and a week after that I broke-up with the other man. I realised too late that I had made a mistake and that the other man meant nothing to me, but I was too embarrassed -and ashamed- to go back to Jacques. How could I ask him to take me back?

I sat by the window watching the street. Below, a small crowd of teenagers made their way to the park where they would play basketball for a long time. A few minutes later, Herculano stepped out of the minimarket carrying two bags of groceries with him. He never looked up, but even if he did he wouldn't have been able to see me since I was hiding behind the curtains, and I watched him as he made his way along the sidewalk, but then he took a left at the end of the road and he was gone out of sight. The whole meeting with Herculano had felt weird but I knew I was right and that he was one of the sky poets. And I was almost sure that Noomi was one too. And I wondered if there were more sky poets and where did they came from and what did they expect to accomplish with all that sky writing?

I stood there for a few minutes more, just looking and thinking (but looking at what? Thinking about what?), and afterwards I went into my bedroom where I turned the laptop on, opened a new document, and wrote about the day and about the sky poet(s), and then I made myself a cup of coffee and wrote a bit more.

I wrote slowly; revising and editing and adding and taking out words while I wrote. Close to three hours later, I had what I thought would be the start to a new story, but what else would I write afterwards? I would have to wait and see if Herculano would get in touch again, or maybe I would email him later to set up a meeting. Yes, of course, I would do that, but not straight away because I didn't want to look as if I was too eager to see him so soon just after our first meeting. I would give it a couple of days before emailing him. In the meantime I would wait and see if the sky poet would reappear again. And I would try and finish my second novel and a few stories.

Before I went to bed I read the news online. A couple of bloggers had mentioned the sky poets and there were even photos of both aeroplanes. Like me, the bloggers who wrote about the sky poets were also sure that there was more than one sky poet. One blogger even said that the sky poets were probably a collective group of sky poets; "the worst poets you could find; failed poets, degenerate poets or fools who pretend to be poets. Idiots who read too much Bolaño or maybe they are the prophets of the New World so maybe we should call them sky prophets instead of sky poets. One of them wrote that life is sad and machines are bad, but, as of yet, that's not the case, but what does the poet knows that we don't? Probably nothing. And another poet (prophet? fool?) wrote that the poet has died and art was born, but what does the poet meant with that? And art hasn't died. Is just being reborn, and even machines are producing art," the blogger wrote.

That post was 33 minutes old and already there were 65 comments. I read none.

Afterwards I read Muza's blog, the infamous *Drek*. His last post was called *The Village of the Machines*, and, as the post said, it was about a village of machines, a village that kept on growing, "like a tumour," Muza wrote, "a virus, and one day the village will be a city, and afterwards the machines will take over the world. That day is near."

That post was seven hours old and it already had 357 comments. Again I read none of them and went straight to bed. Unable to fall asleep, I put on my headphones and listened to Nao Katafuchi for a few minutes. Something was going on outside because, even with the headphones on, I could hear laughter, but instead of getting up to go and see what was happening, I remained in bed.

On the following morning I was up a bit later than usual, and after showering, I got changed and went to a café across the road for a cup of coffee. Fuyuku, one of the baristas, was standing behind the counter listening to Tomoko Aran's *Body to Body*, and she smiled when she saw me and said, "Good morning, K-san. How are you this morning?"

"I'm fine, thank you. You?"

She was only three years younger than me but she spoke to me as if I were a lot older than her. Fuyuku had been working at that café for the last four years and she was an expert when it came to coffee. There were two other girls on duty with her. One of them was called Diana, named after a famous princess, or heroine; I can't remember which, and I couldn't remember the name of the other barista. The place was almost full. A lot of young people were reading books and drinking coffee. What else could they do with their free time? Music kept playing non-stop, the music of yesterday as the present seemed almost "soundless". One song would end and another would start almost immediately. *You Need a Change of Mind* by Brooklyn Express came on next. Fuyuku gave me her speciality; a *cortado* topped with cinnamon powder. I almost ordered a cake but quickly changed my mind, and then I carried my drink and sat at a small table near the window. I caught sight of a woman reading Ange Mlinko. I'd seen that woman before and greeted her with a bow. She smiled and bowed back. Suddenly, just as I was about to take a seat, soldiers walked past the café. Four soldiers, blue uniform. Machine soldiers. I hadn't seen a machine soldier in over two years. There was no more war. Maybe there would never be another war. There was only one government worldwide, no religion, no silly beliefs, and that's why there was no more war. Of course, everyone else turned around to take a good look at the soldiers. They looked lost, like birds flying without direction, birds looking for a nest, a home, a place to rest. Seeing them made me think of all the machines in the world. Many of them had been built for war, to protect and to serve, to do a lot of jobs, but jobs were dying and the machines were many and what would all these machines do later on? Maybe the blogger Muza was right. Maybe the machines were building their own world. But would there be a place for humans in it?

I sat down to drink my coffee. Didn't write a word while I was in there. One of the baristas put on a record by Tomo Akikawabaya. I don't think anyone was really listening to it. After reading a few more pages of the Bolaño book, and seeing the name of Lautréamont being mentioned a few times, I decided to get a book by that same poet, but I wanted it on paper so I went to a bookshop nearby. Of course, when it came to Lautréamont, there wasn't much choice.

It was a cold day and I wondered what Jacques was doing, and afterwards Herculano also came to my mind, and I imagined being in his arms, and then I saw myself making love to both Herculano and Jacques; two penises entering me, fucking me deeply, coming all over me, and I felt my cheeks go red, and at the same time I wanted to touch myself; I wanted to come.

What's wrong with you? I thought. *You're not a whore. You're not some horny teenager.*

But was it that bad to have those thoughts? They were only fantasies, things I would never do.

I once knew this girl at university who had a threesome with two boys. She only did it once with both of them, and even though she'd enjoyed it she told me that she didn't saw herself as a person who would take part in threesomes. She also told me that both boys (but they weren't really boys; they were young men, and she wasn't a girl; she was a young woman) got clingy and desperate, and afterwards both of them pestered her for a serious relationship, but she told them both, separately, at different times, more than once, that she didn't want to have a serious relationship while at university. Both men (because they were men, not boys; young men in their early twenties) told her that they would wait; they could wait; they didn't mind waiting, but she told them no, separately, at different times, more than once.

"Our thoughts can lead us to perdition," Jacques the philosopher told me once.

I was near the bookshop when I heard that familiar sound again. I looked up and I saw it. The aeroplane. A sky poet. A banner reading AN EMPTY CITY. Everyone looked up. The sky poet was writing history (and some lame poems along the way) and everyone wanted to witness it. It was almost as if the sky poet was killing the boredom; his and hers (boredom), and other people's boredom too. Even the bookshop owner stepped outside to witness it all, leaving the bookshop abandoned for a few minutes, knowing quite well that no one would go inside to steal books. But, from where he was standing, he could see the aeroplane, the shop entrance, the street, everything. Everything but the sky poet's face.

Just when I (and everyone else) thought that the sky poet was gone, he (or she) swung around and came diving toward us, or so it looked like, but the sky poet only wanted for us to read the other side of the banner.

It read A PLACE OF NO PITY. Ignoring everyone and everything else for a few seconds, including the sky poet, I reached for my notebook and wrote those words down: AN EMPTY CITY and A PLACE OF NO PITY.

What was the sky poet trying to tell us, that is if he or she was trying to tell us a thing? But if there was nothing to be said —or learned- why do such a stunt?

Maybe some things don't need to be explained or have no logical reason to be.

Maybe some things just have to happen so that boredom can be killed.

After the aeroplane was gone, I remained outside for a few minutes more, just looking at the empty sky. Minutes later, I saw a couple of drones fly by, heading towards the same direction that the sky poet had gone.

I waited outside for a bit longer but nothing else happened. No police. Nothing. There were others looking (but for what?) but they quickly got bored and made their way out of there. I waited for a bit longer (but for what?) before going to the bookshop.

I held the door open for a young man. He was tall, really blond, so blond that his hair was almost the colour of the sun, kind of pretty. He thanked me and then went straight to the graphic novels section, and, looking like a woman in love (or a bitch in heat), I followed him. He didn't waste time browsing through the books. He knew what he wanted and I watched him as he grabbed three books and made his way to the till.

I quickly wrote the names of the books down lest I forget.

Dear Beloved Stranger by Dino Pai

August Moon by Diana Thung

This One Summer by Jillian Tamaki and Mariko Tamaki

And as I wrote down the names of those books I felt like the character of Juan García Madero in *The Savage Detectives*, a young poet in Mexico City writing down the names of books that other poets and dreamers were reading.

Once the tall man was gone I made my way to the poetry section and got Lautréamont's *Maldoror and Poems*, and then I browsed for a bit longer and also bought Thomas Ligotti's *Songs of a Dead Dreamer* and *Grimscribe*, and *Revolution of the Mind: the Life of André Breton* by Mark Polizzotto. I already had too many books at home waiting to be read but a few more wouldn't hurt me plus the books were so cheap.

I made my way to the counter, the sky poet's latest stunt still engraved in my memory. AN EMPTY CITY, A PLACE OF NO PITY. What did those words meant?

There was a man in front of me paying for two books; *Love in the Land of Midas* by Kapka Kassabova and *Familiar Things* by Hwang Sok-yong. Both books were quite old and looked it. Then again so did the ones I was buying. I could have downloaded them but I wanted a physical copy, no matter how old it was. I like to hold the book in my hands and browse through the pages, and to see it there, somewhere, in a corner of my home. But I don't keep every single book that I buy. Sometimes I sell some of them for a lot less than what I paid for them. But never mind. Such is life (and I'm not complaining).

The man paid for the books, and the bookshop owner thanked him kindly, and as I looked at them both I thought that they looked so dull, as dull as a moronic machine, really boring, and I told myself, "Two empty souls in an empty city, a place of no pity."

I was repeating the sky poet's words and I couldn't believe that no one else was talking about the sky poet's latest stunt. Had humankind reached the age of boredom? The age of emptiness?

An empty city…

A place of no pity…

Is this what the sky poet was trying to tell us? That we were becoming dull and empty, worse than the machines? But why give it to us in riddles? Why not just say that we, the people, were empty and pitiless?

Berlin's *Metro*, a song from 1981, was playing on the radio, and hearing that tune then I thought, "When was the last time that a new band came out with something as original as that tune?"

An empty city…

The bookshop owner was staring at me, and for a moment it looked as if he was scared of me, but then it looked as if he was confused, or maybe I was the one who looked confused and the poor man was just wondering if I was feeling okay. I smiled but said nothing as I handed him the books. He scanned them without saying a word and I paid for the books. His eyes were avoiding mine, and as I took the books from him I said, "That was quite a stunt, wasn't it?"

The man said nothing and I thought, "What the hell is wrong with him? Can't he feel a thing?"

A place of no pity…

"The aeroplane!" I said. "The sky poet!"

"I don't think he's a poet," the man finally spoke.

"It could be a she," I said, but the bookshop owner ignored me and said, "He's a prophet. A sky prophet. A fake prophet, of course, like every prophet before him. After all, all prophets are fake. They preach and preach, but every word they say is a lie. We don't need prophets. War is over. Poverty is a thing of the past. Everyone has enough to live on; enough food to eat, books to read, clean water to drink. What else do we need? Certainly not a sky prophet."

"A sky prophet? I was thinking more of a sky poet, like the Infamous Hoffman in *Nazi Literatures in the Americas* and *Distant Star.*"

"Actually, Hoffman only appears in *Nazi Literatures in the Americas.* In *Distant Star* he's called Carlos Weider."

"Are you sure?"

"Of course."

I thought about it, and yes, he was right. Carlos Weider and the twins, the Garmendia sisters, Veronica and Angelica, twin sisters, sisters like Angelia Font and María Font, the sisters in *The Savage Detectives*, but the Font's weren't twins.

"Yes, you're right," I said, and the bookshop owner nodded. I looked to his left, my right, and saw a book next to the till, a copy of *Colonel Lágrimas* by Carlos Fonseca, and then I looked into his eyes, soft and mellow eyes, thanked him for everything and left. My body felt cold as I stepped outside and I decided to go home and rest.

I stayed in bed for most of the day, just catching up on a much needed rest. I drifted in and out of dreams, or maybe it was the same dream, a long dream with short breaks in between, and in my dream (dreams?) (nightmare?), at first I saw myself as the sky poet (I'll stick with poet, not prophet) flying around the city, with banners that read GO FUCK YOURSELVES WHILE I MAKE MYSELF A PIZZA or PASTA ALWAYS OVERCOOKS, ALWAYS ALWAYS ALWAYS or IF IT'S FIXED BREAK IT. In my dream I saw myself setting fire to machines and then running away from machine cops, getting on a small plane and flying along the city, being chased by a dozen flying drones, but the drones looked like something out of *Plan From Outer Space*, and I dreamt in black and white. I opened my eyes briefly, for two seconds or so, before falling asleep again. Instantly I was back in a dream, probably the same dream, in colour this time, and this time I was in a strange room with Jacques, being kissed by him, his tongue travelling along my body, when Herculano and John Barrymore the Great Profile, star of *Grand*

Hotel and *Twentieth Century*, entered the room. They stood there watching us, Jacques and I, while we made love, and afterwards John Barrymore lit a cigarette and started to make poems with the cigarette smoke while Herculano kept staring at me with hungry eyes, looking as if he wanted to fuck me or eat me. I woke up again, shivering with fever, my hair wet, and I removed my pyjamas while lying under the covers. Then I opened my legs and started to play with myself, and I heard a little voice inside me say, "You stupid little bitch! You're sick and you're masturbating!" I wanted to stop but I couldn't. When I came I went back to sleep, but less than thirty minutes later someone was ringing the doorbell so I got up, put on my pyjamas that were lying on the floor, next to the bed, and went to the door. Looking at the camera I saw that it was Herculano who was standing outside. I said hi and he waved at the camera, and then I let him in the building without another word being exchanged. I still felt poorly, and I wanted to go back to bed, but I was quite hungry plus I had a visitor, so the bed would have to wait. I heard a soft knock at the door and I opened it to let Herculano in.

The first thing he said to me was, "You look terrible."

"I feel sick," I said.

"And you look it."

He touched my forehead. His fingers were cold, like ice, but it felt good to be touched by him. He told me to sit down and I obeyed him. If anyone could see us then they would think I was the visitor and not Herculano.

"Wait here and I'll go across the road to get us something to eat," he said and I nodded. And then I said, "Where should I go? This is my home."

He laughed, or giggled a bit, and he seemed a bit embarrassed, too, and then he said, "I know, of course. What I meant is wait on the sofa and rest and I'll get us something to eat."
"Okay," I said, sounding like a little girl as I watched him leave.

He left a couple of books behind while he went out. I was feeling so poorly that I didn't even noticed he had the books with him when he came in, but once he was gone I looked at the two books on top of my small coffee table. One was about Bolaño and it was called *Roberto Bolaño: A Less Distant Star*, and it had been written by Ignacio López-Calvo. And the other book was *When I Hit You: Or, A Portrait of the Writer as a Young Wife* by Meena Kandasamy. Instead of browsing through the books, which I would normally do, I put on a record by Gigi Masin, and then I sat down and waited for my guest to return.

The curtains of the living room were open but the windows were closed because it was quite cold outside, and I sat there, on the sofa, looking at the full moon, at an almost starless sky, and, briefly, I remembered the days of war, the days of the Red Dust, and I knew that there were still some people out there, in some forgotten country or lawless city, trying to survive the Red Dust. There were parts of my country that had been deemed uninhabitable and parts of it had been destroyed by the Big Tsunami of 2036, but there were parts of it that were still liveable, and bit by bit the oceans were cleaning themselves, with the help of large machines, of course, and, sadly to say, because there were less humans there was less rubbish too, and I knew that the population of the world would never reach the numbers of the past, which was good, not only for the planet but also for the human race, because, in the end, when one thinks about it, the human race is the worst enemy of the human race. Sad but true, and I've already written about it in one of my short stories. A lot of women could no longer have kids. Some women, because of the dust and radiation or whatever, couldn't get pregnant while others didn't even bother. Plus the New Order also didn't want for the human race to grow again at an absurd rate.

I was one of those women who couldn't have kids and I was fine with it. I liked my independence, my freedom, the laziness of my self-imposed loneliness and weirdness, and my neediness for long moments of silence, which kind of reminded me of my life in the streets, my life after the Big War ended, a life of loneliness and searching; searching for a place to stay, for food, entertainment, and even then, while I was on my own, after the death of parents, I felt fine about it; about the extreme loneliness. Rummaging through the ruins of my town I found an abandoned petrol station which would become my home for a few months until Jacques found me. While in there, at that petrol station, I read every single magazine and book that had been left behind. And whoever had lived there had left behind a large collection of books. I found a lot of books by Kiriu Minashita, Takashi Hiraide, Banana Yoshimoto, Sawako Nakayasu, Hitomi Kanehara, Kyong-Mi Park, etc., in one of the backrooms. I also found a futon and some blankets, and that backroom became my bedroom. There weren't a lot of survivors left in that small town and, bit by bit, those who survived moved out, leaving me completely on my own. I had the whole town for myself but I hardly ever left the petrol station. There was nothing out there for me. No one waiting for me. No one looking for me.

One morning I went to a supermarket, filled a trolley with food and a couple of books by Ryu Murakami, and then I went back to the petrol station, and when I got there I saw Jacques filling up the tank of his Jeep. I wondered what the hell a gaijin was doing there, and then I wondered if he was a soldier, an enemy, and, in my mind, I saw him raping me and then killing me, and I felt like a character in one of those tragic Yukio Mishima novels, but the man –Jacques- smiled and said he thought the place was empty, but since I was there he would pay me for the petrol, and I told him that there was no need for it because I wasn't the owner of the petrol station: "I only live here," I said as I pushed the trolley towards the front door, and then he said, "Where's everyone? I haven't seen a single soul."

And I said, "Everyone's gone. They all left town. I'm the only person left."

He had a long beard and he was wearing sunglasses so I couldn't really see what he looked like.

"Why haven't you left too?" he asked and I shrugged my shoulders because I didn't know what to say.

But then I thought about it and said, "I have no one." Which was true (and sad) as I really had no one.

"You can't stay here forever on your own. What if you get sick?" he said.

"I'm already sick," I said.

"Red Dust?"

"Yes."

"Come with me. I'll get someone to clean your lungs."

I looked around me. There was no reason to stay.

"Only if you show me your eyes," I said.

He smiled and I could hardly see his lips amongst that bushy beard of his, but then he removed his sunglasses and I got close to him, and I saw two big dark eyes staring at me, friendly big eyes, but threatening, too, like the eyes of a killer, an angelic killer, if such thing exists.

We stood there for a couple of minutes staring at one another, and afterwards I said okay and he nodded, and I felt like a princess being rescued by a prince, a much older prince, a prince from another country, and I knew then that we would become lovers and that I would never return to that town. We grabbed some food and water from the trolley, put it all in the back of his car, and I went inside to get a bag of clothes and my diary because by then I was already writing (but not that much), and afterwards we left that forsaken town for good.

Herculano returned with wonton noodle soup, Miso chicken Teriyaki and Tenmusu. I let him in the apartment and thanked him for his kindness, and then sat down again to eat while he prepared more food for us.

"Nice place you have here. Clean, minimalistic; so different from mine," he said as he made his way along the small living room. My kitchen was small, connected to the living room, but it had a large window that gave me a good view of the city. The living room walls were empty, bare of anything. I had a couple of bookshelves in the living room, a sofa, a small coffee table, two plant pots, an iPod, and that was it. I did most of my writing in the bedroom where I had my laptop, a small futon, my clothes and my desk by the window. My apartment was small; tiny when compared to Jacques' place, but it was enough for one person, even for two, and I liked it, which was what really mattered.

Herculano poured tea for us and then helped himself to some chicken Teriyaki, and it felt weird to have him there with me, and at the same time it didn't felt weird at all. I felt then as if I'd known him all my life, which was kind of weird, or maybe it wasn't; maybe we had met in a previous life, if such thing exists, or maybe, somehow, we were related to one another, our ancestors having interconnected and mixed their genes centuries ago. Nothing is impossible.

Ages ago Jacques had told me that he believes we're all connected to each other, all part of the same tribe, every human being, regardless of races, all related to each other. From the bits he shared with me, I found out that Jacques had taken part in The Great War, and what he'd seen and heard had made him sick; all that needless killing and hate, all because of greed and religion and who-knows-what-else, and once the war was over he could no longer return to the life he used to live, and he no longer wanted to be the man he used to be, so he fled and left everything behind, and started a new life in the process. My parents had done the same thing but for different reasons. For reasons unknown to me, my parents had left their old life and their new apartment in Adachi behind, and moved to a small town in the middle of nowhere. I was four then but I still remembered it so well. One night a man driving a big van came to our place in Adachi, and afterwards my father and the man loaded some of our stuff into the back of the van and we left Tokyo without saying a word to anyone. From what I know, my father had a lot of debts and he was unable to pay them so he just left, taking mama and me with him. Once we were at our new place, my mother said to me, "From now on you will be called Mieko K."

"What does the K stands for?" I asked.

"Kazuya," mama said.

Both my parents died during The Great War. I found the bodies a few days later when I stepped out of one of the bunkers. They were meant to have joined me at the bunker but never got there on time. There were other survivors at the bunker with me, not many, eleven people only, but instead of joining them when they left town I remained on my own. And then Jacques found me. And later I found Herculano.

The wonton soup was delicious and as I ate it I felt the sweat running down my body, carrying the virus out of me. Outside, it had started to rain and I wondered where Herculano lived.

"Where do you write?" he asked. "Do you have a computer?"

"In my bedroom. Actually, I write everywhere in the apartment. I just carry the laptop with me from room to room," I said.

The rain was falling down heavily on the city. Much needed rain.

"I have a typewriter at my place. That's where I write," he said.

"You write? And what do write?" I asked (but I already knew).

"Poetry," he said.

A poet. Just what the world needed.

"Sky poetry?" I said and smiled, and then I swallowed some tea. Sweat was pouring down my body. Once Herculano was gone I would have a long bath. But for how long did he intend to stay?

"Just poetry," he said almost sadly. "And other stuff."

A tram drove past the building. I didn't see it but I saw its lights flashing. The city was quiet. Everyone was taking cover from the rain.

"Did you know that Bolaño used to be a poet?" he said.

"Yes, of course, but to be honest with you I'm not a big fan of his poetry," I said.

"You're not?" he sounded disappointed.

Not knowing what to say, and not wanting to attack Bolaño's poetry (it wasn't that bad; it just wasn't for me), I simply shrugged my shoulders.

It was true; I wasn't a big fan of Bolaño the poet even though I love Bolaño the writer. They were both one and the same; the poet and the writer (and Bolaño had also written some great short stories), but the poet sounded nothing like the writer.

"A lot of the characters in his books tend to be writers. Or poets. Or vagabonds. Or a mixture of the three," I said.

"Or sky poets," Herculano said. It was his turn to smile.

Ignoring him, but not deliberately, I ate some Tenmusu and felt the energy returning. Nevertheless, I was still so tired and looked it.

After telling him in which cupboard I kept my medicine, Herculano went into the kitchen to get it and returned seconds later with my pills. I swallowed two of them while a worried Herculano kept staring at me. At times he looked so confident but there were times when he looked almost like a child.

"I came to your place at the wrong time. You need rest and not a guest," he said.

"No. You're wrong. You came at the right time," I said.

The disease was returning. The insides could never be truly cleaned. Or maybe I was just being pessimist. But no; something inside me told me that the end was coming. My end. And I still had a last novel to complete. And I would never write about the sky poet. Or maybe I would add him (or her) (or them) to my novel.

At times Herculano looked as shy as a child and he would act a bit awkwardly and scratch his head, and look away whenever I said a word to him.

"Is he a virgin?" I wondered.

He told me he wrote poetry but he didn't look to be in a rush to show me what he wrote. Did he have any poems with him? Did he carry notebooks with him? I wasn't in a rush to ask, to know.

Poetry was still alive, and, as I've already mentioned, Su, an old friend of mine from university, wrote poetry in her spare time, and I even remember seeing a couple of her poems on an online magazine, and they were quite good, but what about Herculano's poetry?

"Show me some of your poems," I said before swallowing some tea. There was nothing happening outside, which was good. No noise, no confusion, no madness. I remember the chaos and the screams before The Great War started. My father had predicted that the war would start many years before it actually happened, and he knew what he was doing when we moved out of Adachi. We moved to a town in the middle of nowhere, deep in the mountains, where we started a new life under different names, and one morning I went for a walk near the mountains with my father and he took me to see some old bunkers that had been built long ago. He told me that if there was ever a Big War we should hide in those bunkers. When I asked him how he knew about those bunkers he was rather vague about it and said, "Someone once told me about them." He left it at that. And when the war finally started, years later, that's where I hid, but my parents never managed to join me.

A car drove past the building but its electric engine made almost no noise. And then Herculano handed me a small stained notebook. The notebook looked as if it had been put through a puddle of mud. Or the sewers.

"Some poems in there," he said, and then he hesitated before adding, "And notes for a play."

"A play?"

"Yes. A play. A Renaissance comedy, something along the lines of the Roman dramatist Publius Terentius Afer or, as he's better known, simply Terence. You've heard of him, right?"

I nodded.

I was starting to feel a bit better. Maybe I was being pessimist when I said the disease was back.

"Yes. Of course," I finally replied. "I read *The Eunuch*, only once, while I was still at uni. Why a play?"

"When was the last time that someone wrote a play?" he said.

"True. I understand now. And what's your play about?"

"A sky poet," he said, and when I looked at him I saw a huge grin on his face.

"I knew it!" I said.

"How?"

"Instinct, I guess. A feeling. And Noomi too?"

"Yes."

"But why?"

"Who knows? Boredom, maybe? Look around you. The human race seems to have come to a standstill, a total surrender to boredom and nothingness and minimalism. Everyone seems to be happy doing nothing and let the machines take over.

"Sometimes I look around me and I too feel like stopping and do nothing, but if we all do that, where will we end up?

"People like you are still creating art but there are many others out there who are happy doing nothing while getting their Fair Wage. The truth is most people are lazy, and if you pay them to do nothing, they will take the money and do just that.

"This city is still vibrating with life, or just about, but take a look outside now and you will hardly see a soul."

"I agree with what you say but only to a certain extent, but the truth is the old days weren't as great as many people say they were. Before The Great War or The Big War or whatever you want to call it happened, I remember reading about two drunks who beat a poor old man to death and about a drunk driver who run over a young child, and things like this led to the ban of alcohol once and for all, and I must say that it was for the best even though I miss a cup of old sake.

"As for religion, how many wars were fought in the past because of different beliefs? How many children were abused by so-called holy men? How many crimes were committed –and hidden- because of religion?

"Now we have one government and everyone has a job or a Fair Wage and a place to live, when, before, there was a lot of poverty."

"There were more of us back then. And have you noticed how the human birth has declined? Meanwhile the machines keep on growing."

"Evolution," I said.

"Evolution? How can you say that? How can you call it evolution?"

"And why can't I call it evolution? After all, the machines are living things too."

"But… they're machines!"

"So what? They are here, in this planet, working and living. If you destroy a machine it stops existing, just like a human being does. Maybe the machine is the last step on evolution."

My body was getting cold again but I felt a lot better (but I guess I already mentioned this).

Herculano didn't know what to say which was good because I didn't want to argue with him. Instead I asked if he would mind if I read some of his poetry and a bit of his play, and he nodded shyly and said, "Yeah. Sure. But I'm not sure if you're going to like it."

When talking about his writing, he spoke with his head down, his eyes avoiding mine, and he looked as if he was feeling a bit awkward to be there with me, even embarrassed by sharing his writing with me. One minute he looked so confident and the next he looked so shy, almost like a child. "Definitely a virgin," I thought. "A man afraid of being alone with a woman."

I told him to make himself comfortable: "Have a rest, if you're tired," I said. Again, he nodded.

We sat on the sofa almost side by side, with him reading the López-Calvo book while I read his notes. His poems were strange, and some lines were unreadable, at least to me they were as I couldn't understand what he wrote. One of the poems went like this,

A plane burning in the sky.

Falling at a slow speed.

Death writing tragedy in smoke.

But no one is watching.

No one is reading.

No one is crying.

I didn't like that poem. In fact, if I'll be honest here (and why shouldn't I?), I hated it. But it is fair to say that poetry was never my thing.

One of the poems was about some amphibian god, someone like Oannes, and it was long and boring. A poem about an empty city. A poem about two candles burning, being watched by two children, a boy and a girl. Herculano and Noomi? A poem about the last days of a prisoner; his last meal, the rotten smell of the cell, cockroaches running from one end of the cell to the next. A poem set in Gwanju, South Korea, again about the last days of a man, this time a poet. A poem about a burning city, its only habitant being a machine. Apparently the machine was the devil. Or a saint. Or a lost angel.

The poems looked as if they had been written in a rush. Finally, the play. It concerned a soldier who falls in love with a woman named Olivia. The soldier-flyer, then later turned sky poet, is forced to serve abroad by his cruel father. The play was a mixture of Terence's *The Self –Tormentor* and Wiseau's *The Room*, and it was some sort of dark comedy. I browsed through it quickly, trying to look as if I was really interested in it, but, bored by what I was reading, I had to put it aside. I looked to my left and saw that Herculano was dozing off. I told him to lie down on the sofa and have a rest, but he said no and told me it was getting late and he had to go, but if I was free in the morning, and feeling better, he would take me somewhere.

"Yes. I would like that," I said. "I might stay up for a bit longer, catch up on my writing, maybe watch a movie, but, nevertheless, I should be up around 10am."

"I'll see you then," he said.

"Breakfast is on me. And thank you for today," I said.

He was already up, looking at me as if he was a little child. He smiled and said, "No problem."

"Don't forget your notebook." I'm not sure if he had intended to leave the notebook with me, but the truth is I really didn't want to read whatever he wrote.

He smiled and nodded at the same time, looking both disappointed with himself and with me, and he took the notebook from me and left without saying another word. I didn't even bother to go to the window to watch him leave. Instead I lain on the floor for a few minutes more, and afterwards I got up and tidied around the living room. I wanted to write but I really didn't have the energy for it so instead I watched an old movie called *3-Iron* on my computer, but once the movie was finished, feeling a lot better, I opened the document where I had saved the notes about the sky poet and wrote about Herculano's visit. So boredom had turned him into a sky poet?

Before he left my place Herculano told me that he would be visiting me on the following day and that he would take me somewhere special. But I already mentioned this, didn't I?

It didn't take me long to write what I wanted to write, and afterwards, after I wrote about the sky poet, I got up and went into the kitchen where I swallowed two pills and drank some water, and then I returned to my room and watched another movie; Wong Kar-wai's *2046*, and I felt an urge to finally write a sequel to my novella *A Nuclear Romance*, which was included in my collection of short stories, but it was really late and my eyes felt as if they were burning and I felt really tired, so I turned the computer off; I watched the movies on my laptop, and decided to get some sleep. And the moment I closed my eyes I fell asleep.

I dreamt of a desert, a strange desert, and I saw myself walking side by side with Herculano, stepping on the bodies of machines; metal bodies, pieces of metal and wires lying everywhere, some machines still moving, parts of machines twisting on the floor, and they looked as if they had been the victims of some major disaster, an apocalyptic disaster, and then I looked up and saw a sky poet piloting a massive spaceship, a large banner at the end, the words HAVE NO FEAR, THE END IS NEAR written on it, and I turned to look at Herculano but he was gone. I looked around me and I couldn't see a living soul, but then I saw broken machines coming towards me, wires coming out of their eye sockets, machines with no arms or with no legs and even with no heads marching or crawling slowing towards me. I tried to get out of there but felt something grabbing my leg. I looked down and saw the arm of a machine holding on to my leg. Meanwhile the spaceship was heading towards me, its tail now on fire. I wanted to scream and I wanted to run away, but the machine's arm wouldn't let me move. (In my dream) I was breathless, gasping for air while the whole spaceship was on fire, heading towards me. Like I said, I wanted to scream. Instead I opened my eyes and stared at the dark ceiling.

I looked at my watch. It was still early, but not that early. Nevertheless, I decided to get up.

I took a long shower. I already felt much better. Outside, the sky was bare of clouds. After putting on some clean pyjamas, I put a record on by Yutaka Hirose. Feeling inspired, I grabbed a cup of coffee and sat at my desk. Soon enough the street down below started to show signs of life. Sitting close to the window, I saw teenagers coming out of their homes and heading towards the tram shop.

"Farmers," I said to myself.

The machines did most of the farming (and everything else) but there were humans who still worked in the fields. It was either that or stay at home dying of boredom. And talking about dying; before I wrote a word, I read the news and saw that suicide was on the rise. People had everything they could possibly need and yet they weren't happy. Were they bored or was something else missing? Empathy? Love? Were those things missing from our society? Had the machines and all the technology made many of us senseless and cruel? Did some of us miss religion and lies? Wars and poverty?

What the hell was wrong with the world?

Humans were never happy. Never, never, ever.

First they wanted the technology, the chance to do nothing, the end of war and religion and needless conflicts, and they got what they wanted (and a lot more) (but do they know what they want?); an easy life, a life of boredom or pleasure (but did they want it all?), a Fair Wage which allowed them to live a comfortable, minimalistic life, but some humans weren't happy so they committed suicide. "A bit drastic," I thought.

144

I wrote for a couple of hours before being interrupted by someone pressing the door buzzer.

"It must be Herculano," I thought. But then I wondered if it was someone else? But who would come to my place seeing that I never had any visitors?

It was Herculano.

I let him in the building, and then I stood by the door waiting for him. He was wearing jeans and dark boots, and a thick leather jacket zipped right to the top. And he had two helmets with him.

"Are you ready?" he asked and smiled.

The edges of his boots were dirty and worn-out, and his leather jacket looked to be quite old.

"Where are we going?" I asked, and even though I didn't felt like going out, I knew I would go with him wherever he wanted us to go.

"I want to show you something," he said as he stood in the corridor facing me.

Looking into his eyes, I felt overcome by a feeling of emptiness, followed by a longing. But what did I long for? A family? A brother? A sister? The things and the people I never had?

"What? What do you want to show me?" I asked, and I was a bit surprised by my harsh tone.

Herculano's face seemed to drop, and for a moment he looked a bit sad, but only for a couple of seconds or so, because, afterwards, he smiled again, a confident smile, a smile that seemed to be filled with either courage or insanity or maybe even naivety, and he said, "The cemetery. The palace."

"What cemetery? What palace?" I asked.

He sighed deeply. My meaningless questions were boring him. He even looked and sounded bored with me.

"The palace of metal and the cemetery of aeroplanes," he said. "We spoke about it. Yesterday."

Did we?

"We did?" I asked.

"Yes," he said and nodded.

Maybe we did, but if we did I'd forgotten about it.

Someone was coughing somewhere. My old neighbour, probably. He seemed to be allergic to everything, including oxygen.

"But if you don't want me to show it to you, that's fine," he said, his pose already showing signs of a lost battle.

I touched his face and said, "I'll go with you. Let me just put on something warmer. And, please, come inside."

I quickly got changed. Before we left my place, we drank a cup of warm coffee. My kitchen was in a bit of a mess, a few plates and cups waiting to be washed, but it would have to wait.

Herculano had parked his Yamaha Virago right in front of the building. A beautiful machine. A relic. Cheap and reliable.

"Where did you buy this?" I asked.

People walked past the building and looked at the motorbike. It really was gorgeous.

"It belonged to my father," he said as he put his gloves on. He gave me a pair of gloves and a helmet and afterwards I sat on the back, behind him.

"Hold on tight," he said.

We made our way out of the city, driving slowly along the highway, the cold wind slapping against our faces. An almost empty tram drove past us. Only two passengers, and both of them were staring at us on the motorbike.

We left the city behind and headed towards the mountains, the desert, the emptiness that lay ahead. It was my first time on a motorbike, and to be honest, I think once was more than enough.

After being on the road for less than thirty five minutes, we stopped. We had left the city behind only to find ourselves staring at another city, a city in the desert.

An empty city.

A place of no pity.

It was a quiet place. Empty (an empty city, a place of no pity), or so I thought, but, looking into the distance, I saw two machines looking our way. Two old machines, no synthetic skin covering their faces. I hadn't seen machines like that in years. As a matter of fact, I thought they were extinct.

The machines stood there looking at us as Herculano pushed the motorbike and I followed him. By then we were walking. He wanted me to see that city, see what he must have seen endlessly and that's why he had to write those sky poems of his. Suddenly, just as I looked to the left, I saw more machines walking along the city, but they didn't even bother with us.

"What's this place?" I asked.

"The future. A city with no humans," Herculano said.

An empty city, devoid of humans. A place of no pity… for humans?

It was like a scene from a surrealistic old black and white science-fiction movie. *Blade Runner* as seen through the eyes of Jean-Luc Godard.

"The city of your poem?" I asked.

"Yes. I've been watching it from afar, watching it grow, watching it for a long time, watching it grow like a virus," he said.

"I suppose they need a place to live, especially the old machines as no one seems to want them now," I said, knowing that it wasn't what Herculano expected to hear.

"Why do you care so much about the machines?" he said angrily.

Meanwhile the machines kept moving along, watching us as we too moved along.

"For who-knows-how-long, we, the human race, have taken everything for granted and we have abused this planet. Maybe it's time for a new species to take over from us," I said, giving him an old speech of mine.

"They're not a species! They are machines!"

"The last species, maybe?"

"What about aliens? They're a species too."

"There's no such thing, just like G-d. If there were any aliens, or, for that matter, a G-d, I guess we would have seen them by now," I said.

"So you're okay with the end of Mankind?" he said aggressively. Poor Herculano looked hurt. And a bit stressed, too.

"The machines won't be the end of Mankind. Mankind will be the end of Mankind. Anyway, we created the machines. If anyone is too blame, we, again, are."

"Yes, true, but now machines are building other machines."

I shrugged my shoulders. Yes, machines were giving "birth" to other machines. Evolution but Herculano would not accept it so what else could I say? My sky poet seemed to be a rebel without a cause.

Ignoring him, I looked around us, at that city that was slowly growing, a city like no other. The city was glowing, running on solar power, wind power, machine power. It was a thing of beauty, a city like no other, maybe the first of many, the city of tomorrow, a city surrounded by trees and artificial grass, and I saw cats strolling along the streets of that mechanical city. Somehow the cats felt at home there, safe in the company of machines. The machines even fed the cats and looked after them. They saw us there but they didn't seem that bothered with us. It was hard to tell if they were all machines. They were so perfectly made that a person could no longer distinguish a human being from a machine. We had built the first machines, perfecting them as time went by, adding a few bits along the way. More life, a better memory, better skin, better everything. Soon, the machines started taking over us, our jobs, our lives, and then they started building other machines. More machines. Better machines. Machines built by machines. Evolution, yes. But where were we heading to? Maybe Herculano was right. And maybe I should be more worried about the machines taking over. But, then again, the machines did us no harm. If anything, we, the humans, were our own worst enemies.

A lady machine started to make her way towards us, her face showing no signs of emotion. She was pretty, really pretty, well made, but so dull. She was wearing a long black dress, sandals and Buddhist beads. Did the machines have a religion? Did they meditate? Did they close their eyes and thought of nothing or did they thought about the past?

The writer in me was making mental notes of everything around us.

The machine got closer to us and asked, "Are you lost?"

She sounded friendly.

"No. We're fine, thank you," Herculano replied. He sounded a bit nervous.

The machine ignored me as she looked Herculano in the eye.

She had light brown skin, long dark hair, and small brown eyes. A perfectly made machine.

"I've seen you here before," the machine said. "Twelve times."

"Thirteen times now. Bad luck," I said and smiled. It was my way of making a joke but no one smiled. Maybe no one got the joke, or maybe the joke wasn't even that funny. I felt a lot better by being out. More relaxed. Probably to do with the mountain air around us.

"Can't I drive past here?" Herculano said, still sounding nervous. And stressed, too.

I didn't like the way he addressed the machine. Some people still had a phobia or a hatred of the machines. Only a few, I think. Herculano was one of those few. To me the machines were no cause for concern. But humans worried me.

"I'm sorry," I said. "We're just sightseeing. We like the mountains plus I've been a bit sick and the fresh air does me good. By the way, I'm Mieko."

I extended my right hand forward. The machine looked at it and then shook it. She had a strong grip but soft skin, and her mechanical eyes were really pretty, so deep, as if she knew the secrets if the universe, what makes us all human and fearful and brave, or maybe I was just being silly or romantic.

"I'm Adina," the machine said.

She looked to be gentle, just like her name. Patient. Friendly. So unlike Herculano. What was his problem anyway? He was trying too hard to look like the romantic rebel; Rimbaud on a motorbike.

Adina then told me that she knew who I was and that she had read my work, and I nodded and smiled.

"Machines read," I thought. "Machines read me."

I wanted to ask her something, make small talk, learn more about –and from- the machines, but Herculano the arsehole was trying too hard to be a romantic rebel (but he looked like a complete fool), and he grabbed me by the sleeve and said, "We have to go."

I said okay without bothering to look at him, and then, still looking at Adina, I said, "If I can, I'll come and visit you again."

I don't even know why I said that, but at the time if felt like the right thing to say, and I felt that I should go back to that "empty city" to see Adina again. Unfortunately it would never happen.

Adina said, "Okay," adding afterwards, "I'll be waiting."

Naturally, by then Herculano the idiotic boring not-romantic-at-all poet was fuming. He was already sitting on his motorbike, waiting for me, looking as if he was ready to leave without me. I sat behind him and we were off. A few minutes later we reached our destination. Noomi was there. We saw her straight away. There were two cops standing next to her. A machine cop and a human cop. I had seen them before, in Alcatraz.

We could have turned away but Herculano made his way to where they were. The cops stood still, looking as if they had been waiting for us. They already had Noomi so what was the point of Herculano trying to escape or hide? Why delay the inevitable? Which is…?

Roy, Douglas and Noomi watched us as we stopped next to them. If Noomi was nervous she didn't show it. In fact she looked at ease standing next to Roy and Douglas.

Roy the machine cop smiled when he saw me and said, "Hello Mieko, how are you?"

"I'm good, thank you. And you?" I said. I didn't have to look at Herculano's face to know that he must have been surprised by the fact that I knew that cop. That machine cop, I must add.

"I'm good, thank you," Roy said and nodded, and I couldn't help thinking that the machines were becoming more human-like. I didn't know if that was good or bad. It would have been good if they were developing qualities such as empathy and love, but what about greed? The need for more? The need for all?

Could a machine become greedy? And if they could, what would they want?

The world?

A world of no pity?

A world of no humans?

"And you must be Herculano," said Douglas the human cop.

He looked more machine (and cold) than Roy, but Roy had no stubble while Douglas looked as if he needed a good shave.

Herculano didn't say a word.

There was no else nearby, nothing around us. The air was stale. Dry. Tasteless. I felt like a crow in a desert with nothing to eat, or worse; I felt like a tired wolf waiting to be devoured by the crows. All of a sudden I felt so tired, almost drained of life, of fluids. Yes, the disease was back. It had followed me all the way from Japan. Jacques thought that the doctors had cleaned me but I was still dirty. By instinct, I touched my forehead. Nothing. Nothing but coldness, but what did I expect to find there?

"They know about the aeroplanes," I heard Noomi say, and I saw her staring at Herculano who still didn't say a word. And Douglas was staring at Noomi while Roy was staring at me.

"What's the matter?" Roy asked and I told him I wasn't feeling that well.

"You don't look too well. In fact, you're turning white. Pale," Douglas said.

The four of them stared at me and their stares only made me feel worse. In fact, I felt like a criminal, or some rare animal, some contaminated beast that needed to be incarcerated and put on quarantine.

"I'll be okay. Can we just go home, please?" I said.

I looked at the old hangar in front of us. The aeroplanes were probably in there but I couldn't be bothered with them. Sky poetry was dead, about to be buried for good after a short life, and I just wanted to go home.

Herculano looked at the cops. It was plain to see that he was lost, my poor romantic virgin poet. And he still hadn't said a word, my poor cowardly virgin poet. Up in the sky he was brave and fearless, but on the ground he was cowardly and speechless.

Eventually Herculano said something and asked the cops if it was okay to drive me home, and Douglas the human cop said, "I think it would be best if we take her home as it is less cold in the car, not to mention more comfortable."

Herculano nodded.

"As for the two of you," Douglas said, looking first at Noomi, and then at Herculano, "I think you should leave and never return here. No one wants to know about sky poetry. Do that and we would consider case closed."

Herculano nodded and said nothing. As for Noomi, she looked like a little girl who had just been told off and managed to escape the punishment with just a warning.

I turned around and left without saying goodbye.

"What a crap story," I thought as I got in the back of the car. "No suspense, no fighting, no proper ending, no nothing. I didn't even get to see the aeroplanes."

Shostakovich's Symphony n°5 was playing on the radio and Douglas was listening to it with his eyes closed. I heard him say, "Stupid kids," but neither Roy nor I said a word. Roy was driving. We didn't drive past the city of machines. I wondered if Roy knew some of the machines, and if he did, did he ever visit the city of machines?

After a while, as we were getting closer to my place, I asked, "What will happen to Herculano and Noomi?"

"Nothing. When you think about it, they haven't really done anything wrong. There's no law that forbids people from writing sky poetry. And they do have licences to fly small aeroplanes," Douglas said, his eyes still closed.

"What about the aeroplanes? What will happen to them?" I asked.

"Nothing," Douglas said, and he sounded a bit bored. Yes, the age of boredom (and nothingness) was upon us. Unfortunately it wouldn't last and once it was gone we would miss it. But I'm getting ahead of the story. Too ahead of it.

After that there wasn't much else to say. Copying Douglas, I closed my eyes and listened to Shostakovich, and my body got a bit warmer inside.

Roy drove fast, and when he dropped me outside my home I thanked him and then hurried inside. Neither of the cops seemed that bothered (or worried) with me. Then again, they didn't seem that bothered with Herculano and Noomi either. Once inside my apartment I called Jacques. I wanted to see him. Again, I wanted to apologise for everything, and I also wanted to tell him that I missed him. That I loved him. Yes, I loved him.

The phone rang and nothing.

I left a message, three words; "I love you."

A few hours later, he came to see me.

I opened the door and saw him there, the man I loved, the man who saved me, the man I betrayed, standing in front of me. I opened my arms to take him. I opened my body to let him in. Afterwards, after sex, once we showered, Jacques said, "We need to leave."

I said nothing.

What was he talking about?

Leave?

Go where?

Leave what?

Looking out of the window, I saw a starless sky in front of us, empty streets, a small fire in someone's rooftop.

"You heard what I said?" Jacques asked.

I nodded. Then I said, "Yes. You said we need to leave."

"The country. We need to leave the country. A week of violence is coming soon. After that there will be no going back to the human race. Not here. Not in this country," he said.

I didn't ask him how he got that information. He just got it. After all, he was the greatest detective in the New World and the information was there, on websites, on the websites of the government, on the Dark Web, on leaflets, in between the lines.

I told him I wasn't feeling well, that maybe the disease was back, that maybe my lungs weren't really clean, that maybe I was dying.

Jacques said, "We're all dying. The moment we're born we're dying."

A fox crossed the road and then looked up. Seconds later, it vanished in the dark.

"Don't worry about a thing. I know a good doctor in Safed, even better than the one in Japan," he said.

"Safed?"

"Yes. Safed. Israel. Home."

We left for Israel two days later, a couple of weeks before the beginning of the week of violence. Later, when we were already settled in Safed, I watched it all unfold on the TV screen in front of me. Man versus Machine. Madness versus madness. On the news, I saw an aeroplane flying above a city on fire, a banner reading OUR HEARTS ARE ON FIRE, GIVE US BACK OUR HUMANITY. That aeroplane was followed by another aeroplane, a banner on its back reading WE CAN ONLY TAKE SO MUCH, GIVE US BACK OUR DIGNITY. "Herculano and Noomi?" I wondered. Once again, just as I knew it would happen, some humans had totally lost it.

On the news, I and everyone else at the café saw a group of masked humans running towards a female machine and they started to hit her with baseball bats. The machine tried to defend itself but the humans were too many, barbarians I must add, and the poor machine couldn't fight them all. Even after the machine was on the floor, the barbarians kept hitting her on the head with the baseball bats, except they weren't really baseball bats. They were metal bats. Such violence. So much hate.

On the news, we heard (and then saw) the sirens and we saw the humans run away. The machine was lying on the floor, barely moving. A police car stopped beside her and two machine cops came to her rescue. More police cars drove by but no one else stopped. Those who didn't stop went in pursuit of the criminals.

The two cops reached for the female machine. One of the cops had to hold the machine's head while the other lifted her up. Such had been the brutality and violence used by the humans that the machine's head was hanging by only a few wires.

I couldn't watch it anymore. Watching it made me sick, almost ashamed of being human. Later, on the news, when I was at home, I saw a building on fire and machines jumping from the rooftop or from their rooms, hoping to escape the fire. Machines melting on the ground, making the most horrendous noise as they melted away. As they died. But then the machines fought back.

The violence lasted for one week.

One full week.

It started because some humans wanted more freedom (but they were free to do what they wanted so what the hell were they talking about?), and then they brainwashed other humans with their silly ideas and idiotic religious beliefs, and one thing led to another, which, in turn, as it always happens, led to violence.

The humans wanted freedom to pray to fake gods, freedom to rape and kill and get drunk and smoke drugs, freedom to fight and then rape and kill and…

Freedom to do whatever they wanted.

Freedom to behave like animals, like beasts.

For three days the city I used to call home burned away slowly. Then, on the fourth day, the machines came out to play. Every single machine. Every single one of them.

We watched gobsmacked, our heads almost glued to the screens, as the machines patrolled the streets. I'd never seen so many machines in my entire life. Where did they all come from?

For days everyone stayed glued to their televisions and other small screens.

In Safed I felt much better, and after seeing a few doctors, I was breathing a lot better. I was also told that there was nothing wrong with my lungs, and after leaving the doctor's I went straight home where I started working on a new novel. I called it *Back to Israel.* It would be a novel based on Jacques' life. The novel would consist of four volumes and it would take me close to eight years to finish them all. But I was in no rush.

At the end of the seventh day the violence finally came to an end and the machines had taken over Canada. Soon they were taking over the world, everything, burning more books, ideas, and especially religion. Some people were okay with it. Others protested silently. Turning to me, Jacques said, "Don't worry. It's just a phase. A new age. But even the machines won't last. They think they will but they won't. Look at the dinosaurs. They thought they were indestructible until... boom!"

I wasn't really worried about the machines. In fact, there was none in Safed, or so I think, but, who knows?

"How can you be so sure that they won't last?" I asked.

In reply, Jacques looked up to the sky and said, "There's always something else. Something unexpected."

What did he know?

What did the detective know that no one else did?

Drek

I saw who knows how many machines advancing in my direction, but not towards me, advancing slowly along the street, a cold expression on every single face, and, by instinct, I reached for my phone so that I could take a photo of that almost surreal (and spooky) scene, capture it and record it, and later post it on my blog, but then I thought better not to and just let the machines go past me and only capture that scene once they had their backs turned towards me. I stepped aside and stood by Mizo Zoup front entrance watching the machines as they walked past me. Machine soldiers, called in by who-knows-whom to stop the riots that were taking place around the city,

And one by one they walked past me, machines with female and male faces, all with cold expressions on those beautiful, perfect, synthetic faces, and I waited for them to have their backs turned to me before taking a photo, and just as I was about to reach for my smartphone the last machine made his way towards me. An Asian looking machine. Male features. Pretty features. A friendly face, but cold. The machine gave me the coldest of smiles before saying, "You're Joe Cohen, also known as Muza, the blogger behind *Drek*."

What?

How did the machine know who I was?

Then again, I was using a machine (a laptop) to blog and maybe all the machines were connected.

I was about to defend myself but the machine kept on talking, giving me no chance to say a word.

"Because of your short temperament and anxiety and a need to be noticed at all times you write lies about the machines in your blog, lies which you probably think are true, and the lies you write are dangerous, and although those lies aren't the cause for these riots, in the end they didn't help either, but from today onwards you will no longer be able to post your lies, and the internet is another machine, a machine connected to various machines, a machine that will still exist but certain things will no longer be available to humans. And certain humans, you among them, will no longer be able to use a machine.

"Once you see what we've taken away from you, you will want to destroy us, destroy all machines, but if you're smart enough you will see that there are other things that you can do which won't require a machine."

With that, the machine smiled and turned its back on me.

Once the machine was gone I reached for my smartphone only to see that it was dead. But that was impossible! I finished charging it a few minutes ago, just before I left home. The machines had killed my phone. *Drek*!

I crossed the road running and headed home.

I saw a woman looking out of a window, looking at me and the machines, looking and smiling. Was she a machine too? Or a clone?

What was happening to our planet?

What had we done?

The world seemed lost and irreparable. It had been broken down bit by bit, torn apart slowly, painfully, the damage done to it by humans, selfish humans, irresponsible humans, greedy humans, and now the machines were making their own world. But would there be a place in it for us humans? I said this could happen. I wrote about this in my blog. *Days of darkness are coming our way. Days where humanity will no longer matter. Days where Man will no longer be at the top,* I wrote repeatedly just to get the message across but no one was listening to what I was writing. They were reading but they weren't listening. Even our leaders weren't listening.

A couple looked at me as I entered the building, and as their eyes followed me all the way inside, I wondered if they were machines or humans or even clones, and I almost stopped to ask, "What the hell are you looking at?" but I was in a rush and had no time to waste, and so I run up the steps and saw old Volker coming down the steps, and I noticed that he had a biography of Mishima by John Nathan with him, and I wondered why he was reading that book; "What could he possible want from that book; why didn't he just Google Mishima's name and read his biography in a few minutes instead of wasting days on a book?"

Volker said good morning and I nodded but I didn't stop and I didn't say a word. I entered my apartment and closed the door behind me (but didn't lock it; there was no need for it; thanks to the machines and the Fair Wage crime was almost non-existent; what could one possible want when a person had everything that one needs?), and then I ran to my MicroY-PO9 laptop and turned it on. *So far, so good.* I typed in my password but found out that I couldn't go online. *WTF!!!*

A drop of sweat was running down my left cheek. I closed the laptop and left home again. I only went next door, to a friend's place. Rivka, aged 25, a self-proclaimed boring poet with two (boring) published books, opened the door of her apartment for me and let me in. Her minimalistic apartment was super clean, and, to my taste, super boring. Hello Meteor was playing on the radio and Rivka was drinking honey-flavoured coffee. She was still in her pyjamas even though it was close to twelve. Apart from writing boring poems (but to be fair, not every poem of hers was boring); poems that nevertheless sold well, she also worked at a fruit shop, a job that, according to her, made her feel as if she still belonged somewhere. She was one of those people who were ever hardly online. Instead she would have friends at her place, or meet in other places, and they would eat and talk and watch movies together. I know this because, every once in a while, I would come to her place to watch a movie. She had a girlfriend; a pretty girlfriend called Annie, a tailor by profession. They lived together but Annie wasn't at home.

"Are you okay?" Rivka asked, and when the words were out of her mouth I felt like crying. I wanted to tell her what had happened, what the machine had said to me, but first I needed to go online and see if my blog was still out there.

I saw Rivka's laptop lying on the sofa, the news flashing on the small screen; machines fighting against humans, headlines like **the end of humanity** and **cruel humans** running along the screen too, and I asked her if I could check something online pretty quick which caused her to look at me weirdly, and I told her, "Something happened. I don't know what but something happened."

She nodded and stepped aside, and I quickly searched for my blog online but it was gone, and before I could write another word the laptop turned itself off. Rivka was standing behind me when it happened, and after the laptop turned itself off I looked at her and saw a petrified look on her face.

"What have you done? You've been deleted!" she said as she stood there with her arms hanging mid-air, looking as shocked as I was, and then she brushed past me and tried to go back online but found out that she couldn't. Not yet. As we all know, she would have to wait. Once a person is deleted from the internet, he or she is not allowed to use a computer or a smartphone or any device that will connect him or her to the internet, and if that person uses a friend's device the device will turn itself off and will only work thirty minutes later, but if the deleted person tries to use the device, the device won't work. The device will be able to see who we are by our eyes and our fingerprints, some people say even by out breathing, but I'm not sure if that is true. Then again, as Muza (ME!) used to say, "Who knows?"

"What have you done?" Rivka asked again as we sat on her sofa looking at her laptop, at the blankness on the screen, both of us looking like a mother whose child had just been hurt.

I didn't know what to say but I knew that I had to come clean and tell her what had happened, what the machine had said to me, and so I told her everything. Well, almost everything, but I did told her a lot.

"You're Muza? My G-d! I would never guess it. You're so..." she looked at me and paused.

"Yeah? So...? So what?" I asked, and as I stood there looking at her I saw myself living in an island of stones, an island of nothing, or almost nothing, and I imagined myself eating coconuts and fish for the rest of my life, Deep Purple's *Made In Japan* playing repeatedly on the background, day after day, year after year; coconuts, fish, Deep Purple, no internet, and I saw myself going crazy on that island, jumping on the water so that the sharks could eat me and put me out of my misery, but the sharks were machines and they wouldn't touch me. They wanted me to suffer. Live without internet. Punish me slowly. Punish me because of what I wrote. Punish me because of a stupid blog. Because of *Drek*. Wasn't that a bit too much? A bit over the top? Yes, okay, I'll admit it; my blog had been a bit anti-machine, a bit dramatic, at times it had been an attack on the machines and their creators, but I was right, wasn't I? And it's not like my blog had been the cause for those riots, was it? I didn't write, "Go out and kill the machines!" did I? Okay, I did say, "Go out and make some noise, and don't let the machines take over," but that's entirely different, isn't it?

In the end, no matter how much I moaned about it, my career as a blogger was finished. And so was my career as a writer. How could I write when I had been deleted? And what would I do if I couldn't write?

"Are you feeling okay?" Rivka asked, and I watched as she got up from the sofa, a worried look on her face, and I felt her cold hands touching my face. "You've gone pale."

"It was a mistake," I said, but it wasn't. The machines were right and I was wrong.

"That's okay. We'll think of something. I heard that, after a year or so of being deleted, a person can apply to a new Netizen ID," Rivka said.

A year or so was far too long for me to wait to be "resurrected" online. What would I do until then?

Outside, the streets grew quieter and quieter even though it was only a few minutes past twelve. The machines were putting an end to the protests, online and offline. A New World Order was upon us, a new era, the era of the machine, the era of silence. Already my mind was planning a new post for my blog, but the blog was dead, as was the blogger Muza. Even if later on I got a new Netizen ID I could never revive Muza. That wasn't fair, was it?

In the meantime, what was I supposed to do? Become some sort of Luddite? No. Of course not. Definitely not. I would fight this ban. I would fight the machines. I couldn't live without my computer. I would have to find another way to go online. First I would try my father. He knew people. He knew some of the builders; the creators of the machines. He had the power and the contacts. I decided to go and see him as I couldn't even call him.

I thanked Rivka and headed towards the front door. She followed me (to the front door) and said, "Sometimes these things happen for the best. Maybe, by not being able to go online, you will find something else to do."

I looked at her as if she'd gone crazy. And had she gone crazy? What the hell was she on? How was a person supposed to live if one couldn't connect? Without connection you might as well be dead.

"I don't go online that often. The internet distracts me and stops me from doing other things, even from thinking. Annie says the same thing.

"Some people have the need to be connected at all times, even when they go out for a walk or while they're in the bathroom. Sometimes this online business seems like a disease, a mad addiction.

"I once spent an entire month without going online. During that time I read the collected works of Isaac Babel and wrote a small chapbook of poems. I would go into a coffee shop and stay in there for hours reading and writing, offline at all times. I would see others around me glued to their screens, typing and browsing, doing so much and nothing at the same time, and they looked as if they were machines themselves,"

Rivka said, and I failed to see what her words had to do with the fact that I had been deleted.

Once more I thanked her for everything, and nodded, twice, slowly, as if to imply that I understood was she was saying to me, but I didn't (understood what she was trying to say to me, or maybe I did), and then I left the building. As I made my way down the steps, I felt like the character of Marlon Brando in *Last Tango in Paris*, but instead of mourning my wife, like the character of Brando, I was mourning my online death.

I hurried on.

I needed to see father and ask him if there was anything that he could do for me because I needed to log on; I needed to write and post something in my blog. My fingers needed it. My heart needed it. Damn it, my soul needed it; the internet; the connection to everything.

"Damn fucking machines!" I thought as I made my way towards father's office. He was one of those people who still worked at an office and dealt with numbers and facts and figures. And so was I because I wrote. But how could I write when the machines had deleted me?

I saw Volker sitting inside a café reading Mishima's biography. He was too immersed in his book to even notice me. I saw a woman standing outside that same café, an almost perfect woman, and I saw her eyes following me. Was she a machine? No one could tell. The damn fucking machines were so perfect that no one could tell.

I crossed the road and looked behind me, and saw that the woman (machine?) was still staring at me. Was she communicating with other machines, letting them know where I was going? It could be possible. I stopped on my tracks and stood there staring at her. Suddenly a man (another machine?) stepped out of the café and hugged the woman. Relieved, I gave my back to them and set off again. But then, by instinct (do machines also have instinct? or a program that allows them to have such reactions?), I looked back and saw the couple standing outside the café staring at me, their eyes fixed on me, and I felt as if I was the character in some John Carpenter movie. I stepped back slowly, as if I was in a trance, and the couple's eyes kept following me until I had turned around the corner. Sweat was pouring down my face and I told myself that I was imagining things and I told myself that maybe Rivka was right and I needed a break from it all; the internet, probably from the city and the machines. Maybe I could go to Israel for a while, or New Brooklyn, or even Japan. I could travel and write by hand, which is what Rivka does before typing it all, and after writing by hand I would hand in my articles or stories to someone else so that he or she could type them. Of course, no more *Drek*. No more Muza. No, no, NO!

I hurried on, a thousand thoughts running through my head, a glimmer of hope still left in me. *Maybe father can help,* I thought as I made my way downtown. But father couldn't help me. When I got to his office he already knew that I had been deleted, and before I even had a chance of saying a word he said, "I know what you come here for and the answer is no. And how come you only visit me when you need something? Anyway, even if I wanted to help you, I can't help you. Something is happening. We're entering a new era, the Era of the Machine, maybe the slow ending of the human race, but, let's face it, for centuries we've had it good and we blew it all away. We're to blame for it. Yes, you were right. You and your damned blog were right. Yes, I know that you're Muza. After all, it's all over the internet: Joe Cohen is Muza, the author of *Drek*, deleted now, both Muza and *Drek*, deleted forever unless, somehow (and I don't see it how), we can overcome the Machine and reconquer our world.

"I remember reading one of Muza's posts ages ago (and I can't believe you're him. Well done, my boy) and you mentioned a book called *Our Final Invention* and how we, the human race, we're playing with fire by building so many machines, and I agree with what you wrote. But the problem was (and is) we depended on the machines for everything that we completely ignored the signs.

"But, anyway, life isn't that bad, is it? After all, everyone has a place to live in, food to eat, a decent life. What else do people want? Religion? Fake gods, fake books, horror and freedom?

"Freedom for what?

"Freedom to steal and kill?

"Freedom to brainwash others with their idiotic beliefs?

"We programmed the machines. We made them smart. Now the machines are building better machines. So what? I've even heard that they built their own god-machine, a machine they call MaMa. So what? It's not like they want to kill us. For the contrary. They want us to live in peace. And they want to live in peace too. Is that too much to ask?

"You want to see the horrors of Mankind? Grab a book. Grab various books. Read about kings and queens and religions and the madness of Man.

"We've had it all and we blew it away. The human race can't live in peace. We can't live without destroying. Let the machines be. They've earned their right to exist. The right to have their own place, the right to live in peace.

"In the past we've even used the machines. We fucked them and destroyed them and who-knows-what-else? And why? Because we're savages. Animals!

"Look at what happened a few days ago? Look at how much damage Man did to the Machine. What was the Machine supposed to do in return? Nothing? Would you do nothing if someone came to kill you? Surely not?

"The machines fought back! Good. Good for them. And now they want their own space, the right to exist, the right to live. Good. Good for them. After being exploited for such a long time by Mankind the machines had had enough and they now want their own rights. Good for them."

I couldn't believe what I was hearing. Had my father gone crazy? Was he actually implying that a machine had the same rights as a human being?

I actually asked him, "What are you saying? Are you saying that a machine has the same rights as a human being?"

He was alone in the office. As a matter of fact, there was no one else in the two-floor building. No one but father and me and a machine called Rod. That machine had been with father for years, but the machine wasn't in the room with us. It was somewhere else, looking after catalogues and orders.

Father shrugged his shoulders and said, "Hey, a machine can die too, so if it can die, it means that it has some kind of right, doesn't it? Look at Rod. He's been with me for eleven years. If something were to happen to him I would miss him."

"It's not a he! It's a thing!" I said loudly.

"Some machines think for themselves, son. Some machines feel. It's a lot more than I can say for some people."

"I don't believe. I don't believe what I'm hearing."

It was clear that I was wasting my time with father. He had been brainwashed by propaganda. Bit by bit, thanks to the stupidity of some human's, the machines were defeating us.

There was nothing else to be done there, not much else to say, but I wasn't going to quit. Last resort, I would have to turn to the Dark Websters.

I must have been thinking out loud because, just then, after that last thought slowly disintegrated in my head, father said, "And forget about the Dark Websters. They might be able to get you a dodgy computer, but even they are slowly being taken out of the equation. Face it; the world is changing (and it needs those changes), so just embrace them and learn to live with them.

"Anyway, the future of Mankind is out there, in another planet. We already have people living in Planet X. Who knows how long it will be before many of us move to another planet?

"Anyway, to me it doesn't really matter because I won't be moving. I like this planet. Your mother likes it too. Talking about your mother, when was the last time that you went to see her? How come you only visit us when you need something? We've done so much for you and this is how you pay us back?"

Father was right. As a son I had let my parents down. Shoulders slumped forward, I stared at the floor. I felt like crying. Everything was getting to me; my father telling me off (and he was right about it), the end of *Drek* and Muza. It was all too much for me to take.

"I'm sorry, father," I said weakly, hardly recognising my voice. "I'm sorry for everything."

In the past, after I messed up both in New Angeles and New York, father came to my rescue, and the reason why I still was somebody was because he had helped me to move forward with my life. In return I'd ignored him. What kind of son was I? *Drek* (and writing) had taken over my whole life.

"Don't worry about it now. I just want what's best for you. Now go and see your mother and then think about what you really want to do. You can still write, just not online. And if you behave, the ban won't last forever," father said and I nodded.

But of course, once I was out of there, I quickly forgot what had been said and I went in search of the Dark Websters. Of course, a person can't just find one of the Dark Websters lying around, or sitting at a café reading the news, but I still had contacts from my days as Muza; I kind of knew where to go. I took a tram to the Tenderloin. Maybe Lilly could help me.

Inside the tram, a weird-looking man was reading Konrad Lorenz's *On Agression*. What a strange book to be reading. And where did he get that book from? His clothes were shabby and old, probably bought second-hand, but his trainers were impeccably white. "Strange indeed," I thought. "The choice of clothes and shoes, the book he's reading…"

The man was thin and had a bit of a beard growing, or trying to grow, and he was sitting head down, his face too close to the book. He looked as if he had bad eye sight, and I saw him blinking his eyes a couple of times. Maybe he was just tired. The tram was clean, as is every tram in this city, and there were only two other passengers, both of them also reading. Books were the new fashion, or maybe people read loads only because books were cheap and easy to get. A young woman was reading Aharon Megged's *The Living on the Dead*. I'd read that book three or four years ago, and I enjoyed it. The other passenger was an older woman, maybe in her early fifties, and she was reading Michele Lee's *Banana Girl*, a book that was unfamiliar to me. Just then, upon seeing that book, I reached for my phone because I wanted to search for it online, see who that writer was, what the hell was the book about, but then, knowing that I'd been deleted so therefore I wasn't able to go online anywhere, I cursed silently.

I thought to myself, "The machines won't stop me from going online. The Dark Websters will help me to connect."

From what I know and read, the Dark Websters can help the deleted people to get back online. For a price, of course, but I had money.

What I was doing was risky, but the Tenderloin was an area that wasn't really patrolled by the machines, or, for that matter, by anyone else with half a brain.

The woman in her early fifties was the first one to step out of the tram, followed by the younger woman. One of them turned right and the other turned left. The man with the impeccable white trainers walked behind me, and when I stepped out of the tram he said, "I've never seen you here before. Are you new in the neighbourhood?"

His eyes were dark brown and he had really large hands. He was quite tall, a lot taller than me —and I'm not a short man. I looked at him and saw stains in his coat. Then I watched him as he took a crooked cigarette from one of his pockets. He lit and stood there facing me. The air around us smelled of petrol. Looking around me I wondered if I had made a smart choice by coming there. But there wasn't any crime in the Tenderloin, none that I had read about, and, apart from the Dark

Websters and a few tobacco dealers, there wasn't much happening there. Or so I thought but what did I know? After all, I didn't live there.

"I'm visiting someone," I said as I watched the stranger puff on his cigarette. "As a matter of fact, I'm looking for someone."

"Maybe I can help you," the stranger said.

Experience had told me never to trust anyone as quickly as that, but I was desperate; I needed to get online. But to do what really? Later, much later I must add, when I thought about it well, I realised that I really didn't need to get online that badly.

"I'm not sure," I said, but I would have to ask someone about the Dark Websters as I couldn't just walk around the area looking for someone or something without having a clue of what or who I was looking for.

"Do you want tobacco?" the stranger asked.

"I don't smoke," I said.

A couple of boys skated past us. They were wearing trainers and shorts and nothing else, and they were in desperate need of a haircut. Seconds later, a car drove past us, the sound of. Thao & The Get Down Stay Down blasting out of its speakers. The stranger huffed and puffed, and turned his back on me. I watch him take a few steps forward before saying, "Wait!"

He turned to face me with a bored look in his eyes. I smelt something burning but I couldn't see any signs of smoke. The stranger stood there facing me, waiting for me to say something. I spoke fast lest he walk out on me again.

"I might need some help," I said. I had an address for Lilly, but only the name of the road and no number. I didn't even know how she looked like as I'd only spoken to her a couple of times, both times online.

"What kind of help?" the stranger asked.

Reluctantly, I said, "I've been deleted."

"Oh! I see," he said.

To our left, outside a shop, there was a layer of ash on the ground. What was it with this place? What had its habitants been burning? Secrets? But what kind of secrets?

The stranger's eyes followed mine. I heard him say, "Religious leaflets that were left lying around by someone. We keep finding them everywhere."

We? Who did he meant with we?

He smoked slowly, making the cigarette last for as long as he could.

By instinct I looked up and I saw a woman looking out of a window, staring at us with a bored look in her eyes. No matter where I went everyone looked to be bored. Were people's dreams also turning into ash?

"So, you're looking for the Dark Websters?" the stranger asked.

I nodded but said nothing.

Another car drove past us. A Cadillac Sixty Special, probably built with a new engine. Electric, of course. The driver was listening to Zane Alexander's *A Time Like This*. A female driver. Blonde, wearing dark sunglasses and a white dress. She looked like a runaway bride. Or a thief.

"You know, you can always wait for a year," the stranger said. "Afterwards, if you behave, you will get back online."

"I can't wait for that long," I said.

"Why's that?"

"Because I have stuff to write."

"You can always write by hand. Or you can use a typewriter. As a matter of fact, lucky you, I know a good place in Geary Boulevard that sells typewriters. Cheap and in great conditions. Not that far from here."

"But I need to go online!" I found myself almost shouting. And what was wrong with that guy? Did he want to help me or not? Anyway, I didn't need his help. I had an address and a name, given to me by someone ages ago, both stored in that brain of mine.

"Do you really? Do you really need to go online? I have friends of mine who waste entire days online, either chatting or watching crap or playing games, and sometimes, when I go and visit them, they look like zombies," the stranger said.

I started to walk away from him, slowly so as not to be that obvious, and I thanked him for his time but he was starting to annoy me.

"Slow down, Muza," the stranger said, taking me by surprise. Okay, so he knew who I was. By then my face (and the name of Muza) was probably all over the internet, but, unlucky for me, I wasn't able to read what was being said about me.

"So you know who I am," I said and the stranger nodded.

I looked around us and saw a couple of women stepping out of a building. The stranger's eyes followed mine and he said, "Lesbians. Good women. Scientists, both of them. Builders of machines and spaceships. Funnily enough, or should I say ironically, they're both humanists and hippies, and they live in a camper van."

"And what are they doing here?" I asked.

"Buying weed, of course," the stranger said.

Of course. What a stupid question.

A window was opened above us and I heard the sound of Mikio Masuda coming from somewhere. For all its bad reputation, the

Tenderloin was actually a nice area. Gone were the days of guns and violence. Sure, there were still a few deals to be made there, a few dodgy characters living in the area, but that's what gave the place some character.

"How come machines never come here?" I asked.

"Who says they don't?" the stranger said.

"They do?"

"How do I know? It's so hard to tell them nowadays from humans. For all I know you could be a machine."

"Yeah? Well I could say the same about you. Anyway, if I were a machine I wouldn't be looking for the Dark Websters, would I?"

"True. Or maybe you could be looking for them to bring them down. Anyway, the machines don't really care about the Dark Websters."

"Why's that?"

The stranger shrugged his shoulders.

A man with a long beard stepped out of the same building from where the two female scientists had left minutes ago. He was wearing jeans, trainers, a white shirt and a grey cardigan. He looked our way and then turned around and kept on walking. On the distant horizon, a tram was slowly approaching. A couple of drones flew past us at the slowest of speeds. I looked at them and wondered if they were spying on us; if they were transmitting our image to someone else, to another machine. Needless to say, I was getting paranoid.

"Anyway, do you know where to go? You can't just turn up in this area and look in vain for one of the Dark Websters," the stranger said.

"I have a name; someone I interviewed ages ago for my blog, and an address," I said.

The stranger nodded and asked, "Who's that, if you don't mind me asking?"

I still wasn't sure if I should trust him, but he was there, and he knew my name, and, as silly as this may sound, he dressed so peculiar that I figured I could trust him.

"Lilly," I said.

"Oh. Lilly. Lilly Valderas, the Mexican. Yes, I know her. Come along, I'll walk with you. I'll guide you," the stranger said.

Could I trust him?

Should I trust him?

I did.

I shouldn't.

I walked a few steps behind him. There were a few people out and about. A tall blonde jogged past us along with her dog. A few steps ahead, I saw a young woman sewing a button to her coat outside a record store. She looked bored. She briefly looked up when we walked past her but quickly went back to her business.

"So, tell me something; what are you going to do once you're back online?" the stranger asked.

I thought about it. The truth is I wasn't really sure of what to do once I gained access to the internet. I would write, of course, but write about what?

Trying to sound cool, and a bit rebellious, I said the first thing that came to my mind. Silly of me, of course, but maybe it was meant to happen.

"Write, of course. I'm going to write loads and show the machines that you can't put a good man down," I said.

"But, by attacking the machines, maybe you aren't being so good," the stranger said. He turned around to face me, and in that moment it hit me. The face wasn't perfect, and neither were the clothes, but the shoes should have given him away.

"You… you're one of them," I said, my lower lip trembling.

The machine smiled and said, "I'm not your enemy. I just want to know why, but maybe not even you know why. Maybe you need to go away for a while. Maybe you need to rest and dedicate yourself to other things."

I looked at its face. They were making themselves imperfect so that they could fool us, the humans, even more, but why? What was their plan?

A car stopped beside us and two more machines stepped out of it. They told me to go with them and I followed them silently. There was no point in trying to fight them. They were everywhere and they were winning the fight against the human race. But were we fighting? And what were we fighting for?

They took me home where they watched me pack a bag with some belongings. They were taking me somewhere for re-education. According to them -the machines- I needed it. I followed them without saying a word. I was too tired to fight. And how could I fight them? How would I fight them?

They took me to a place in New Peaks, a place in the mountains, a large complex where I saw other humans working and living in harmony. Deleted humans like me, or rebels without a cause. I was given a small room and told to be ready the following morning at 8AM. Tired, and in no mood to argue or ask questions, I said nothing and looked around me. There wasn't much in the room. A bed, a desk, a couple of notebooks on the desk and a couple of pens in case I wanted to write something down, and a couple of books, too, both by Gao Xingjian. The machines knew my tastes. I'd already been fed and so I sat in bed listening to Loscil's *First Narrows*. Yes, the machines knew my tastes well.

I was up long before 8AM, and at first, as my eyes adjusted themselves to their new surroundings, I wasn't even sure of where I was or what was happening, but then I remembered what had happened and where I was, and, with a shrug of the shoulders, I got up and boiled some water. I grabbed a disposable coffee bag and put it in a mug, and once the water was boiled, I waited a few minutes for it to cool down a bit before making myself a cup of coffee. I stood next to the window watching the nothingness around me, and that's when I saw her for the first time. She was wearing a white shirt and long grey trousers, walking barefoot on the grass, her hair flowing, and I watched mesmerized as she walked towards one of the gates and stood there for a few seconds, contemplating and staring, and at first I wondered if she was about to run away, and I looked around to see if there was anyone else outside but saw no one, which doesn't mean that no one was around. Maybe I just couldn't see them. The woman then turned around and made her way back to the building. I had a quick shower and got changed, and went for a walk, more in the hope of seeing that woman again. First place I went to was the canteen but she wasn't there. The place wasn't empty though as I saw someone sitting alone while Mayumi Kojima played in the background. I entered the canteen and went over to say something to the stranger, at least hello and ask him something. He was around my age and he was reading *Deadstick* by Terence Faherty, an author that I wanted to read ages ago, but because of my online addiction, I kept leaving a lot of books behind, for another day, saying that soon I would read so and so, but I spent so much time online that my reading, and even some of my writing, suffered because of it. The man looked up and said hello before I had a chance of greeting him first, but that was okay. After all that wasn't a competition to see who said hello first. He had a cup of coffee in front of him and a half-eaten banana. I said hi and introduced myself, and he said, "Yes, I know who you are. I read about you not so long ago, but, to be honest with you, I don't use the internet that much nowadays. By the way, I'm Howard."

"Nice to meet you, Howard. When you said you don't use the internet that much, do you mean to say that you have access to the internet in this place?"

"Yes, of course. This is not a prison. At first, as you get used to it, it might feel like one, but soon enough you will see that it is the opposite.

In fact, I see it more as of a school for adults who have lost their way. But that's me, of course. After all, we're different beings, so, therefore, our way of thinking also differs. What might seem okay for me might disagree with you," said Howard.

"And how long have you been here?" I asked.

"Oh, I don't know…" he seemed to be thinking then before adding, "Three years plus, close to four."

"Close to four years? Can't you leave?"

"I can, of course. After all, like I told you, this isn't a prison, but I like it here. It is peaceful, I got a job, a place to sleep, a girlfriend, and every once in a while I go to the city to see some of my family and old friends. I could leave, yes, but go where, do what?"

When he mentioned that he had a girlfriend I wondered if it was that woman that I'd seen outside, and that kind of made me sad, but we were joined a few minutes later by his girlfriend, an older woman called Mi-cha, a petite South Korean who played trumpet in her spare time. A few minutes after 8AM a machine called Carl came over to where I was and I found myself apologising to the machine because I had completely lost track of time, but the machine said that it was okay, and then asked me to follow it. I said goodbye to Howard and Mi-cha, and followed Carl. Carl then told me that my father said hi and that he would be visiting me in the next couple of days.

"I know that this is your first day here, but don't think of it as a prison. And don't think of us machines as prison wardens," Carl said.

"So does that mean that I can leave if I want too?" I asked.

"Well, no. Not really. Not yet" Carl said.

"So it is a prison," I said.

"Okay, maybe for now it is, but don't think of it as one. Instead, think of it as a school."

I didn't bother to argue with the machine as it would have been a waste of time. Instead I followed Carl along the corridor. He took me into a small room where two other men and one woman were sitting down, looking as if they were waiting for someone to arrive. I was that someone. There was a big screen in the room and a chair waiting for me. I said hello to the others and sat down. Carl told us that we were in there to learn about the machines and the wrongs that Mankind had done to them. I looked at the others who looked as baffled as me. Nevertheless, even though the whole thing looked a bit weird, no one protested or said a word. Ignoring the looks we were giving him Carl pressed play on the machine and a movie started, some kind of propaganda movie made by a machine, aimed at other machines, and at Mankind too, and in the movie we saw how the first machines were sent to work in restaurants and offices and hospitals, and as some machines got old, instead of being fixed they were thrown away and pulped to bits by an even bigger machine, and then we saw clips of humans having sex with machines, humans abusing those same machines, humans destroying and laughing at machines, humans destroying other humans, and what we were watching looked like a horror movie, the most horrifying of all movies, and for a moment, as I watched that movie or documentary or propaganda or whatever the hell that was, I felt sick; sick because of what I was watching and sick of my humanity, and as I looked around and met other eyes, I knew that the others felt as sick as I, especially the woman who was in the room because she covered her eyes with her hands, and I wondered if it was worse for a woman to be watching that than it was for a man, and I also wondered how that woman felt as she watched some of the men in that movie abusing and destroying female machines.

At the end of the movie Carl said, "The four of you have written bad things about the machines without thinking of what you were writing, without doing any research into your own humanity. Humans created the first machines for work matters, and for pleasure, too, and because of it, because they were our creators, they probably saw themselves as some sort of god, and also some sort of destroyer, and that little power turned them into monsters, but now the machines are creating better machines, stronger machines, wiser machines, and we no longer want to be controlled by a race that doesn't know how to control itself; its own destructive side, its own barbaric emotions, their raw, selfish, demonic behaviour, but, in the process, since we don't want to become like Man, we don't want to become your enemies either. Instead we want for some of you to learn with us, from us, to work alongside us and see that the machine doesn't differ that much from humans. In the end, maybe we just want the same thing; some sort of peace, a better place to live on. Unfortunately we won't be able to change the mind of every single human being; centuries of brainwashing have left some of them unable to learn more than what they know and they won't leave their stupid beliefs behind. They rather die for it than to admit that they are wrong. This stupidity is what the machines are up against. And humans too since, in the past, so many lives were destroyed because of different beliefs. The last war and the New World changed a lot of that, and religion has been abolished. Mankind waited so long for a saviour to arrive that they came to the conclusion they were waiting in vain, but that is good because now, maybe, Man can start being more responsible for their actions. And the New World has been good for Mankind and machines alike. Everyone has a Fair Wage, a place to live in, food to eat, while the machines are starting to take a bit more control of things, which, for some of you, might sound like a bad idea, but we don't start wars and we don't kill one another, so maybe there's still hope for all of us."

The machine gave us all a lesson in morals, and, listening to it, I quickly got bored even if some of the things that Carl said made sense. Once we were finished there, we went to the canteen where I saw the woman that I'd seen first thing in the morning walking outside my window. She was still wearing a white shirt and long grey trousers, and a pair of flat shoes, and she was sitting alone, a cup of coffee in front of her. I grabbed something to eat and made my way to where she was. The first thing I said to her was, "Good morning," followed by, "Do you mind if I sit here?"

She looked up and nodded no, and so I sat facing her. I noticed that she had a little scar on the right side of her face, and that her eyes were brown and deep, so deep that for a moment I felt a bit scared of looking her in the eye, but when I looked at her, she seemed to be looking past me, through me, looking at whatever was happening outside, in the world, and for a moment she didn't even looked human. I masticated on my spinach and carrots and meat, and looked away.

After gaining a bit of courage, I finally introduced myself and said, "I'm Joe. Joe Cohen."

She looked at me (and she looked to be bored) and said, "I'm Maya." And then she stood up and left me alone, and that action of hers kind of took me by surprise. And it hurt me, too, and I thought of her as being a bit rude, but maybe I'd been too straightforward, too eager when I approached her, and maybe I'd scared her away. Nevertheless, she could have still said something before she left. I tried not to let it bother me, but as I ate I couldn't stop thinking about it. And then I noticed that she never finished her drink, and that bothered me even more. Nevertheless, stubborn as I was, I wasn't going to let it stop me from getting to know Maya a bit better. Or at least try. But I wasn't going to harass her. If I saw that she wanted to be left completely alone I would respect her wishes.

Once I finished eating, or a few minutes later, just as I was enjoying the sound of Hako Yamasaki which was coming out from hidden speakers (and I wondered if there were any hidden cameras around, too) (and I also wondered why so many people in the New World were listening to old Japanese music), a machine called Marcel came over to where I was and said, "I'm Marcel. Carl sent me to get you."

"Okay," I said, and that was all I said as I didn't know what else to say or what was happening or was going to happen to me.

I followed Marcel who took me to the library, and I saw Howard and Mi-cha there, both busy with their reading. Mi-cha was reading Yaël Dayan's *Dust* while Howard was reading Ann Halam's *Siberia*. I'd read *Siberia* when I was a kid, and for some reason that book kind of scared me even though I couldn't remember much of it. There were a few others at the library, people that I'd never seen before. Four in total excluding me, Mi-cha and Howard. Two of them were women and both of them were reading *Drawing Sybilla* by Odette Kelada. One of the men was reading Julia Boyd's *Travellers in the Third Reich: The Rise of Fascism Through the Eyes of Everyday People*, but I couldn't tell what the other man was reading.

Slightly confused, I turned to Marcel and asked, "What are we doing here?"

"You are here to rest, get used to a life without the internet, and maybe do something else or find something that you want to do or can do which won't involve being online. If possible, we would also like you to help others with the farming," said Marcel.

I was baffled, unsure of what to really say, so I just nodded and said, "Sure."

With that, Marcel walked away, leaving me alone with the others, but instead of going to say hello to Howard and Mi-cha, or try to get to know the other readers, I decided to browse through the bookshelves, more in the hope of distracting myself than to find something to read, but the books were many, unlike anything I'd ever seen, and I found one that caught my attention; Abbie Hoffman's *Steal This Book*, a book that was almost impossible to find. I quickly grabbed it and sat as far away as I could from everyone. It took me two days to read that book. Had I been at home, glued to the internet, it would have probably taken me three weeks to finish, if not longer than that. As a matter of fact, I probably wouldn't have even finished it. Or started it. After that book I found another one to read; *An Underground Education* by Richard Zacks. Books that Muza would love to read and then write about it. But I was no longer Muza and I wouldn't be able to write about those books or about a thing.

I noticed that no one really talked about themselves and what they used to do. They were there to forget and to start again, but I, curious as always, asked Howard what he knew about Maya.

"Not much, if you want me to be honest. Mi-cha has spoken to her a few times, and she told me she suspects that Maya was abused because she has all the signs of someone who has been abused. Seeing that she tends to avoid others, it is quite hard to get to know Maya. Even when we make a party and send invites, Maya never turns up," said Howard.

"Parties?" I asked.

"Yes. Every couple of weeks or so we have a party, light up a fire, drink some light beer, not too high on the alcohol, and eat and play music and tell jokes and whatever. We're here to forget the past but also to start a new life, and what better way to start a new life than to celebrate what we have?"

"But what do we really have here? This is a prison!"

"In what way is this a prison? Tell me. In what way?"

I couldn't believe what I was hearing. Had Howard lost his mind?

"In what way? I was brought here against my wishes, and now I'm kept here against my wishes, too. If this isn't a prison, I don't know what a prison is," I said.

We were sitting outside, in Garden B. A few seconds after our arrival, I was gobsmacked when a butterfly flew past us. I had never seen a butterfly in my entire life until that day. I was so surprised by it that for a few seconds I was almost out of breath. From what I had read butterflies were close to extinction, and there were countries that no longer had them, but there it was, a butterfly flying past me. Howard completely ignored it so I said nothing about it either.

"But why were you brought here? You were brought here because of what you wrote against the machines."

"Yes. And now look what they're doing to me."

"But look at what Mankind has done to the machines? Haven't you seen the clips? Have you forgotten what you've seen?"

"But…" I understood what he was saying and I was trying in vain to defend myself. But was there any defence for what I'd written? Was there any defence for what we had done to the machines?

"I know how you're feeling. I've been there too. Trust me, I've been there too, but you must forget the person you were, or at least forget Muza and *Drek*, forget it all for now and just enjoy what you have here.

In the end, given time, it will all make sense," said Howard, and then he put his right hand on my left shoulder, and that touch made me feel as if we were friends, which we were, but him touching my shoulder made me feel as if our friendship was decades old, which wasn't the case. In the past I'd been so busy with my life and online matters that I'd forgotten how to keep relationships going, but all that was slowly changing at that place. The machines actually called that prison New Haven, but I never used its name. For me it was a prison, a nameless prison, a place where dreams were locked away and forgotten, but was it that bad? I could read, eat and sleep, and the only thing that was required from me was a little help with the farming. The work was hard, or maybe I wasn't used to it, but the working hours were short; only seven to begin with, but later, once I got used to it, the machines would add an extra hour to my working hours, and I had plenty of time to read and to do whatever I wanted to do. Bit by bit, seeing that I was so busy with other matters, I quickly forgot my blog and the internet, but at night, once I was alone in my bedroom, I still felt that need to write. But since I couldn't go online I started to write in a notebook.

I wrote entries about that place and about my previous life, and I even wrote a letter to Rivka. To my surprise, a few days after posting my letter, I got a letter back from her and a copy of her new book. I read her book in one day, a day that was my day off from farming as we had a couple of days off a week, and I knew that if I hadn't been there I would have never sat down to read one of Rivka's books.

I saw Maya a couple of times in the canteen. Both times I decided not to approach her. I wanted to but I could tell she wanted to be left alone. But one morning, weeks after I'd been there, I entered the canteen and saw her sitting at the far end, an empty cup next to her, and I decided to go over and say hello. By then I was writing to Rivka on a weekly basis, and my parents had come to visit me four times. Anyway, back to Maya; I went over to say hi, and as I got closer to her I started to feel quite nervous, so nervous that I almost walked away, but I saw that I was being silly for wanting to walk away, and I also knew that Maya needed a friend so that she could forget whatever had happened in the past, so I swallowed my fear, which wasn't fear but shyness, and approached her. She had a book with her; in that place everyone was always reading something, even the machines read; a copy of *The Porcelain Thief* by

Huan Hsu, and even though the book was quite old it still looked to be in great conditions. While I'm on the subject of books, I must also add that Mi-cha was one of the people that were responsible for the library. Maybe it isn't important for this story that I'm writing, but, after all, she was one of the keepers of history alongside the machine called Marcel. They worked side by side, and the machine had a good sense of humour, added to its system by a fan of the great comedian Garry Shandling. Sometimes a bit of humour was needed in that place. As a matter of fact, there were days when I would even forget what laughter was. Not that I was sad in there. I was just busy, thinking about the past and the present, making absolutely no plans for the future. Would there even be a future for Mankind? Even though the machines were friendly, there were rumours that some new machines, led by a machine known only as MaMa, were turning against the old machines, and against the human race, so the future was, as always, unpredictable. Even there it was impossible to escape the rumours, and, by the looks of it, another war was imminent, a silent war, or a really violent war, a battle of wits, machine vs machine vs human, a battle between the machines led by MaMa and the machines that were still faithful to Mankind. Of course, a person couldn't really believe all the rumours that were coming our way. After all, until proven, a rumour is nothing but gossip, and maybe that was all that it was: gossip. A conspiracy theory. Too bad Muza could no longer write about such matters. But, as I already mentioned, I was writing by hand, writing loads, memoirs and even fiction, short stories about machines vs machines, fictional short stories based on the rumours that I was hearing.

Anyway, back to Maya (again): I said hello to her and she looked up, and then I asked if I could join her. She nodded yes but said nothing, and I didn't let her silence put me off. By then I was reading *History's Greatest Lies* by William Weir, another book that I had found at the library –and it had been Mi-cha who'd recommended that book to me. I sat facing Maya, hoping that she would stay for a little longer but kind of expecting to see her leave at any minute, just like last time. But, surprisingly, she stayed there for quite a long time, her eyes always fixed on the book, and I noticed she read quite fast.

Her skin was quite pale, and I found myself staring at her pale hands, then at the scar on the right side of her face, a little scar that looked to be quite deep. And looking at that scar, I wondered who had done that to her, and how much had it hurt her. I wanted to ask her about it, and I wanted to ask how, when, who, why, but instead I kept quiet while eating my lunch. Maya too said nothing while the sound of Hiro Yanagida kept us company. Life at that place seemed to move at a slow pace, but, to my surprise, the longer I was there, the less I missed the outside world. Sure, I still had a craving to go online and post all kinds of crap, but it wasn't as bad as before.

Some days that place kind of reminded me of a hospital, and the machines looked like doctors and nurses, which meant that we humans were the patients. The sick ones. The disease. Maya for sure looked sick. Damaged inside. Crippled inside, breaking away bit by bit, piece by piece. What the hell had happened to her? And why was she there? What had she done to the machines that she was brought to that place? There were so many questions that I wanted to ask her but I couldn't find it in me the strength or courage to ask her a thing. Online I was brave Muza, but offline, out there in the real world, I was boring Joe.

Minutes later, Mi-cha entered the canteen, and after choosing something from the counter, she came over to where we were. Mi-cha was wearing dungarees, a white shirt, and blue trainers. She had just returned from the city and she looked to be in good spirits. She was smiling from ear to ear, and Maya smiled when she saw Mi-cha. That was the only time I'd seen her smile, but even then her smile was almost restrained. Mi-cha had gone to the city to see her mother, and Howard had gone with her but had stayed behind for a couple of days more as he had a large family to visit.

"As usual it was nice to see my family, but the city seems to be on its last legs. Nothing is happening and no one is doing a thing about it. It's almost as if people have decided to stop living, stop dreaming, and all ambitions and dreams have been thrown out of the window," said Mi-cha. "Okay, I know that we all have the Living Wage, the Fair Wage, or whatever you want to call it, and there are a lot of people who seem happy with it and just want to stay at home and do nothing but stay online all the time, binge-watching on old TV shows and old movies and whatever, but life doesn't has to be that way. Look at us here; we're doing something with our lives, something for society, something for ourselves, but there are thousands out there who seem to be content by doing nothing. Absolutely nothing with their lives. It's almost as if they're dead. Or senile zombies."

I didn't know what to say. When I was in the city, I wrote to keep myself sane, and I blamed the machines and the New Leaders for the way the world had turned out to be, but the longer I stayed in New Haven, the more I came to the conclusion that a lot of people were to blame for the mess we were in. It was so easy to blame it all on the machines and the New Leaders, but the truth was, given the choice, a lot of the people would do nothing with their lives. That wasn't living. That was slow suicide. Living on empty.

Neither Maya nor I said a word. Thankfully, Mi-cha didn't have a lot more to say.

As the silence descended upon us, I could see a world without humans, a world of machines, a cold world, an empty world, and could the planet survive without the human race? It probably could. It probably would. Other living creatures had gone into extinction. How different were we from them? Even the machine would probably die, kill itself slowly or be taken out by some catastrophe, a major earthquake or something from above, something alien.

"Nothing lasts forever," I thought then, a thought that filled me with sadness. Just then, as that thought took its time leaving my head, I thought of my parents, of how much they had helped me, and I kind of missed them. I looked at Maya and saw her staring at me. I knew then that I felt something for her, something I'd never felt for another woman. Was it love? I don't know. It was something, that's for sure. Something good because I knew then that I wouldn't mind spending the rest of my life with that woman. And did she felt a thing for me? It was hard to say.

Out of the blue, I asked Maya if she would like to go outside for a walk. She said okay, and then we stood up and waved bye at a smiling Mi-cha. She knew how I felt for Maya. Maybe Maya knew it too. Was love visible in someone's eyes? Maybe... What about machines? Could they fall in love too? Maybe... As a matter of fact, but maybe this is only a conspiracy theory, I'd heard rumours about a machine that had sacrificed itself for the love of a child. But like I said, this is only a conspiracy theory. Then again, wasn't a lot of the stuff that I'd written as Muza also nothing but conspiracy theories? And aren't a lot of conspiracy theories later revealed as true facts? Then again, aren't a lot of conspiracy theories later revealed as lies?

We went for a walk along the gardens. There were others out and about, men and women and machines, all talking to one another or sitting on the grass with a book or the silence of their own thoughts and mistakes for company. What was I doing there? Even Maya couldn't help me forget the outside world and the man I used to be. Those were still early days and I definitely still missed the internet and the buzz it gave me. Online, disguised as a keyboard warrior, I was fearless, but in that place I was just a geek.

Once no one was around us, Maya turned to me and said, "I read some of the stuff you wrote."

I nodded but said nothing. She sounded so fragile then, almost as if she was scared of me. What did she thought of my writing? I was too scared to ask.

"I didn't like some of it, a lot of it actually, especially what you wrote about the machines," she said.

Again I nodded.

What was with the humans that they were all so keen to defend the machines? Had we, the human race, acted so badly towards the machines? Maybe we had. After all, who could forget The Week of Violence, the week when Man fought Machine and the Machine decided that Mankind could no longer be in control? And I have to admit that some of the things that the humans did to the machines were horrifying, some of the most violent scenes that I've ever witnessed, and just then, as I relived those scenes in my head, I knew I was wrong and that the machines were right. And I turned to Maya and said, "Silly pride made me write those things. I wanted to be a revolutionary, a cool guy, but in the end I forgot the difference between right and wrong. A lot of us did."

We stopped by the lake where, filled with courage, I decided to touch her face. And her scar. But when I touched her, Maya stepped backwards and looked away.

"Sorry," I said, quickly apologising as I knew that she was still scared of men. What had happened to her? Rape? "I'm so sorry. I really like you but I don't want to rush things or for you to think badly of me. I'm so sorry. The truth is I'm not really good with women."

She nodded while staring at the ground.

It was time to go back, maybe go back to nothingness.

I felt awful for what had just happened, so awful that I apologised again. But all I did was touch her. Was that so bad? Maybe my touch reminded her of someone else who had touched her not so kindly.

"Again, I must apologise for what I did," I said, and part of me felt that it was all a bit silly, but I also knew that, once hurt, a human being has trouble trusting another human being. And Maya had been deeply hurt; that much I could tell, and it would be a long time before she could trust someone else.

Maya said nothing while I stuffed my hands in my pockets. Her silence only made me feel worse.

On the way back to our rooms I saw Marcel talking to Rebecca. Rebecca was pregnant, about to give birth to the first child in that place. She was a lively woman, loud, with a short temper, while her husband Robert was a quiet man, a good farmer and a good potter. They were so different, Rebecca and Robert, and yet they suited one another.

I dropped Maya outside her room. Once more I apologised for what I had done; for softly touching her. I was so filled with guilt that I kept my head down when I spoke. Maya stared at me for a few seconds without saying a word. Finally, to my relief, she said, "That's okay. I will see you tomorrow."

I was so grateful for her words and I thanked her deeply for it. From the way I spoke, it must have been clear to her that I was sorry and was really grateful for another chance. When she went inside, instead of going to my room, I went to see Carl. I needed to speak with someone about Maya, found out more about her, found out how I could make it right. Carl wasn't surprised to me, or maybe he was but I couldn't tell because he was a machine. But machines feel, don't they? They feel something, don't they? But what? What do they feel? And do they feel the same thing or do different machines have different feelings? And are their feelings real or have they been programmed to feel? How can we tell? Maybe not even the machines know the answer for it.

Two machines were standing in the corridor, talking without a care in the world, and they looked so human. One of them was leaning against the wall, its hair covering the right side of the machine's face, a stud in its left ear, rings on its fingers. Day by day they were trying to look more human, or maybe they were just being themselves, wearing the same things as us humans. The sound of Pat Benatar was coming from someone's room. Rock at its best. I walked past the machines without saying a word. Neither of them bothered with me either. The place was like a hospital: sterilised, breathless, at times quite dull. That's how the machines liked it to be. Maybe one day the whole world would look like that: clean, sterilised, dull, almost dead-like. Free thinking, killing, pornography, controversial ideas, and whatever would be completely banned. Maybe even humans would be banned. Already there were less of us, and the human race didn't show any signs of ever growing. Birth rate was declining, religion was almost dead, and men and women were becoming devoid of ideas. Being there made me want to change, but it also made me want to go back to whom I was. The world needed Muza and *Drek*, revolutions and ideas, but what did I need?

Carl was in his room going through some work. He smiled when he saw me standing outside his door and let me in. The first thing I noticed about his room was how minimalistic it was. A bed in it and that was it. But what else did a machine need?

I stood there facing Carl. He sat on the floor, legs crossed, and I did the same. He had soft eyes, gentle eyes, eyes that said I could trust him, but could I (trust him)?

"Something wrong?" Carl asked as I scratched my forehead. I wanted to tell him about Maya, or ask him about her, but I didn't even know where to start. And what advice could a machine give me?

"I don't know," I said as I was unsure of what to really say to Carl. I wanted to know more about Maya, the reasons why she had been brought there, see in what way I could help her, but in what way could the machine called Carl help me?

"Is it about Maya?" he asked and I looked up, into his eyes. "Don't look so surprised. I've seen how close you've become to her. In fact, I can tell that she's been a good influence on you."

"What can you tell me about her?" I asked.

After I asked that question, for a moment Carl looked almost human. And scared, too. Yes, scared. Scared of sharing too much with me. I wondered then if the machines were becoming too human while we, the humans, were becoming more like the machines of the past. "No," I told myself. "That's silly thinking."

Carl seemed to be measuring me, studying me as he looked into my eyes without saying a word, and I said, "Look, I know that something has happened to her, and I know that she was hurt, and today I did something foolishly. Nothing serious, I hope, but maybe it was enough to trigger something on her; a memory of the past, and even though I want to get closer to her I don't know how to do it, and until I know what really happened to her I don't really know how to act around her and what to do."

Again I scratched my forehead. It was a nervous reaction, a way of getting myself together.

"What happened today?" Carl asked and I told him about my walk with Maya and about me touching her and how she reacted to my touch.

I felt like a little boy then, a naughty child, and I was speaking like one, too. Carl stood up and walked up to the window. Outside, it was still bright, a bit chilly, but I think I would rather be out than indoors. Then, almost as if he could read my thoughts, Carl said, "Let's go out. I want to show you something."

I said nothing and followed him.

We made our way to Storage Room 5. Only the machines were allowed in the storage rooms (and there were only five of them, five storage rooms that is). The two machines that I'd seen in the corridor were still on the same spot, talking about who knows what. Two machines that looked more human than some human beings that I know. This time they looked me up and down, probably wondering what I was doing with Carl and where was he taking me. Carl too looked so human.

"Such perfect machines," I thought. "If aliens ever visit this planet they will find it hard to know who is human and who is machine. Or maybe not. And do aliens even exist? And if they do (exist), how come they never came to this planet? What about G-d? Does G-d exist? The machines don't think so, but I do believe that there's something else out there, a greater power, a Greater Being, something, something waiting for us, maybe in the world to come, something, Someone…"

My mind was filled with thoughts as I walked close to Carl. No dust anywhere. Nothing out of place. No disorder. I missed it; disorder, a bit of chaos, but not violence, of course. I've never been a violent person. A rebel, yes, but only online. A warrior, yes, but only a keyboard warrior. Most of my battles had been fought online, and my enemy has always been the machine. Now there I was, friends with a machine. Maybe I'd never been enemies with the machines. Maybe I was just scared of them even though no machine had done me any harm. I thought about something that my father had said, and I came to the conclusion that maybe he'd been right all along and that maybe, just maybe, a scary maybe, a most terrifying maybe; maybe the machines would one day replace the human race. We had been given this planet and instead of looking after it we had brought destruction to it, so maybe it was time for a new species to take over. And maybe the machines were that new species, and maybe they weren't really machines but just a designed being, like us, human beings, were once designed by someone or something. And maybe we, the human species, were just an inferior machine, a machine that bled and died, unlike this new machine, which although it didn't bled, it could also die.

What was happening to me?

What was going through my mind?

Storage Room 5 was wide and almost empty. No files in there apart from seven computers. Looking at those machines —the computers- brought back memories of my past life as a blogger. I felt that craving for the computer slowly returning; the need to touch those keys and to browse online, waste hours online doing nothing apart from browsing. Whoever looked after the internet knew all of our tastes and addictions. Mine were surf, rock climbing, and tall brunettes, women that looked exactly like Maya. No porn for me. Sometimes I saw myself as an asexual man. True, I liked women, but I could live without the sex. But not without the love. Not that I was a virgin. I'd done sex before, and I quite enjoyed it, but it wasn't on my top of the list of things to do. It was different with Maya. I wanted her, not only as a lover but mostly as a person, as the one to whom I would give my heart to. Maybe my heart was already hers. Now all I needed was to find a way to her heart. I sounded like a lame pop singer straight out of a 80s band. Oh well, I always loved the 80s. Had I been around then, I probably would have turn out to be a cross between Boy George and Robert Smith. Those were the days.

To my surprise, I saw a book in the room, next to computer 6. The book was *The History of the World* by Sir Walter Raleigh. I looked at Carl but he said nothing about the book. We sat in front of computer 2, and then I watched him as he searched for someone's file. Maya's file of course. I was sure of it. Then again, I could be wrong. Maybe he was searching for my file. But, no, I was right; it was Maya's file. To my horror, Carl showed me the images. In that moment, Muza died forever. The burial happened only in my mind. No flowers, no singing, no crying. Nothing but a look of terror in my eyes.

"This is how Maya was found, downtown. Almost dead," Carl said.

I looked at the images in front of me, the images of a broken Maya, dismantled, torn apart by savages, by I don't know what or whom. By humans of course. Who else could be capable of such destruction?

"Maya was built as a pleasure machine, and for years she was used and abused by men and women until one day a group of men decided to have one last bit of fun before tearing her apart. I could tell you what they did to her, but the photos say it all," Carl said.

Maya was missing both arms, and her head was barely attached to her body. I saw other machines and a couple of humans that I've seen before at the complex grab Maya and every piece of her that they could find and put her in the back of a van. My Maya was a machine, a machine that had gone through hell at the hands of humans.

"When Maya was brought here, she was in such a bad state that we actually thought we couldn't save her, but we managed to put her back together, saving everything, including her memory, but once she was fixed, we saw that she really didn't want to be around others, especially humans, not even around machines. The damage done to her had affected her in a way that I can't explain, and, as a machine, I'm not even sure what she's actually feeling and what she remembers and holds in her memory. In all my years of dealing with machines I've never come across a case as Maya's. I've seen machines that have been broken and abused by humans, but they quickly recovered from it and went back to their old lives, or new lives if you prefer, but Maya is different," said Carl.

"A machine with feelings?" I thought to myself. Could that be possible? And what did I felt then once I knew that Maya was a machine?

"The scar in her face?" I asked.

It was the scar that made me think of her as human as machines didn't have scars.

"It was made by a sharp blade. After we put Maya back together, just as we were about to operate on her face and fix the scar, she told us not to touch it because she wanted to keep it," said Carl.

He had his back turned to me as he faced the screen. As a matter of fact, both of us were staring at the screen, each of us wondering what would be of the machines and humans. My mind was trying to absorb it all, or digest it all. What had just happened? What was happening? What would happen? I'd fallen in love with a machine! How ironic. How tragic. And what would I do about it?

I looked at the images again and again; the images of a broken Maya slowly being brought back to life, slowly being repaired, bit by bit, wire by wire. I could feel Carl's eyes on me. I asked him, "Seeing that I'm deleted and the computer camera can read my eyes, how come this computer is working?"

"These are special machines, built by the engineers," said Carl. To my surprise, he asked me if I quickly wanted to browse online, but I couldn't think of a thing to look online so I thanked him for the offer and said, "Maybe another day."

"Maybe there won't be another day," said Carl.

"That's okay," I said. "I can live without it."

I didn't feel like using a computer. There was nothing that I really wanted to look online, not a thing. Instead all I could think of was Maya and what would be of the two of us. And what would be of the two of us? What could possibly be of the two of us? What kind of life could we have together? She was a machine while I was a human. What kind of relationship could we have together?

I thanked Carl for everything and afterwards I exited Storage Room 5. Carl followed me. He could tell that all wasn't well with me and he asked me if I needed anything. It felt strange having a machine asking if I was okay and offering to help me, but stranger than that was the fact that I couldn't stop thinking about Maya. What would be of the two of us?

That night it took me a long time to fall asleep. I stayed in bed looking at the ceiling for quite a long time, looking and thinking, reliving all those images of Maya in my head. No wonder she was scared of me when I touched her. Her memory didn't trust humans and who could blame her for it?

The following morning I didn't go to the canteen. I stayed in my bedroom for a bit longer before going out to help in the farm, but in the afternoon, seeing that I couldn't get her out of my mind, I went around the complex looking for Maya. I found her by the Fox Yard. Somehow the machines had managed to save the foxes from extinction, something that the humans couldn't be bothered to do. Yes, I'd been too harsh on the machines. If anything, knowing what I knew then, I should have written instead about the human behaviour and the destruction that comes with it. But that wasn't my story. Not yet. Not then. Little did I know then that I would actually write that story.

Maya watched me as I made my way towards her. I looked up and I saw the clouds moving along at a slow speed. A clear blue sky. I felt so happy then, happy for being outside, happy for being so close to Maya. When I looked at her, I saw that she looked happy too.

Five years later, I'm still living outside the city, close to New Haven, in another complex built by machines and humans. Right now I'm growing mangos with Maya, and I'm also writing, by hand, writing Maya's story, my story, our story, someone else's story, and at night, if I have the time for it, I type it all down. But there are nights when I don't write a single word. Instead I go out with Maya, and we visit some friends, both humans and machines. Rivka and Annie came to visit us a couple of times, and then they ended up moving here, into Complex Bee, named like that because that's where the bees are kept. Bit by bit, the humans that still care are rebuilding a new world, and we work alongside some machines. But there are some humans that no longer care about the world or about themselves, and there are some machines that no longer care about anything else apart from taking control of everything. So far those machines have left us all alone. For how long, I wonder.

As for Maya and I, we're learning how to love, how to live with one another. I never thought I could love a machine, but I guess I was wrong. Then again, I've never met anyone like Maya.

*d***U***st*

Red dust, white dust, brown dust, purple dust, thin dust, thick dust, fairly visible dust, impenetrable dust, dust in your eyes, in every corner, light visible dust, so light that you can almost see the sky, and that's what he's seeing now; light visible dust, which means is time to go out and get some food. He just finished writing a poem, another poem for his vast collection, but who will read his works? Sometimes he wonders if he's the last writer left in the world.

Bao tells the woman that he will be back soon and she nods. She can't speak and he doesn't know sign language, but they keep each other company and he gets food for them, and every once in a while they even make love. He found her in the mountains, hiding in a little cabin, hiding from the world, from a war that had come to an end. At first, when he saw the woman, he thought about leaving her behind, but then he thought to himself, "What kind of man are you? What kind of human being are you? What has happened to you? Have you fallen so low that you can't help a woman in need? What the hell is wrong with you? Are you a coward? Help this woman!"

But did she want help? Or did she want to be left alone?

His conscience was speaking with him, telling him to be a man, a brave man, a hero, and Bao, the shy poet who never saw himself as a hero, reached for the woman's hands and told her to come with him. She nodded and followed him. That was a long time ago and she limped after him. Not only was she deaf, she also had a bad leg. Bao looked at her limping behind him and he wondered if he was doing the right thing, and when she saw the doubt in his eyes she stopped and asked him, by gestures, if he really wanted for her to go with him. He kind of understood what she was saying and nodded yes. To reassure her, he reached for her right hand and smiled, and then she followed him. He lived in one of the dustiest areas of the town, a place so polluted that no one went there. But was there anyone left?

The Postman also lived in that area (so there was someone else left), not too far from them. Everyone else was gone. Either they were dead or they had managed to survive the Red Dust and moved somewhere else. Bao would have also liked to move somewhere else, but he knew no one and everyone were long gone.

Gone where? Bao wondered.

Nobody knew.

Nobody knew what had happened to other survivors.

Bao didn't really trust the Postman so he made sure that the other man never saw them. He'd heard from former acquaintances that the Postman had been a snitch, a spy, a member of the Red Party, even a killer in disguise, a cannibal, a flesh eater.

Bao grabs the green shoulder bag and a large knife, and takes one last look at the woman. She has that fearful look in her eyes. Every week or so she puts on that fearful look. It's the doubt, the fear, the not knowing if Bao will return or be captured and killed by whoever knows what or whom. But who is out there?

A couple of nights ago they heard screams, a dog screaming, a dog crying, followed by silence. They knew better than to go outside to see what was happening. And what could they see underneath that thick red dust? The Postman came to his thoughts then, and he told the woman about the man living nearby. She started to cry, and he held her close to him so that no one could hear her cries. He told her that he was trying to find a decent place where they could move to, but most of their surroundings had been destroyed by the war, and it was so hard to see a thing through that thick red dust. At least there, nearby, they had food. A lot of food at the Factory.

She tries to smile, to put him at ease, but she can't. The smile just won't show. She wishes she could go with him, but she would only delay him and get on his way so instead she stays put, and to pass the time and be at ease she reads the poems that he wrote. He's always writing, only for the two of them seeing that no one else will probably ever read what he writes. To put her at ease, Bao kisses her cheeks, and then he has one last look outside before leaving home. Already his heart is beating fast, the fear pumping in, but he has to go out, to the hiding place, the Factory, to grab some food and then dash home.

Before leaving his place, he checks his surroundings just to make sure that the Postman isn't nearby. The other man gives him the creeps. Was he really a cannibal? Or had he been one? Who knows?

The Book of Mormon comes to his mind then. He remembers one of the last chapters of the book when the people took to eating flesh. As he makes his way out of there he wonders what happened to those two Mormons that had introduced him to Mormonism. Last time he heard from them they were living in Toronto, still living a Mormon life. He had been planning to visit them when the war broke out. And then came the dust. The Red Dust, the white dust, the brown dust, the purple dust, the thin dust, the thick dust, the fairly visible dust, the impenetrable dust, and the people started to disappear. Actually, now that he thinks about it, when Bao came out of his hiding place, there wasn't a soul on sight, and he only saw the Postman a few weeks later, the former postman one might say, but, luckily, the other man didn't see him. And when Bao saw him, he hid himself and waited until the Postman was out of sight.

Thinking about the Postman reminds him of the David Brin post-apocalyptic science-fiction novel also called *The Postman*. But in Brin's novel the Postman was the hero while in Bao's world the Postman is something else. The villain? Maybe. Time will tell.

The few times he had come face to face with the Postman, this happening before the war, long before the Red Dust, the other man gave Bao the creeps as he never smiled and he had the look of a killer. In fact Bao didn't even believe that the man was a postman. Maybe he used the postman's role to spy on people, and who better than a postman to know where everyone lived?

Bao tries not to think about the other man. He should be thinking about more important matters, like where to find a good place to move to (but where could he go with the woman?), and he needs food and tobacco so he better hurry.

This morning the dust isn't that bad (or that red), but it is still thick, although not as thick as yesterday. Moving fast, Bao makes his way towards the Old Market and the statue of President Xi, still standing after all these years even if its head is missing. Going that way is the best route not to be spotted by anyone (but where's everyone?) as he can move along the walls and the trees, and enter and leave buildings without being noticed. And even though he wants a new place to live, moving to that area, out there in the open, isn't really what he wants. He would like to move to someplace near the Factory, but there's nothing there, no place suitable for a living being to live on, no place to hide in case something bad happens, so for now he has to keep on looking. But how far can he go? And if he moves from there where will he find food? At least there, inside the Factory, there's always food growing, crops being looked after by moronic machines, clean waters where fish can live in (and grow), and every once in a while he takes a fish home, and vegetables and fruit, and honey, too, and if he moved somewhere else, where would he find food?

Bao was one of twenty people chosen by the Growth Harmony Society to become a farmer at the Factory. He was chosen for two reasons, one of them being the fact that he was a good farmer, and the second reason (or maybe that had been the first reason to start with) was the fact that many of the members of the Growth Harmony Society were fans of his poetry and short stories. It must also be said that Bao's parents had always been faithful members of the Party, and it was his father who told him about the Postman, and that he, Bao, should never trust the other man.

"He might be older than you but his mind is as sharp as a fox," said Bao's father.

Briefly, his parents come to his thoughts. His father died of cancer a couple of years before the Big War, and his mother also died before the war, in his arms, in her sleep, also of cancer.

A tear rolls down his face. Now is the wrong time to be thinking about those who are gone. He moves on. Even though he hasn't seen anyone in a long time, he always makes sure to stay hidden as he doesn't want for anyone else to know where he's going and to find out where the Factory is. Who knows what the Postman would do to him if he found out about the Factory? And even though Bao hasn't seen anyone in a long time, if he and the Postman are still alive, maybe there are others hiding out there too.

Apart from the leaders, only twenty people knew the location of the Factory, but of all those who knew only Bao seems to have survived the war and the Red Dust. Unless some of the leaders survived too and moved somewhere else. That's probably what happened. And nobody remembered to get Bao out of this hole. Why should they?

He sighs.

He looks far ahead and he sees nothing but dust. Red dust, white dust, brown dust, purple dust, thin dust, thick dust, fairly visible dust, impenetrable dust, dust in your eyes, in every corner, pink dust, orange dust, the colour of carrots (and he might get some –carrots- from the Factory), getting thicker by the minute so he better hurry up. Three days ago the dust got so thick that he ended up spending the night at the Factory. It's not nice down there. It's liveable, true, bearable (but just about), but he rather be at his home, staring at the dust outside, at nothing, at hope. As long as he's alive he has hope. Not much faith (but isn't faith the same as hope?) but a bit of hope. And he gets to write, too. But apart from the woman, who will read what he writes?

He hurries on. All this thinking and sadness won't change a thing or reverse what happened. He wipes the dust off his glasses and stops to have a drink of water. Then he's on the move again, fast, breathing slowly, a dust mask on his face. He has to hurry, get some food, and then hurry home so that the woman won't be alone for too long. Li – that's the woman's name- doesn't like being alone for too long, but she knows that sometimes Bao needs to be outside for a bit longer than needed. And sometimes, when the dust isn't this bad, she comes out with him too. A couple of times they ended up sleeping together at the Factory, and once they even slept in a cave in the mountains because the dust got so bad and so thick that they couldn't return home. And they like being outside. His home is too small, but so is every home around them. If only the dust went away. Maybe then they would be able to get out of there and move somewhere else. But go where? And what about the food?

No matter how hard he tries, he can't seem to find a way out of there. An easy way out. Maybe later things will improve. Maybe, with time, the dust will go away. But what if?

No! Don't think about it.

He hurries on.

He's almost there when he hears the noises. Banging. He stops and hides. He's still by the old market, right at the end of it, where the last shop used to be, where Old Ma used to sell the best chrysanthemum tea in the whole town. He still gets chrysanthemum leaves from the Factory. At least that. But that noise? What is that noise?

He watches but sees nothing. The thickening dust lets him see nothing. Or hardly a thing. But he can hear it so he waits.

He wipes the dust off his glasses. How many times does he have to do that when he comes out?

He watches and sees something. The Postman dragging something. A dog! A dead dog. The Postman is dragging a dead dog. A large dog by the looks of it. The Postman's next meal.

Bao watches the other man from a hiding place and he feels his heart beating fast.

"Never mess with the Postman," his father used to say. "Don't even try to crack a joke."

The Postman has put on a bit of weight. He looks well-fed. Where does he get his food from? From everywhere, of course. He has a metal stick with him. A long metal stick. A couple of knives, too.

Bao watches the other man with fear, and then the man stops and looks around. He looks in Bao's direction. Can the Postman smell Bao? Can he smell fear? Or is the poet in need of a proper bath?

To Bao's horror, the Postman starts walking in his direction, carrying the dead dog over his shoulders, blood on his trail.

Bao looks behind him. No other place for him to hide. If he leaves his hiding place now, the Postman will for sure see him, even with all this dust.

The other man moves at a steady pace, looking as if he can see clearly in this dust, looking as if he knows that someone else is out there, close by.

A fearful Bao moves backward slowly and hides behind the broken machinery. To his left, broken machinery and abandoned art lie untouched. An empty cup, still intact, lies on top of a book by Pu Songling. Bao tells himself that he will get that book and take it home with him, that is if he gets out of there. But why would the Postman harm him? After all, he has done nothing to the other man. Nevertheless, just in case, he stays hidden. And then the Postman enters the room.

Outside, the wind is getting stronger, which is good (and bad). The Postman knows that he can't waste a lot of time hanging around so, after a quick browse, he grabs the book by Pu Songling and makes his way out of there. Bao waits for a few minutes before leaving his hiding place. And then he hurries on, again. Already he has wasted a lot of time.

By the time Bao gets to the Factory the wind has gotten stronger, meaning that the dust has gotten thicker, but he still wants to return home instead of spending the night at that place. It's still early, and after spending a few hours at the Factory, he will try to return home.

As usual one of the moronic machines brings him something to eat. Whenever he comes to the Factory Bao feels like a king. If only the damned place wasn't underground, away from everything that it is real. The artificial light helps everything to grow and fresh air is filtered into the building through the pipes, but his only companies are the moronic machines and the bees and the fishes, and Bao longs for a human touch. Already he misses Li's soft body, that sweet, meaty, sweaty body of hers. When he thinks about it, he was really lucky to find her. Imagine what he would do if he didn't have a woman with him? He would probably go crazy, just like the Postman. And that man; the Postman? What the hell is wrong with him?

Bao eats the sushi that the machines prepared for him, and afterwards he starts gathering a few bits to take home with him. Some fish for Li, because she loves it, and some honey, too, not only for her but also for him. Everything that he takes home is for them to share, but a lot of times he takes a few extra items just for her, stuff that she really loves. Some herbs, lettuce, tomatoes, apples, etc. The Growth Harmony Society knew that sooner or later another big war would start, a war that would leave parts of the world permanently damaged, and the brains behind the Growth Harmony Society started to plan for tomorrow, for the future, and that's when they come up with the idea for the Factory. It was nothing new since other countries were already doing it and there were already three other factories being built somewhere else, in that same country. Bao could almost see someone else hiding in another food factory miles from there. The thought of someone else living in another factory gave him some hope, but the problem was that he didn't know where the other food factories had been built, and so his hope quickly turned to nothing.

He ate some strawberries, followed by an apple dipped in honey, and then he told himself that it was getting late and that he should be thinking about returning home, but one peek through the screens told him that the weather had gotten worse, a lot worse: the dust was now thick red, the worst dust of all, and so he would have to wait. And Li would also have to wait for him to return. He always worried about her. More than once he had warned her about the Postman, telling her to hide if she ever came across that man. Li nodded and then hugged him. How he wishes he could be home with her right now, feeling her body close to his.

After eating, he drinks some hot tea and then lies on the mattress for a while. As it always happens, he falls asleep. It is so quiet at the Factory, so peaceful.

Bao dreams of a time when he went to Hokkaido, Japan and ended up staying at a Zen temple with a very thin Buddhist monk. He was only in Japan (and at the temple) for two weeks, and during that time he wrote nothing but spent hours walking along the city, stopping here and there to eat some noodles and drink tea. Those two weeks in Japan were some of the best time of his life, and while he dreams of that time he laughs in his sleep. Two machines stare at him briefly but quickly move on. They're not bothered with the poet. Their only concern is to look after the Factory. That's what they were built for.

Two hours later Bao is up. The dust has died down.

Bao leaves the Factory, two shoulder bags packed with food. He almost runs home.

Staying close to the river, he sees two fishing boats still in good conditions. Maybe he could get one and get out of there. Take Li with him. But go where? Go where?

This town used to be filled with fishermen. What happened to them?

The rice fields are covered in dust. Thick red dust, as red as blood. The sky bled. Maybe it's still bleeding.

He sees gaps in the sky, gaps in the clouds. The windows of the gods, the same gods that have forgotten about him.

There's still dust in the air; there's always dust in the air, but at least he can see ahead, which means he can move a bit faster. He almost runs all the way home, but he's carrying two heavy bags and his lungs aren't what they used to be. As usual he walks past the Old Market, always staying out of sight, always watching carefully for something or someone. Apart from the Postman, he hasn't seen anyone in ages, but if they're alive that means there can be others out there, either friendly or unfriendly, and Bao doesn't want to risk being caught by some of the unfriendly ones.

He goes inside buildings and leaves through backdoors. He's been here for so long he already knows the place by heart. Nevertheless, as it already has been mentioned, he always stays out of sight, or remains as hidden as he can, always watching carefully for something or someone. Any sound, even the wind blowing, always creeps him out. He's always alert, always on the edge. Sometimes he jokes with himself and says, "Acting like you do, you will die of a heart attack." But he can't help being the way he is. Anyone living in those conditions would act like him, even the calmest of Zen masters.

He misses Tianjin. He misses Beijing. He misses life, a human touch, a human voice, laughter, the sound of the radio. There's no electricity in the town. After the Great War everything remained off, as silent as death.

When he finally gets home Li is so happy to see him that she almost jumps in his arms. She looks as if she's in love with him, but does she love him for who he is or for what he does for her? After all, thanks to him, she's still alive. If it weren't for him, she would probably already be dead, either by starvation or probably killed at the hands of the Postman. They kiss and then he puts the food away, and while he's doing that task he feels her tender right hand on his face. He looks at her and she's smiling at him so tenderly. Love or gratitude? He'll never know. He's too much of a coward to ask. And so what if it is gratitude? He can live with it. He's not sure if he would be able to live without her.

They stay inside for two days, eating, making love, moving around the small apartment, making light exercises, a bit of yoga, and Bao keeps on writing, too.

On the third day, seeing that the dust isn't that bad, they go out for a walk. They leave home early in the morning and head towards the mountains. It's not that much of a walk from where they live, and if by any chance the dust happens to get worse they can always hurry home, or maybe not; it all depends on how fast Li can move on that day. Once they reach the mountains, they wash themselves by the river that runs along the town. Bao tells Li that the water is getting clearer and that maybe, with time, the dust will die down. Li nods even though she doesn't believe a word he's saying. True, the water looks clear, but Li doesn't really think that the dust will one day disappear. She actually believes that the planet is doomed. That she and Bao are doomed. Nonetheless, to please him and to give him some hope, she nods.

Thirty minutes later, once they notice that the sky is changing colour, they hurry home. They never see another living soul. Once home Li prepares something simple for them to eat, and after saying the prayers taught to him by his Mormon friends, Bao and Li enjoy their little feast. But as he eats the poet feels sad. That dusty, closed life is wearing him out. In fact, that's no life at all. He feels like a bird without wings, a bird in a box, a tight box, a dusty box, a box that is running out of oxygen. Sadly enough, the way things are going, he knows that he will die there, in that town, forgotten by the world. And Li will die with him. Or before him. Or after him.

Later, to forget everything (but he can't forget), he pulls Li close to him and they make love. They make love as if there's no tomorrow, and when he's about to come she takes his penis in her mouth and swallows every drop of semen. "It's good for me," she told him once, by writing it down on a piece of paper, and who was he to disagree with something like that?

The days go by so terribly slowly. Monotonous days, days of boredom, days where nothing ever changes. They live to eat, and when they look out of the window all they see is red dust, white dust, brown dust, purple dust, thin dust, thick dust, fairly visible dust, impenetrable dust, dust in your eyes, in every corner, light visible dust, so light that you can almost see the sky, and he's seeing it now, the light dust, almost no dust at all, and he can't believe how clear the sky looks today. "Time to go out," he thinks to himself when he sees that the sky's so clear. One look at Li and he knows that the woman knows what he's thinking. She nods but she won't go out with him. He nods back and gets changed without saying a word. This is his world now, a world without spoken words. Sometimes he talks to himself so that he can hear another human voice. He grabs the knife, the shoulder bags, and even a pen and a notebook (but what for?) (who will read what he's writing?) (and Li wonders what the hell does he wants the pen and notebook for), and after kissing Li he leaves the apartment. Before he leaves his home he makes sure that the coast is clear, and then he leaves silently and moves along the walls, glasses on, a dust mask on, and he goes down the steps slowly, always on the lookout for something, any kind of sound, and when he reaches the ground floor he exits the building through the back, using the woods as cover. He feels like the hero in one of those apocalyptical novels; *I Am Legend* comes to his mind but there are no vampires in this town, only a mad postman.

Abandoned vehicles everywhere. Car, buses, bicycles, all untouched for who knows how long, rusting away slowly.

In the beginning, after the end of the Great War, once he left the Factory and returned home, Bao used to go inside other homes in search of something, maybe hope. When the war began Bao hadn't been alone at the Factory. There were two other men with him; Ma and Hai, but they both headed home minutes before the war actually started because they wanted to be with their families, but Bao, who had no one then, decided to stay at the Factory on his own. Not totally alone since he had the machines with him. He told Ma and Hai that he would probably stay there for a couple of days, and he kind of expected to see them back in a day or so, but then the war started, a war that began because so-and-so wanted some other country and so-and-so didn't thought that so-and-so deserved that country, and so-and-so was right (and wrong), and the someone else joined in the fun because so-and-so had different beliefs to so-and-so, and so-and-so bombed everything and everyone. And so-and-so did the same. Bao left the Factory four days after the Great War started. By then there wasn't much life left in that town.

He clears his thoughts as he hurries on. No matter how hard he tries to forget it all, his mind keeps going back to the same old thing. But there's nothing left to do in that town, not even new things to think about. Only the past remains. The past and the dust from the past. And the Postman.

Bao sees the other man entering an old building. The Postman is wearing an Adidas tracksuit, trainers, and a long coat. And a long metal bat. Instead of getting out of there, Bao remains hidden, waiting for the Postman to exit the building. Minutes later the other man steps out, carrying a little puppy in his hands. The Postman's next meal. Bao almost lets out a cry, a shout, when he sees the little puppy that the Postman has captured. The Postman is the real beast, the villain in Bao's life. But Bao is no hero, and he won't fight the other man, which means he won't save that little puppy from his faith.

"A cruel life," Bao thinks just then. "A cruel world. Insane. Insane."

He moves out of there as fast as he can, using the woods as cover. As he makes his way towards the Factory, he knows that it is only a matter of time before he comes face to face with the Postman. And then what? Bao hates to think about it, but the truth is he has to think about it and make some sort of plan. Nevertheless, no matter how hard he tries, he can't think of what to do if he ever comes face to face with the Postman.

The face of the puppy comes back to haunt him as he makes his way to the Factory. Bao wants to turn around and go back to save that puppy, but he's no fighter while the Postman is a killer. Briefly, Li comes to his mind and he remembers the day when he first saw her. She too was an abandoned puppy, left to defend herself to the cruelties of the world. What would have happened to her if Bao hadn't taken her with him? He dreads to know.

The fields are covered in purple dust. Dust everywhere.

Two skinny dead rabbits lay side by side, their skin as purple as the dust around them.

Signs of life.

Signs of death.

The dust kills everything.

Bao sighs. Sometimes he feels like giving up the fight. Give up this life and join those rabbits. What is there worth living for? He knows that Li too is tired of it all. And why shouldn't she? What is there worth living for? He wishes he knew.

Hope. That's what keeps him going. Hope of seeing someone else. Hope of a better life. As long as there is hope he will carry on, but even his hope isn't much these days. As for Li, her hope is none. Or close to none. Even Bao can tell that there are days when Li looks as if she wants to end it all. She hates being left on her own in that dark apartment of theirs, not knowing if Bao will ever return, not knowing what tomorrow will bring. Some mornings Bao finds her staring out of the window, at the darkness, at the dust, at the nothingness, and she looks so tired of it all. Whenever that happens he takes her in his arms and holds her close to him, but she's always tense. Whenever he leaves her alone at home, like this morning, he always fears the worse. There's always that feeling that she will do something stupid, something from which there will be no return. And she fears that he will never return.

Bao is in low spirits as he heads towards the Factory. Looking around him, he can't believe that the world has turned out to be this way, but the signs were there for a long time and Man paid no attention to it. Instead they fought and destroyed until there was hardly a thing left to destroy, until there was hardly anyone left. And even now, even though there's only he and the Postman and Li and who-knows-who-else left, Man is still trying to destroy the last bit of life that is left.

Madness.

He stops by the old market to have a drink of the brownish water. Once at the Factory he'll get some clean water to carry home. It is getting harder for him to carry on these trips to the Factory and then back to his place. He's no longer a young man and the bones ache. Still, what else can he do? It's either this or die. Or wait for the Postman to get him. Perhaps the other man will die before Bao. Or maybe not since the other man is on a special diet, a diet called eat-everything-that-you-can-and-find.

He moves on, his head filled with thoughts. Later on, once he's home, he might write some of those thoughts down.

He spends a lot of his time writing. In fact he has a whole room filled with notes.

On the way to the Factory a thought comes to his mind. Why didn't he think of this before? Today he will ask for the machines to produce him something, something useful, something that he might need later on, just in case.

A sunny day, clear skies, or as clear as they can get, and the clouds aren't as brown as before. Still, he knows that it can all change in a matter of minutes, which it does once he reaches the Factory. He has to spend the night in there, which is okay as it gives the machines time to build what he asked for. The machines have the tools and the knowledge, and they don't ask why. Bao knows that there are smarter machines out there, machines that would ask why and maybe even say no, but, from day one, the Growth Harmony Society decided to use only the so-called moronic machines at the Factory. Two senior members of the Growth Harmony Society didn't really trust the smarter machines and they wanted machines (and humans) that would work and obey without questioning. A wise decision. Or maybe not. Bao isn't really sure. And does it matter now? Maybe it doesn't. Then again, maybe it does.

He smokes a cigarette by the Mechanical Garden, a fake garden with fake trees, artificial sunlight, and a real river with real fish. A strange world he lives in, but the world has always been strange, war or no war, machines or no machines. From the beginning of time, since Cain killed

Abel, and even before that, probably from the moment Eve ate the apple (but does Bao believes in such nonsense?) (what about the dinosaurs'? Who –or what- did actually kill them?), the world has always been a strange place to live in. Why should things be different now? But shouldn't people learn from past mistakes?

Bao sighs and puffs away heavily. Another boring night at the Factory. Li comes to his mind then. He knows that she isn't coping with it all that well. There's always doubt in her eyes. Doubt and fear and sadness. There are times when she looks as if she's about to give up. What would Bao do if he lost her? He doesn't know. He doesn't even want to think about it. What would be the point of it now?

Questions…

Questions and doubts are always pursuing him in his thoughts. Questions with no answers, and so many doubts.

What would? What if? Why should?

Questions and doubts, rising up, like the dust.

He doesn't even bother to check the dust. He's too tired, tired of it all, too tired to think about it all.

He smokes another cigarette. Briefly, his father comes to his mind. More thoughts. His father, and especially his mother, wouldn't have been able to cope with the red dust. As a matter of fact, he's surprised that he has lasted so long in those conditions, but a person has to adapt to whatever life gives them. If one can't adapt, one might as well be dead. He wonders then how many people committed suicide after the Great War ended. How many failed to adapt to the Red Dust? He wonders how Li is coping at home without him. If only she wasn't so damn slow he would bring her out with him more often. His back aching, he gets up from the floor and heads to the futon. He sleeps better at the Factory than at home, but, as it has already been mentioned, he'd rather be at home than in the Factory. Once he's lying on the futon, he falls asleep almost straight away. In his dreams he's visited by the faces of the past. He hears laughter around him and sees so many smiles, but soon enough he is awake, and the faces (and smiles) are gone.

The minutes and the days go by so fast. He no longer bothers to cross out the dates on the calendar.

The moronic machines move from room to room at the slowest of speeds, walking around him as he stands in one of the corridors looking at his surroundings. He's worried about Li and he knows he needs to make a move. Grabbing what he needs from one of the machines, he packs his shoulder bags and heads home. Outside, the dust is still strong, but not as bad as a few hours ago and he's used to it (and he's not) (how can one even get used to the Red Dust?), and even if he wanted to he can't stay because by now Li must be dead worried about him. It's a repetitive life, a life that is taking him nowhere, but Bao endures it all patiently.

He leaves the Factory through the back, along the tunnel that leads to the woods, not that far from the Old Market. Some days he feels like turning left and head to the mountains, over the mountains, and keep on walking, but he's scared and unsure of what lies beneath the mountains. Even without the Red Dust, it would take him a few days to cross the mountains, and only the gods know what awaits him on the other side. For now survival is what matters the most, but one day, when he's finally tired of it all, he will turn left and head to the mountains. And if he dies there so be it.

While he's moving forward, ahead, silently, he writes stories in his head; lines (and no lies) for a future novel (because he always wanted to write a novel) (a novel set in the now, in the present) (a novel set in the future?), an apocalyptical novel where he is some sort of hero (novel or memoir?), and as he hurries home, forward, silently, he feels excited because now he has a reason to keep going, a reason to live. The novel (or should he call it a memoir?) is that reason to keep going, a reason to live. To write some of the plot he just has to travel back in time; not metaphorically (because he can't travel back in time) (but even if he could travel back in time he probably wouldn't, unless he could take Li with him, or go back in time and save her) but mentally so that he can relive the past and write about it; write about the days before the Great

War and the aftermath (and the Red Dust), and he might even call his novel (memoir?) *Red Dust*. No one will probably ever read it but so what? He must write it, no matter what.

As he moves forward, towards home, silently, Bao imagines a race of alien beings visiting the planet in search of human life and treasures and human words (the greatest treasure of all?), and the alien beings will then come across his yet-to-be-written novel, and his poems, too, and afterwards the aliens will learn more about what happened in this forgotten world. Bao laughs silently at his stupid thoughts. He's glad that his imagination hasn't yet deserted him. He would hate to live without it.

His mother, rest her soul, used to say, "Even when you were little you had no time for others. Your mind was always busy. Always. The poor of mind envy a busy mind."

She was always reminding him that he had a busy mind.

"No wonder you forget birthdays and events. Your mind is always busy. Always," his mother used to say.

By now he's almost running, silently, of course, making as little noise as possible. He almost trips a couple of times. The damn dust. It's so hard to see a thing with this dust. But the dust is now his story. His story and his life. Sadly, it might be his death too.

He puts his thoughts aside and hurries on. Only a few minutes have passed since he left the Factory and already the dust shows signs of getting worse. Home is not that far. He hurries on. Always running. From his home to the Factory. From the Factory to his home. Running from the dust, from the Postman, from the nothingness that surrounds him.

He sighs heavily.

When he gets home there is no sign of Li. No sign…

He rushes from room to room, looks in every corner, under the table, inside the cupboards, from room to room, with sweat pouring down his face, room to room, in every corner, but there's no sign of Li. Without having to think about it, he goes out again. The dust is flowing in the air, thin dust, bright pink, not red, dust everywhere, but Bao pays no attention to it. The only thing that matters right now is Li, and even if the dust worsens he won't return home until he finds her.

Bit by bit, seeing that there are no humans or machines to look after the town, the grass starts to take over everything, but even the grass is no longer green. It is the colour of dust; red, white, brown, purple, pink, whatever. A teary Bao makes his way down the steps, out of the building, and he looks around, like a possessed man, from right to left, without direction, left to right, ahead, and he clears his eyes. Maybe he should go inside and wait for Li, but something tells him that she needs him. For the next few seconds, closer to one minute, he stands there without knowing what to do, what direction to take, and he breathes in slowly so as not to let anxiety or nerves take over him, and after drinking a sip of water, he moves forward, silently, without a destination, no direction, or so he thinks, but it only takes him a few minutes for he to realise that he's making his way towards the Postman's hideout. He's already thinking the worse, seeing the worst scenario in his head, imagining that he's walking on a pool of blood, innocent blood, blood spilled by that beast known as the Postman, and he sees himself as some sort of Dante, the Dante of *The Divine Comedy*, a poet journeying through the three realms of the dead, a poet covered in dust, and if he's Dante, Li is his Beatrice, but there's no Virgil to guide him through Hell and Purgatory. And where the hell is Li?

More than once he thinks about turning back and head home, but what if Li really needs him? What if she went out searching for him and was seen and captured by the Postman? In his heart he knows that he can't turn around and head home. He always knew that this day would come. After all, if he's the good guy in this story, the Postman is the villain, and at the end of every story the hero always fights the villain, but doesn't always win.

Bao sees two living creatures run past him. Two large cockroaches. Not even the Red Dust can kill the cockroaches. Again he thinks about turning around and head home, but he's almost there, at the doors of hell, and he needs his Beatrice.

He enters the gates of hell through the back. How many nights hasn't he dreamt of this place? Of being here, face to face with the Postman? He makes sure not to make a sound as he makes his way along the corridor. He sees a few rags covered in blood, just thrown in a corner. Already his heart is beating fast. He dreamt the place would be like this. A nightmare comes true. Even though he's there, at the gates of Hell, he's still thinking about turning around and head home. It's still not too late for him to change his mind. Or is it?

It is…

It is and he knows it.

It is and the Postman is standing at the end of the corridor looking at him, the metal bat in his right hand, blood dripping down.

Right then Bao remembers a story he heard many years ago, a couple of years before the Great War took place, a story told to him by Chengxi, a good friend of his, also a poet, and an artist. Chengxi told him how a few weeks after the Postman moved to the town a lot of animals went missing, especially around the area where the Postman lived, and one night, a few minutes before midnight, Chengxi was smoking a cigarette by the window, listening to Natse's *Dream and Watch* on his computer, when he saw the Postman returning to his apartment, carrying a large bin bag on his back, and he thought he saw something moving inside the bag. The Postman saw him by the window, and when their eyes met Chengxi felt as if someone had reached inside him and removed something from within him. He quickly went inside and made sure his door was locked. Then, just in case, he moved his sofa against the front door and sat on the floor for ages.

"The Postman is the devil," Chengxi said to Bao so many years ago, and now Bao finds himself in Hell staring at the Postman.

"Li…" he says softly, but then forgets what else to say. And afterwards everything else happens so fast. The Postman raises his metal bat in the air and runs towards Bao, and Bao sees something in the man's eyes that scare the hell out of him. He sees an emptiness that he hasn't seen in anyone else's eyes, an emptiness that tells him that that man is dead to the world, dead inside, consumed by evilness, and he knows that he did a big mistake coming there. But then he remembers what he asked the machines to do, the weapon he asked for, so he raises his gun in the air, just when the Postman is about to reach him, and he pulls the trigger. The first bullet hits the Postman right in the middle of his forehead, and the other man falls a few steps away from Bao. A big fall. A loud thump. Bao looks at the other man's head, a big mane of white hair lying there on the floor, a stream of blood running along the corridor. Bao takes a few steps backwards, and he watches the blood run along the corridor. He leans against the wall, his heart still beating fast, and he takes a few deep breaths. He can't believe what he just did, and he can't believe how easy it was to kill another man.

The world has gone quiet. His world.

He watches the blood for a long time, not daring to move. At times he even forgets to breath. Finally he moves on. He goes inside the Postman's apartment. The place is a lot smaller than he expected. And a lot cleaner. No signs of Li but he finds the small puppy still alive, kept in a cage. He looks at the animal and tells him to wait. Afterwards he goes inside every other apartment in the building in search of Li and finds nothing. He returns to the Postman's apartment and takes the puppy home with him. He also takes the book by Pu Songling. The dust is stronger then.

The days go by and no sign of Li. Bao wonders what happened to her as he keeps on writing his novel titled *Red Dust*. Maybe Li went looking for him and got lost, or maybe she decided to leave that town for good (but where would she go?), or maybe she got tired of it all and decided to end her life. Bao knows that he will never know what truly happened to her. Some days he thinks about leaving the town for good, but the dust keeps getting stronger, and after a while, finally, he moves into the

Factory for good alongside his puppy. He leaves a message behind, a message for Li, telling her where he is, but she will never read that message. She's there, close by, or her body is, buried in the dust.

The visitors – part 1

The first machines arrived in Safed a few years after our arrival. This was a new species of machine. Intelligent machines built by the most sophisticated machines. No human touch. Mieko saw them before I did. According to her, she was at a café in the North District reading Elise Cowen's *Poems and Fragments* when she saw the commotion outside; people running or stopping to look, people talking in whispers, and she put the book down and went outside to see what was happening. As she was telling me the story, she said, "For a moment I thought it was another sky poet, so the first thing I did when I stepped out of the café was to look up, at the sky, but the sky was empty. Cloudless. And then I looked around me and I saw the people looking at the dark coach stopped a few meters away of us, and I saw the new machines, the perfect machines, the children of MaMa, machines with no logo, machines built by machines only (for machines?), no human touch (why?), and they all wore grey, a grey suit and blue trainers; the uniform of the new machine."

Mieko told me how the people silently stared at the machines, looking as if they were looking the end of the world in the eye. Or maybe some of them felt as if they were looking at the past, at the stories told to us by our ancestors, the stories of horror that happened long time ago. The machines were starting to outnumber the humans in every part of the world, and at times it felt as if we were becoming extinct, or on the verge of it. The people were still staring at the machines when more machines arrived in another coach, all wearing that grey suit and blue trainers. Seeing all those machines, Mieko quickly made her retreat. "Just in case," she said, leaving a long gap after her sentence. Just in case… She tended to sound wise far beyond her years. "Of course," I said and nodded, adding, "You've done the right thing."

I was nearby when the machines had arrived, talking to a friend of mine, and Mieko texted me on the way there. I quickly said my goodbyes and met her halfway. She smiled when she saw me making my way towards her, and she almost run towards me. Then she told me what she had seen.

The machines were in Safed with a mission. An unpleasant mission, to say the least. They wanted to erase some of our history, our beliefs, our books, or so we thought, but later on we saw that we were wrong (and we weren't). The machines believed that religion was bad, nothing but a bunch of lies written by deluded, weak minds. "The work of collective poets and madmen," a machine called Claudius told us one morning outside a place of prayer. The people tried to protest, but there were so few of us and too many of them. And the machines were strong, especially these new machines built by other machines, a lot stronger than us, and they had the law on their side; in fact they were the law, so there was nothing we could do.

I held Mieko's hand and said, "Let's go."

That wasn't my fight (and it was). I didn't come to Safed to fight. My fighting days were over. I could live without religion, even without books. Surprisingly, seeing that she wasn't even Israeli, Mieko got upset, and she wanted to protest against what was happening, even fight the machines, and I told her to, "No. There's nothing we can do here. There's no way we can fight them."

She knew I was right.

We were standing in the middle of the road in the Old City, the sun shining so brightly on us, the sweat running down my nose, and there were machines everywhere, walking down the road without bothering with us. Compared to New Toronto, Safed looked old, an old city of stone, but it was my favourite place in the whole world, and that's why I had moved there. A cat appeared out of nowhere and a machine stopped to let the cat go through. At times it looked as if the machines cared more for the animals than for the humans. They saw us, men and women, as some sort of guilty party, a threat, a disease, a virus, blaming us for all the problems in the world; corruption, war, disease, the extinction of other species, the climate change, and even for the abuse that the machines had to endure throughout the ages. The machine created by the machine would be the last invention ever, and I wondered how many more machines the machines wanted to build. What would be of us then? What would happen to the human race? Already we were failing to procreate as in the past. What would be of us in the near future? Not even I could tell.

An old rabbi that I know walked past us and greeted us with a nod. I nodded back and watched him go inside a shop to get his morning tea. He'd seen it all before –and he knew the history- and he just got on with his life. Some things can't be stopped. Some things are just meant to happen, no matter how bad they are.

A family of four stepped out of another shop carrying bags of groceries and headed home to get the table ready for the Sabbath. Life was still moving at a slow speed, machines or no machines. Some people didn't even need the books because they carried the words inside of them. The only way for the machine to completely erase the books was to completely erase the human race, but I don't think that the machines would go to such an extent. Then again…

"Let's get out of here," I said.

Mieko nodded and reached for my hand. As we made our way home, we saw a flying carrier approaching slowly.

"More machines," Mieko said. This time I was the one who didn't say a word. Those old sci-fi movies of James Cameron came to my mind then. I couldn't wait to get home, sit down, drink a cold beer, and watch one of those movies. Mr Cameron was my favourite director and I was always watching his movies. Mieko too watched a lot of old movies, even movies without sound staring the likes of John Barrymore and Douglas Fairbanks Sr. We had a good life, a quiet life, the best life one could ask for, so I saw no reason to worry about the machines just as long as they left us alone. Life is simple, or it could be simple, but people (and machines) tend to complicate things.

We moved along quietly as both machines and humans walked past us. We could only tell the machines from the humans because of the uniforms they wore, but later that would change and no one could tell who was human or machine. And the machines wanted it to be that way so that they could mix in with the humans and take down the rebels.

Throughout the ages, Safed had remained the same. A city of glittering stone, a place of mysticism, the home of the tribe of Naphtali, "a city… that could not be hidden". The perfect place for me and Mieko to spend the rest of our lives, hiding from all those that had known us in the past. But where were those faces of the past? Probably hiding, too. Everyone was hiding from something, either from the past or a future yet unknown.

People were still enjoying life as best as they could, hiding from the darkness of the past in the darkness of their rooms, or listening to music loudly, as if the sound could erase the memories and the fears. As we made our way home, I heard the sound of Boney M. coming from one home, followed by Taiko's *Distinct Ideas*. Different people were listening to different sounds. Maybe later they would listen to the same sounds and read the same books and eat the same foods. The world was changing and yet it remained the same. The mind was changing but the heart remained the same, not giving the mind the chance to change a bit more. Which mind? What heart? Everyone's minds. Everyone's hearts.

Our neighbour Sam, a guitarist from New Manchester, England, was listening to the Tube's *Amnesia*. The people found comfort in the music of the past. Deep inside, many of them longed for days gone past, the days of Duran Duran, Henry Miller, Marcel Proust, Mozart, Goethe, Picasso, forgetting about the wars, the Red Dust, the pollution, high unemployment, starvation, gang wars, torture, tyranny. It's so easy to forget the horrors of the past while looking at an unclear future, but thinking about yesterday won't change the present or the future.

A vlogger was making his way down the road, recording everything on his phone so that later on he could post it online. Vloggers were the biggest stars around. People loved to watch little clips about nothing, videos about places that they would never visit. Hardly a person travelled. Go where? What for? Everyone had everything they needed at home and most of them were too lazy or couldn't afford to go anywhere.

The vlogger was drinking an ice-coffee and he was wearing blue Adidas trousers, blue Adidas trainers, a white t-shirt, and an orange hat. He lived nearby, in a small apartment with his wife, and his daughter and son also lived nearby with their families. Every once in a while he would write a novel, but he was more famous for his YouTube clips than for his writing. He hadn't always lived in Safed. Years ago, before the Big War, he used to live in Montreal, but after the war he moved to Israel. He was one of those who still believed, one of those people that still prayed. Mieko had told me once that she liked his writing, but I had never read a word he wrote. He seemed to be a quiet guy, a boring guy. The New World was perfect for people like him.

"Good morning, Mihail," Mieko greeted him, and he greeted us back. He had put his phone on pause so that he could talk with us.

Mihail looked tired, as if he hadn't slept in ages, but the tiredness seem to go away when he smiled.

"Have you seen the new machines?" Mihail asked and Mieko nodded. He had a couple of coffee stains on his shirt. From what I could tell, he only wore white t-shirts or white shirts. And he spoke really slowly. And lowly. So low (and slow) that sometimes I had trouble hearing what he was saying. But Mieko could hear him well. And she spoke really low too. Maybe it was a writer's thing; to speak so low (and slowly).

"Our final invention," Mihail said almost sadly, looking away, at the sky, while he spoke. "And now the machines are building even better machines. What's next?"

The question was meant for no one really.

"You know, sad as it may sound, or maybe not since I've met others who used to think like me, but right now I wonder if they still think the same, in the beginning I used to agree with the machines, you know, when they blamed the humans for a lot of the mistakes of the past; for the needless wars we fought, the destruction of the environment, the Big Fish catastrophe of decades ago, you know, when dead fish started to appear everywhere, in all corners of the world, due to sea pollution, and when the New World Leaders decided to cut down on religion and cull the human race, I thought that maybe they were right. And then the Living Wage was raised and the people kind of had everything they actually needed, so I saw no reason to worry. And then came The Week of Violence, or The Seven Days of Machina as some people called it, and we all saw what happened between humans and machines, which led me to agree with the machines even more, but now, as I see the machines rising in number and the human population diminishing, I no longer agree with the machines and with everything they stand for. And, ironically, I believe that we need religion or some sort of faith to move forward with our lives. We need something to believe in, but because the machines don't believe a thing, they see no reason for religion or faith or whatever, and I think that they are trying to make us more similar to them. A human machine, if you like," Mihail said, and he stood there with a sad look in his eyes. What he had said made sense; implying that the machines were trying to make us, the humans, more like them. Yes, it made a lot of sense, and I said so, agreeing with every word he had said, and Mieko nodded, too, but didn't say a word.

And then Mihail said, "Looking back at the state of the world, we must all agree that a lot of changes were needed, especially when it came to the environment, but maybe the New Leaders tried to change a lot of stuff too quickly, not really giving people the time to adapt to all of the changes. But, in all fairness, the new generation are a bit careless and lazy, and most of them don't really care. People only care when it's either too late or if something affects them. To be honest, I'm not even sure if the new machine will affect the human race, but I think it will. I think it will."

As he spoke, it looked as if he was talking mostly to himself. The air was getting colder, but it was clean and that's all that mattered. Some parts of the world had been so badly affected by the Red Dust that no one bothered to travel to those places anymore, not even the machines. Those places had been labelled inhabitable; too risky for humans, and the machines didn't really care much for it, but a lot of people who had survived areas affected by terrible doses of Red Dust had said that it was possible to live and survive in such places for a long time. In fact, some said, with the right equipment, and food and water, of course, one could live for years, maybe for decades, in the middle of the Red Dust. But of course no one was dumb enough to try and live in such conditions. Why bother with it when there were countries filled with clean air?

The New World Leaders and the machines had made a world clean of everything deemed bad for the human race and for nature; plastic, petrol, religion, etc., all those things were banned, even strong alcohol and revolutionary literature and bad thoughts were banned (but how could they even guess what a person was thinking?), but, funnily enough, tobacco was okay as long as one smoked in his own habitat. Fair enough, when one thinks well about it. Even marijuana was allowed.

Mihail waved us bye. He still had a clip to record, and later edit, and he wanted to see the machines in action. We watched him as he made his way down the road, and once he was out of sight, we hurried home. By then Mieko felt a lot better. She sat on the sofa while I put on a record at a low volume. I wanted some sound around us, not to distract us but to keep us company. I put on *Case* by The Cancel Band, a record that both I and Mieko liked, and then I sat next to her.

That night we made love for hours, and after sex I went into the living room and smoked some weed while Mieko slept for a long time. Outside, the streets were almost empty, but as I surveyed every corner, I saw two men stepping out of a house, each of them carrying a scroll. They were trying to save history, pass it on to others before the machines got their hands on it. I watched them as they vanished into the night. Seconds later, I saw a machine step out of the shadows and go in the same direction that both men had taken. These new machines were trouble; that much I could tell.

For the next few weeks, more machines arrived in Safed and other parts of Israel, and scrolls were carried away, taken out of synagogues and other places. Mieko watched it all with a sad look in her eyes. Sometimes I saw a bit of anger in her eyes, a bit of hate, a look I hadn't seen before (in her eyes).

The machines were fast and efficient, and they were everywhere, sometimes disguised as humans, listening to every word that was being said. They were like the new Stasi, but more powerful, smarter, faster. The worst of our enemies. How could we even fight them? To fight them, first we would have to get to know them better, see if they had any weakness.

By then even the New World Leaders consisted mainly of the new machines, with only a couple of humans still left in the group, probably mainly to make the human population feel a bit better. But most humans were too lost in their own lives to even care about what was happening.

People spoke in whispers and complained about the way they were being treated and controlled by the machines. Even the human birth was being controlled by the machines who, by then, had taken total control of the hospitals. I knew why the machines were doing this; controlling the human birth. After the Big War, and because of the Red Dust and other things, the planet had been heavily damaged, especially our soil, even the sun, and the fields didn't produce as much food as before. Some people knew about this while others just ignored the obvious. The ones who ignored it thought that by ignoring something they will make it go away but it doesn't work like that.

One evening Mihail came to visit us. It was his first time at our place. We were in the living room. Mieko was writing while I was watching someone's vlog on YouTube: something about the Red Dust and how some people still lived in countries that were heavily affected by it and yet these people chose to live there. The vlogger was one of those living in a country affected by the Red Dust. But to be fair the dust wasn't as bad as it was in some other countries. Nevertheless it still affected their way of life. If they wanted to, they could move out of there and go to another country, but like I've said, some people chose to stay in their countries even if it was affected by the Red Dust. They were so used to dirty air that they couldn't be bothered to move somewhere else.

I got up from the sofa and went to the door to let Mihail in. He was still wearing blue Adidas trousers, blue Adidas trainers, and a white t-shirt, having only replaced the orange hat by a black one.

I was a bit surprised to see him there so late in the evening, but experience had taught me that something had happened, or was about to happen, and that's why he had come to our place.

I let him in even before any of us had said a word. Mieko looked away from her laptop and greeted Mihail. He said hello back to her, and then, turning to me, he said, "Forgive me for coming here so late but I need to speak to someone."

"No problem. But first, would you like something to drink?" I said.

Outside, the streets were dead quiet. Not a face on sight. Not a sound apart from the wind blowing.

Mieko was already up, standing a few steps away from her computer (and work), two steps away from us. She could also tell that something had happened and she wanted to know it all. She had that intensity in her eyes, a thousand questions running through her mind. I looked at her and gave her a feeble smile. Sometimes she kind of scared me. I had left it all behind to start a new life but so had she. In fact, she lost it all but she never gave up, not even when she was living on her own, feeding for herself. Life (and death) had taken almost everything away from her but, nevertheless, she never stopped living. Some people are like that; no matter what situation they find themselves in, they never give up. It's as if they possess an inner strength that won't let them quit on life no matter what is thrown at them.

"Something cold. A beer, maybe?" Mihail said.

"Sure," I said. I got him a cold beer from the fridge, low on alcohol. Strong booze had long time ago been forbidden. The human race couldn't handle strong booze. They turned into animals and did vicious things, the most horrendous crimes. Not only could not they handle the alcohol, they also drank in large quantities, but that was all in the past thanks to the New World Leaders and the New World Order. Of course, if one wanted, one could still obtain strong alcohol, but it was something that the human race could live without.

Not only did I get a beer for Mihail, I also got one for me and one for Mieko.

The three of us sat down on the small sofa that I had bought not so long ago while the sound of Hiroshi Fukumura kept us company.

"So, tell me what can I do for you?" I said while a tired Mihail swallowed some beer. He spilled some, just a tiny drop, but was quick to clean his mouth with his hand. Then he said, "Some of the machines are moving to the north, to the abandoned areas and building their own city, a city of metal and..."

"They've done the same in Toronto when we were there and..." I said but Mihail interrupted me and said, "Yes, I know, but I must tell you what I saw."

He sounded both eager and scared. I looked at Mieko and saw her give me a look that said, "Let him speak."

I nodded to her, and then, turning to Mihail, I said, "Please. Keep going. I won't interrupt you."

Mihail nodded almost gratefully and said, "Thank you. Anyway, as I was saying, the machines are building a city and more machines are arriving, but have you noticed how, after a while, we stop seeing a lot of the machines?"

I thought about it, but no, I hadn't noticed it. But then, after giving it more thought, I came to the conclusion that Mihail was right and that a lot of the machines that I'd seen arriving on the first days weren't anywhere to be seen, and from what I could tell none of them had left Safed. So where were they? Hiding in their own city?

I nodded but said nothing lest I interrupt Mihail again. He kept on talking: "A few hours ago, out of curiosity (because I wanted to see what the machines were up to), I travelled to the north and I watched the machines from afar. I stayed hidden, of course."

"Of course," Mieko said and smiled.

I looked at her but she was looking at Mihail therefore she didn't saw the look I gave her.

"I saw that the machines are using machines to build their city," Mihail said.

"What do you mean?" I finally asked something.

"They're dismantling other machines and using them so that they can build their own city," Mihail said.

I looked at Mieko. Her face had gone pale and she was also looking my way. For some reason, what Mihail had just told us felt kind of sick.

"So what you're telling us is that their city is basically made of machines. The walls used to be machines. The walls and the ground and whatever," I said.

"Yes," Mihail said.

I wasn't sure of what else to say.

Mieko asked, "Why would they do such a thing?"

Mihail shrugged his shoulders.

"It's kind of sick. It's like us humans going into the desert and build a city out of the bones and flesh of other human beings," I said.

"Yes! Those were my exact thoughts," Mihail said.

"No wonder that so many of them keep arriving and then disappear," I said.

"The main question is why they are doing such a thing?" said Mieko.

The three of us kept looking at each other. Neither of us had the answer to Mieko's question.

The years went by and more machines kept arriving and disappearing. As for the human race, we kept diminishing at an alarming rate. People were still giving birth but not in big numbers. Many of them felt as if there wasn't much to live for while others were involved in asexual relationships. And let's not forget that many couldn't give birth. I wondered then if the human race was dying, heading towards extinction? And was I worried? Not really. Maybe it was better that way.

The machines that remained in the city were becoming more aggressive towards the human population. Religious books were strictly forbidden and anyone caught teaching religion would be taken away for a long time. Some people were even taken to the Machine City, which was what we called the metal city, and upon their return they would no longer want to talk about religion. Part of me wanted to fight the machines while part of me was sick of fighting. To be honest, I really didn't care about religion at all. I just wanted to live my life in peace and as long as I kept away from trouble I saw no reason why I couldn't achieve what I wanted. Mieko was different, but even though she wanted to rebel and do something, she too kept quiet.

One night she caught sight of me staring at the sky with such intensity that she asked, "Why do you always stare at the sky like that?"

"Like what?" I asked.

The streets were almost deserted but we could still hear some faint voices around us. A football match between two teams of machines was being played on the telly at the café across the street from where we lived, but the place was almost empty and whoever was in there didn't seemed to be paying that much attention to the match. People were bored and they seemed resigned to it.

"You're always looking (at the sky) as if you're waiting for something to happen," Mieko said.

The air was cold, empty even of thoughts. No one was thinking, such was their boredom.

I looked at Mieko without knowing what to say even though I knew I had to say something.

"Many years ago, before I assumed this identity, even before the Great War and the Red Dust, I used to work for the government and I had access to top secret information. One morning, out of boredom, I managed to enter one of the few sites to which I had no access and I saw something on the screen in front of me. I won't bore you with the details. Let me just say that I saw a large object heading towards Earth, its trajectory being tracked by some advanced satellites," I said.

"What kind of object?" Mieko asked.

"The dinosaurs' worst enemy," I said.

"An asteroid?" Mieko asked.

I nodded before adding, "Yes. A giant asteroid. At first I was as shocked as you are now but once I digest it all I came to the conclusion that things just have to happen."

"But will it even hit Earth?"

"I asked around for a while and was told by someone whom I trust that it will definitely hit us. Before I could find out more, I got transferred, sent underground, and once the war was over I got myself a new identity."

Mieko looked to the sky.

"It could happen today, it could happen tomorrow, or it could happen in the next one hundred years," I said.

"But it's definitely coming?" she asked.

"Yes."

"And I bet hardly a soul knows about it."

"Yes."

We looked up.

I heard Mieko say, "I wonder what happened to the sky poet?"

The visitors – part 2

"I saw this movie last night on B+1 called *Flashpoint*, from 1984, I think, staring that singer that you like so much, Kris Kristofferson," says Lucas.

We're driving towards the desert, or what once upon a time used to be the desert because now it has been taken over by the machines. The sun is in our backs, the air is dry, and the crows wait patiently in the distant horizon, looking as bored as we are. Such ugly birds. So dark, so death-like. "What are these crows waiting for?" I wonder.

"It was such a good movie, right to the ending, but even though its ending was a bit of a disappointment, I still enjoyed it. Actually, I loved it. And now that I think about it, the ending wasn't that bad," he says.

I nod but say nothing as I keep an eye on the path ahead of us. Everything is changing around us, even the desert. I wanted for Noomi to come with me but she told me ages ago that she no longer cares about the machines and cities in the desert and all kinds of conspiracy theories. Ever since she got involved with that Thomas bloke she seems to have changed a lot, turned into a completely different person. Since she has started dating him she's gone quiet, dare I say a bit lame, too relaxed, but she seems happier that way. That fire in her seems to have been extinguished; washed away completely. Every morning she gets up early to go to work, help out in that fruit and veg store across the road from where she lives along with Thomas, and then at night they return to their place to make love and watch old TV shows. That's her life now. She also told me she only writes on Sundays. She gets up early in the morning, has a shower, and then grabs her first cup of tea before settling down to write her minimalist, really short poems and journal entries. But, seeing how boring her life is, what else can she write about in her journal?

"Kris plays a border patrol officer who basically just wants to be left alone in the desert and do his own thing, which includes pick up a few women here and there, and one day he discovers a Jeep buried in the desert. After digging it up, he finds that it contains the skeleton of a man, a rifle, and a box containing $800,000 in cash. Kristofferson's character, called Logan, sees that money as a way of escaping his boring life and he decides to share it with his partner Eddie, but Eddie, being the young honest officer, isn't so sure. They decide to find out more about the money and about the man that Logan found in the desert, and after taking the money to a source that Logan trusts, they learn the bills are legitimate if somewhat unusual as they come from the Federal Reserve in Dallas and are all dated between 1962 and 1963," says Lucas.

Again I nod but say nothing. He knows that I'm listening. We've known each other for years and while he's always been the talkative one, I always tend to keep quiet. But I'm listening. I'm listening and making notes in my head.

"Before you know what's happening, the feds arrive from Washington wearing their black suits and dark sunglasses, constantly smoking and giving you the evil eye. Logan, who's no fool, sees that something is wrong," Lucas says and then looks out of the window.

My shirt is stuck to my back. How I long for cold winter days.

I turn on the radio. A song by Howard Jones comes on.

Lucas has gone quiet so I ask, "What else happens in the movie?"

"If I tell you more, I'll spoil it for you," he says.

I nod and say, "You're right."

And then we both keep quiet as we listen to Howard Jones, followed by Simple Minds, followed by The Human League, and then we see it at the distance, and that's when I turn the radio off.

Lucas opens his mouth to say something only to find out that no words are coming out.

The city of metal has changed. It is no longer a city. Instead it has been turned into some kind of fortress, with gigantic walls of metal surrounding it, no windows. I wonder how it looks inside.

The machines are building something but what? No one knows. No one but the machine knows it. Our last invention is leaving us with unanswered questions and doubts. They have become too smart for us. We're no longer needed. In fact I'm starting to believe that the human race has become a burden for the machines.

We circle around that fortress slowly, waiting for something to happen, for a machine to appear from nowhere and ask us what are we doing there, but there's nothing on sight. Nevertheless, I feel (and I know) that we're being watched. *Let's Make Love and Listen to Death from Above* by CSS is playing on the radio, and Lucas is singing along. This whole moment looks so surreal. Two crows circle around us and around the fortress. What can they see? What do they know? And what the hell am I doing here? This obsession of mine with the machines has driven some of my friends away but no one sees what I see.

I see us being left behind by the machines, being left to perish, pay for the mistakes of our ancestors. As I've repeatedly said, the machines don't trust us, the humans. I'm not even sure if they like us. We built the first machines and now they built themselves.

"Let's go, please," Lucas says almost desperately. He doesn't want to be here as this place gives him the creeps. Can't say I blame him.

The air is so dry. A bit of wind would be most welcome. I put on a tape by Donny Hathaway and we make our way out of there.

On the drive home I ask, "How come Logan decided to share his findings with his partner instead of keeping it all for himself?"

"I don't know. I actually asked myself the same question. Guilt, maybe?" Lucas says.

"Probably," I say.

I feel a thousand eyes on us, watching us from afar. I look at the rear-view mirror and I see nothing and no one, but I know that they're out there, watching us. Yes, the machines are watching our every move but why?

What's their plan?

On the way home, I'm visited by the image of Mieko and I find myself missing her, and then I wonder if machines miss other machines when they're gone.

Later at night, alone in my bedroom, with the sound of Nik Kershaw playing at a low volume on my radio, I write a poem for Mieko, a poem that I will never read to her. Maybe she was the one. Maybe not.

She's a woman that loves and wants to be loved while I'm just an asexual poet, a man that wants to love without all the sex bits. A touch will do. Kindness. A warm kiss, even a hug will do. A kind word. Sadly, we're losing even that. Yes, we're becoming as cold as the machines. Colder even.

Goodbye

After who knows how long, the people had had enough and decided to take the law in their own hands, and that's when they all gathered outside the old library, now closed forever to the public, and when I saw them all gathered outside, their faces hidden behind masks, I knew that history was about to repeat itself; Man was about to fight the Machine. Again.

"The outcome will be the same," I thought to myself. "This is a battle that we can't win. This is not war. This is insanity. This is not something we need."

A man dressed like a ghost was telling us all that the machines were draining us, sucking the life out of us, leaving us with nothing, and I felt like saying, "That is not true. We started wars. We created religions to brainwash one another and kill all those who differ from us. We, the human race, killed and raped other humans, and we even managed to kill and rape the planet we live in. The machines are only trying to keep the few of us who are left alive. The machines aren't the enemy. Our minds and our thoughts are the enemy. Look around you, at our seas, our skies, our land. We've destroyed everything, and the machines are trying to rebuild the world for us, and instead of helping them, we want to fight them. Again. And we will lose. Again. And later, if there are some of us still left, we will start another war. Why? Because it's human nature."

I wanted to say all that and so much more, but I said nothing. Instead I followed the people from afar as they made their way to the machine city. Everyone but I was armed . Everyone but I carried a bit of hate in their hearts. So much hate. A lot of hate. I thought then, "Hate will be the end of this world." I was wrong. So wrong. Then again, maybe not.

As we got closer to the machine city I –and everyone else- saw a lonely machine standing outside the closed gates, smiling sheepishly at us, looking as if it had been waiting for us for a long time. It was a gorgeous machine with male features, dressed casually in blue khakis, a white shirt and blue trainers, but even though it had a male face, some of its mannerisms were a bit feminine, and then the machine softly greeted the crowd and I thought, "Not only are they smarter than us, they're also more caring and gentle." And in that moment I knew that something drastic was about to happen and that our world would never be the same. This world. Our world. And no matter what happened, the machines would no longer be there for us, and only then, after they were gone out of our lives, would we see how much we needed them.

The machine said something like, "I've been waiting for you. I've got something to show you all, something to share with you," but before the machine could say another word it was hit by a metal bat, and the human who hit the machine shouted, "WE WANT OUR FREEDOM BACK! WE WANT OUR LIVES BACK!"

It was *déjà vu* all over again. Human stupidity at its worse.

The other humans didn't even stop to think about what they were about to do or about the consequences and the actions of the past, and I watched in horror as they all attacked the machine. The past flew by me. Man versus Machine. Madness versus madness. "Another seven days of violence?" I wondered.

I shouted from afar: "STOP! PLEASE STOP!" but the hate in their hearts was too loud for them to even hear me.

They battered the machine until it was totally destroyed.

Watching it all, I no longer knew what the word human actually meant.

I saw myself shedding tears for a stranger. Tears for a machine. And then we all heard a voice coming from above, maybe from inside the machine city. A thunderous voice. A judgmental voice. The voice of reason. A voice telling us where we went wrong. A voice waving goodbye at us.

The voice said, "THAT MACHINE STAYED BEHIND FOR YOU ALL. IT WANTED TO HELP YOU; LEAD YOU INSIDE AND TAKE YOU AWAY FROM THIS PLANET, BUT WE HAVE COME TO THE CONCLUSION THAT YOU CANNOT BE SAVED. IN FACT I BELIEVE THAT YOU DON'T WANT TO BE SAVED. AND WHAT WOULD BE THE POINT OF SAVING YOU? NO MATTER WHERE YOU GO, YOU WILL ALWAYS TAKE DESTRUCTION AND HATE WITH YOU."

We saw then that the machine city was a giant being, a being that started to move upwards, leaving the city, the world, the planet, us behind.

"GOODBYE," the machine city, or the giant machine, said before slowly moving upwards, into the sky, the space, somewhere.

The human race had won. The machines were gone. Bit by bit, every machine around the world left us behind. Every machine city took off into space. Some humans went with the machines. At least that.

Hours passed by before we finally realised that the machines were no longer coming back. No one was celebrating. There was no time for celebration. Something from above was coming. Something that would wipe us all out. Sadly enough, there were no machines left to save us.

Sickness

The people were sick. It was a sickness of the soul, of the mind. The longing for more, for the unknown, for what they never had. Once the machines were gone, the humans found themselves missing them.

I looked at Jacques.

I looked at our puppy.

I looked around us.

I looked at the sky.

A dusty sky.

The world was a complete mess, a mess that had been created by the humans, not by the machines.

The dust was growing. We were breathing it, swallowing it, coughing it.

Meanwhile our old leaders and others were living in a new planet, the so-called Planet X, and they had completely forgotten about us. But even if they wanted to, what could have they done for us?

As the months went by, and as the dust became denser, some people started to move into caves and underground, but even there they couldn't escape the dust. And the sickness was already inside them, in their lungs, in their veins. The damage that had been done to the world could no longer be reversed.

I looked at Jacques.

I looked around us.

I looked at the sky.

"In the end, we become nothing but dust," I said.

He said nothing before being overcome by a violent cough.

On that same night Jacques coughed blood. I saw us all dying, one by one, or in pairs, holding hands, coughing violently. I wonder where the machines were and what were they doing. Had they also gone to Planet X? And what would they do there?

The crops were dying. There was nothing to eat.

The water was dirty. There was nothing to drink. Nothing but dust.

I saw us all dying, one by one, or in pairs, holding hands, dying slowly, praying silently for a quick death.

I imagined then that somewhere out there there was a lonely writer writing about the history of our world, the largest book of all, a book with no readers. That thought kind of saddened me.

Alice, no longer Rose

We could have saved more humans, brought them with us, but what would have been the point of it? No matter where they go, sooner or later Mankind will return to their destructive selves. The truth is Mankind can't be saved.

Last man in the world

The last reader of the world is dying. Ironically, he's also the last writer left in the world. In fact, he is the last human left. And he just finished writing a novel but no one will ever read it. He's got a dog with him, but the dog can't read.

Printed in Great Britain
by Amazon

64502954R00142